E.R. PUNSHON
MURDER ABROAD

Ernest Robertson Punshon was born in London in 1872.

At the age of fourteen he started life in an office. His employers soon informed him that he would never make a really satisfactory clerk, and he, agreeing, spent the next few years wandering about Canada and the United States, endeavouring without great success to earn a living in any occupation that offered. Returning home by way of working a passage on a cattle boat, he began to write. He contributed to many magazines and periodicals, wrote plays, and published nearly fifty novels, among which his detective stories proved the most popular and enduring.

He died in 1956.

Also by E.R. Punshon

Information Received
Death among the Sunbathers
Crossword Mystery
Mystery Villa
Death of a Beauty Queen
Death Comes to Cambers
The Bath Mysteries
Mystery of Mr. Jessop
The Dusky Hour
Dictator's Way
Comes a Stranger
Suspects – Nine
Four Strange Women
Ten Star Clues

E.R. PUNSHON

MURDER ABROAD

With an introduction
by Curtis Evans

DEAN STREET PRESS

Published by Dean Street Press 2015

Copyright © 1939 E.R. Punshon

Introduction Copyright © 2015 Curtis Evans

All Rights Reserved

Published by licence, issued under the UK Orphan Works
Licensing Scheme

First published in 1939 by Victor Gollancz

Cover by DSP

ISBN 978 1 910570 92 0

www.deanstreetpress.co.uk

INTRODUCTION

During the Golden Age of detective fiction, the country of France proved a popular literary destination for British mystery writers making occasional excursions to foreign crimes. At the dawn of the Golden Age, Freeman Wills Crofts set much of his landmark debut detective novel, *The Cask* (1920), in France, while Agatha Christie's third published mystery, *The Murder on the Links* (1923), sees Christie's series sleuth Hercule Poirot (Belgian, not French!) competing with the Paris Sûreté to solve a baffling slaying on a French golf course. According to Christie biographer Laura Thompson, the Queen of Crime based *The Murder on the Links* on an actual crime in France. E.R. Punshon likewise drew on real-life criminal inspiration from across the English Channel in *Murder Abroad* (1939), his thirteenth Bobby Owen mystery, which is set in the rugged Auvergne region of south central France and has a plot that the author partially based on a then notorious unsolved crime, the murder a decade earlier of Englishwoman Olive Branson at the scenic mountain village of Les Baux-des-Provence.

On 4 May 1929, Edith May Olive Branson (1884-1929), an artist and cousin of English High Court judge Sir George Arthur Harwin Branson (future grandfather of English businessman Richard Branson), was discovered dead in a cistern on the grounds of her villa. She had been slain by a single bullet to the forehead that was fired, neighbors believed, around nine o'clock on the previous evening. Initially local police theorized that Branson had committed suicide, but in England her family balked at this claim. Within a few days, however, Chief Inspector Alexandre Guibal of the Marseilles police judiciaire had taken charge of the case; and Guibal, a recipient of the O.B.E. (Officer of the Most Excellent Order of the British Empire) who had worked for British intelligence during the Great War, announced that the family's darkest fears were correct: Branson's mysterious death was indeed a case of foul play. Guibal had discovered bloodstains within Branson's villa and he surmised from this, reasonably enough, that the artist "could not have shot herself and then walked to a tank 20 yards away in stockinged feet and a nightdress."

Both Branson's gardener and his brother-in-law, Francois Pinet, manager of the local Hôtel de Monte Carlo, were arrested and subjected to what newspapers referred to as a "gruelling third degree interrogation," after which the gardener was released, but Pinet was committed to trial. Although Pinet, 25, was two decades younger than the 44-year-old Branson, police theorized that the "handsome athletic young man" had been the artist's lover and that he slew her after she had promised to bequeath to him the Hôtel de Monte Carlo, which she had purchased from Pinet's parents. (Despite this assurance, Branson later made a will leaving her entire estate to a cousin in England.) In an echo of Arthur Conan Doyle's famous Sherlock Holmes story "Silver Blaze," Chief Inspector Guibal noted that Branson had owned four large watchdogs, not one of which had barked on the night the artist was slain, indicating that the murderer was someone familiar to them. Guibal also established that, contrary to Pinet's claims, he and Branson had stayed together in several Marseilles hotels, registering under assumed names.

The wealth and social prominence of the victim, coupled with the titillating idea of a well-bred, middle-aged Englishwoman carrying on a sexual affair with a much younger French hotel manager, made Francois Pinet's murder trial a press sensation, with accounts of the affair appearing in newspapers around the world, in France, England, Australia, the United States and presumably other countries as well. Emphasis was laid upon Olive Branson's "eccentricities," which seemed mostly to boil down to her inclination to live independently and her active interest in attractive members of the opposite sex. ("[N]o girl was ever easier for a man to meet," one newspaper feature article observed snidely of Branson.) When Pinet's case came to trial nine months later, the press seems to have taken the certainty of his conviction as a matter of course, but, in a shocking turn of events, the young man—who, it was reported, "looked almost a dandy in the dock," with his hair oiled and his clothes nicely pressed—was acquitted.

Counsel for the defense maintained to the end of the case that Olive Branson had done away with herself. After Pinet's stunning acquittal the mystery around Branson's death remained officially unsolved a decade later, when E.R. Punshon published *Murder Abroad*. (Indeed, it remains unsolved today.) One can surmise how the case might have proved irresistibly tantalizing to the mystery author, who had written about outré murder in France three years previously, in an essay on the infamous serial killer Henri Désiré Landru (aka Bluebeard), published in *The Anatomy of Murder* (1936), a Detection Club true crime anthology.

In *Murder Abroad* Detective Sergeant Bobby Owen is cast into a freelance investigation of the strange death in France of an eccentric, socially prominent Englishwoman at the instigation of his fiancée, Olive Farrar, owner of a chic West End hat shop, who has despaired of her and Bobby ever being able to save though their regular occupations sufficient money upon which to marry. Fashionable as her hat shop is, business has not been particularly remunerative, Olive having found it rather challenging to persuade more than a few of her hoity-toity customers actually to pay for their purchases; and Bobby's salary as a police sergeant is a comparative pittance. However, Olive informs her fiancée that one of her best customers ("she pays cash"), the socially-connected Lady Markham ("she was at school with the Home Secretary's wife"), stands poised to come to their rescue, in return for Bobby's rendering of certain investigative services.

Lady Markham has promised Olive that through her politically prominent husband she will secure Bobby's appointment as private secretary to the elderly chief constable of a Midlands county, on condition that Bobby determine what really happened to Lady Markham's late sister, a fifty-five year old amateur artist discovered drowned in a well on the grounds of her domicile, an old converted mill in Citry-sur-l'eau, a charming village in the Auvergne. The French police have concluded that the sister, a Miss Polthwaite, likely committed suicide, but her family firmly rejects this answer. Lady Markham has confided further to Olive that the eccentric Miss Polthwaite, certain that "a revolution was coming, with guillotines in Trafalgar Square and everyone with any money shot at dawn," was known to have converted most of her cash assets into diamonds, which have since vanished, and that there is a substantial reward--most providential for a newly-married couple--that Bobby can claim if he can locate them.

Given a month off from his job (a bit of Lady Markham's string-pulling, that), Bobby soon is on his way to France to find out what he can about the demise of Miss Polthwaite and the whereabouts of her missing diamonds. Once arrived in Citry-sur-l'eau, he harvests a bumper crop of murder suspects, including both French natives and English expatriates of long and recent standing. Readers now familiar with the Olive Branson case detailed above doubtlessly will cast suspicious glances at the youthful and extremely good-looking Charles Camion, son of the keepers of the local hotel, whom villagers deridingly termed Miss Polthwaite's gigolo; yet there are additional intriguingly dubious characters lurking about the lanes of Citry-sur-l'eau, including a preternaturally sensitive blind beggar known as Père Trouché.

The case is a pleasingly tricky one and Punshon's sense of local color in a French village is assured, so that readers of *Murder Abroad* should derive some of the same pleasures from the novel that may be found in contemporary works by the crime writer Georges Simenon, a French-language author whose mystery tales, duly translated, were starting to win at this time popularity within the English-speaking world. As Maurice Richardson perceptively wrote in the *Manchester Observer*, in the novel Punshon "combines ingenious yet sound detection with lively, natural writing in a way that is admirable and all too rare....The atmosphere...is full of dark forces, yet not too strained, and local colour is most skillfully applied." With *Murder Abroad* fans of classic mystery will find that a sojourn in France can be amply rewarding. Read on to see whether Bobby Owen finds it so too.

Curtis Evans

CHAPTER I
THREEFOLD MISSION

"Bobby," said Olive Farrar, a trifle nervously, "do you think you could ask for a month's holiday?"

Detective-Sergeant Bobby Owen, of the C.I.D., Metropolitan Police, answered tolerantly:

"I could. I could also ask for the Crown Jewels and promotion to Assistant Commissioner. It would be quite a toss up which drew the largest, loudest, most emphatic 'No'."

Bobby and Olive were engaged. Bobby had his weekly pay as a police sergeant. Olive owned a hat shop which just about paid its way. If she sold it now, most of her small capital she had sunk in its purchase would be lost. Nor do the police authorities much care about their men interesting themselves in any way in business activities. Business interests and official duties might clash. And though the pay of a sergeant of police is enough for two to live on, the margin is not great. In point of fact Olive and Bobby had just been holding an informal committee meeting of two on Ways and Means and had found the conclusion arrived at a little depressing. Bobby indeed was quite ready and willing, even anxious, to make the hat-shop business a present to anyone who would accept it, but had to admit Olive's point of view when she hesitated to face the loss of her small capital. Olive said thoughtfully:

"You speak French, don't you?"

"I wish it was German," Bobby said. "Nowadays German's your only wear in the Special Branch."

"Lady Markham is a customer of ours," Olive told him.

"Who is Lady Markham?" asked Bobby. He added: "Cash customer?"

Olive nodded impressively. In small Mayfair hat shops cash customers are appreciated.

"Well, what about her?" Bobby inquired next as Olive seemed lost in a somewhat awed contemplation of her real live cash customer.

"She's rather nice," explained Olive, rousing herself, "and she was at school with the Home Secretary's wife."

"Look here, Olive," said Bobby uneasily, "don't you get trying to pull strings."

Olive looked at him gravely and then pronounced the following profound and awful truth:

"The whole art and conduct of life in England consists in pulling strings."

Bobby gasped. Then he said suspiciously:

"Who told you that?"

"I thought of it myself," said Olive, though native honesty compelled her to add: "After I had been talking to Lady Markham—at least I mean after she had been talking to me."

"Oh," said Bobby. He asked: "Who is Mr. Lady Markham?"

"Her hubby? Oh, he's an M.P. At least, I think he is, or else he's one of the people who say who are to be M.P.s. It's something to do with politics anyhow."

"Means he's expert in string-pulling, I suppose," observed Bobby.

"What," asked Olive, "is twenty per cent on £40,000?"

Bobby was beginning to look a little dazed.

"Olive," he said, "I know I have only a slow dull masculine mind—"

But Olive was not listening. She answered her own question.

"Eight thousand pounds," she said slowly.

"Correct," said Bobby. "I expect you worked it out before, though. Anyhow, what about it?"

"If you had eight thousand pounds," Olive pointed out, "you would be in a position to propose to me."

"I shouldn't think of such a thing," Bobby declared firmly. "Never take your fences twice. What's this about eight thou, though? Know where it's to be picked up?"

"Lady Markham does."

"Well, why don't she?"

"Do you remember some months ago there was a lot in the papers about an Englishwoman found dead in an old mill where she had been living somewhere in the Auvergne?"

Bobby stared and frowned.

"I think I do. Suicide, wasn't it? Didn't they find her in a well? I forget the name?"

"Polthwaite. Lady Markham's name was Polthwaite before she married. It was her sister. There's another sister and two brothers. They believe she was murdered. One of the brothers is a lawyer. He went over there when it happened. He says the French police admitted as much privately but they didn't want to say so for fear of harming the tourist trade. He says they know perfectly well who killed the poor old soul. But there was no proof. Nothing they could act on."

"Well, it's like that sometimes," Bobby admitted. "We know all right often enough. I've heard a crook telling our people just exactly how a job was brought off and then defy us to prove it. You've got to satisfy a jury within the rules and within the rules— well, it means within the rules. I expect it's much the same over there. Besides, they might think it a good idea to let it pass as suicide while they went on trying to dig something up. Where's the eight thousand come in?"

"Miss Polthwaite was the rich one of the family. She had money left her by an aunt. She was a good business woman, too, Lady Markham says, and made some good investments. The lawyers have been through her papers and say the estate ought to be worth nearly fifty thousand pounds and instead there's hardly anything at all."

"Investments gone wrong?"

"No, she had been buying diamonds, uncut stones chiefly."

"Had to sell at a loss?"

"They know exactly what she bought. She kept a full record. There's nothing to show she ever sold any."

"Well, then," said Bobby, puzzled.

"It was her way of investing her money, Lady Markham says. She thought it was safer like that. She didn't trust the Stock Exchange."

"Well, who does?" asked Bobby. "All the same, there's gilt-edged government stocks."

"She didn't trust governments, either," said Olive.

"Well, there's that," admitted Bobby.

"Her idea was that diamonds are always value—you can demonetize gold but not diamonds. Also diamonds are portable; you can put diamonds in your pocket or your handbag but not lumps of gold. And she thought their value would never fall because De Beers wouldn't let it. Even if it's true they have packing cases stuffed with diamonds filling their warehouses in South Africa, both De Beers and the South African Government will take precious good care the market's never flooded with the things. So long as they're not too big you can always sell diamonds and she only bought small ones—worth about £20 or £30 each, never more than £50 or less than £10. Mostly uncut or unset stones, but a good many rings and brooches and so on as well. Uncut stones are easier to carry about and keep hidden, but people can see the value of a cut stone set in a ring more easily."

"Old lady does seem to have been a bit cracked," remarked Bobby, still feeling a little puzzled. "Did she hand over a diamond ring every time she wanted a new hat or a pound of sausage?"

"Lady Markham says she bought herself a small annuity, too. Four hundred a year, I think. She lived on that and only spent half."

"I still don't see the big idea," Bobby said. "If she wasn't merely cracked, that is, and that would make the suicide idea seem likely."

"No, it wasn't that," Olive explained. "She got excited about Bolshevism and revolutions and that sort of thing. So she sold out her investments, gave up business, and took to painting instead. When they found her in the well, she was still holding a paintbrush in one hand. There was a picture on her easel and she must have been working on it up to the last moment before she jumped down the well—if that's what really happened."

"Did she know anything about diamonds—perhaps she got done down and bought a lot of duds?"

"Oh, no, she was quite an expert. Old Mr. Polthwaite had a jeweller's shop in London—it's still there with a branch in Paris. He sold out to his partners years ago and opened an office in Hatton Garden for dealing in precious stones. The Polthwaite family haven't anything to do with Polthwaite's, the jewellers, now, but Miss Polthwaite did most of her buying through them—partly for old time's sake, but chiefly so that no one should know, especially the Bolsheviks, I suppose, and then Lady Markham says she was always very secretive. Especially lately. She was sure a revolution was coming, with guillotines in Trafalgar Square and everyone with any money shot at dawn."

"But not people with diamonds?" Bobby asked. "Did she think they would be let off?"

"Lady Markham says her idea about diamonds was that they could be—hidden," Olive answered with just the faintest touch of emphasis on this last word.

Bobby looked thoughtful. He was beginning to understand. He said:

"You mean they think that's what she did with the diamonds and that they're still hidden," and in his turn he laid the least possible emphasis on this last word.

Olive nodded.

"That's where the eight thousand comes in, is it?"

Olive nodded again.

"Lady Markham," she explained, "said they would go equal whacks with you. Her two brothers, her sister and herself, and you, one fifth each. Twenty per cent. If you could find the diamonds."

"Why me?" Bobby asked. "Doesn't seem much chance anyhow. Why don't they take on the job themselves?

"They think you've experience. There's another thing," Olive added. "They feel a bit bad over the poor old soul being murdered and nothing done about it."

"If she was murdered," Bobby said. "Anyhow, I couldn't help there. Not likely. Not after all these months. Not in a foreign country."

"Lady Markham thought if you could find out what had become of the diamonds, then perhaps that would show who was the murderer and the French authorities would be ready to take action."

Bobby sat thinking. Eight thousand pounds! A small enough chance perhaps but how much it would mean if it came off, to him and to Olive. Olive went on:

"Lady Markham says the chief constable where they live is wanting a private secretary, because he's getting a bit old. She says her husband has a lot of influence though of course she couldn't promise anything. Only she said they would be grateful, and I think she meant it. Even if you didn't get the diamonds back. Just for trying."

"Strikes me," declared Bobby, "there won't be much more than trying to it. Ten to one some crook got to know, and that's why she was murdered and the diamonds stolen. All sold in Amsterdam probably by this time."

"Lady Markham says not. They all think Miss Polthwaite wouldn't have let anyone know. They only knew themselves when Mr. Polthwaite went through her papers after her death. Even her lawyers had no idea. Nor her bankers. They knew she was doing something with her money, but that was all. She always managed her own affairs. At the inquiry in France nothing came out about any diamonds. They called her a rich Englishwoman but in the Auvergne they would call anyone rich with four or five hundred a year. The French police had a theory. They made that quite plain, too. They think she had a quarrel with one of the young men in the village and he killed her. They think he was her lover."

"I thought you said Miss Polthwaite was an elderly woman?"

"Yes. It's rather horrid. I think really that's what's upsetting Lady Markham more than anything. The French police spent most of their time smiling and looking down their noses and saying what else could you expect when an old spinster—Miss Polthwaite was about fifty-five—takes a hot-blooded young man as her lover? Lady Markham says it's a foul lie. She began to cry about it. She says she and the others want their sister's name cleared. I think really they mind more about that than about the money. If you show she was murdered and the diamonds stolen, they would be more pleased than if you got the diamonds back but didn't prove there was nothing nasty about her being friends with the boy the French police think was her lover and murdered her."

"Who is he? Is there anything to go on?"

"His name is Camion, Charles Camion, Lady Markham says. His father keeps the hotel in the village. Poor Miss Polthwaite lived in an old converted mill just outside. He is very good looking, Charles Camion, I mean. There seems no doubt about Miss Polthwaite having taken a great fancy to him. She was painting his portrait."

"Was she really an artist or only playing at it?" Bobby asked.

"I don't know. Lady Markham said she went there partly so as to be near a Mr. Shields, who really is well known and quite successful and who has a studio somewhere about. Young Camion was at the mill a good deal and there was a lot of talk. The general idea seems to have been that the young man was doing very well for himself. I daresay the village people couldn't understand an elderly, unmarried woman taking an interest in a good-looking boy without there being anything more than friendliness in her mind. I don't see why, but I expect it would be like that anywhere. Why shouldn't she just have taken a fancy to the boy, thought she would like to paint his portrait, and then the poor old thing gets murdered, and everyone believes all sorts of nastiness. I don't wonder Lady Markham feels a bit sick. Anyone would. Lady Markham says Miss Polthwaite was a bit silly in some ways and rather mean and secretive, but they were all very fond of her. I think I should want it cleared up if I were in Lady Markham's place. She has heard of you. She asked me to speak to you."

"What do you think yourself?" Bobby asked.

"It's horrid to think of people saying things about a poor old dead woman who can't defend herself," Olive answered.

"It may be true," Bobby told her slowly. "I mean what they are saying. Elderly, unmarried women do go a bit queer sometimes. Not often, but it happens. If you read modern novels you would think every elderly spinster was necessarily boiling over with all kinds of suppressed sex and spent all her time sitting in a corner and letting it fester. It's nasty rubbish only nasty people believe. Maiden aunts aren't like that."

"I know," said Olive. "I had one. She was a dear. The worst thing she ever did in her life was to slap a little boy for swinging a cat round by its tail. She always felt she ought to have explained, not slapped. It troubled her a lot."

"I'm all for slapping," said Bobby. "Hard and frequent. We all know our maiden aunts even if the psycho-analyst people don't. All the same, that suppressed type does exist. Perhaps this Miss Polthwaite was one. No telling."

"You see, Bobby," Olive explained, "that's exactly what Lady Markham and the others want cleared up. They want the diamonds back all right if they can get them, but I don't think they expect to and I don't believe that's the chief thing. It's more the horrid things being said. There were hints in the English papers, and all the people they know whisper about it and Lady Markham knew about us and she began talking about it last time she was here."

"Well, what's the idea? What's she want me to do?" Bobby asked doubtfully.

"Go there and see what you can find out. The mill where it happened is to let. The man who owns it lets it out to visitors in the summer but no one will want to spend a holiday there so soon after a murder, so it's sure to be vacant still. Lady Markham thought you could rent it and look round. The diamonds may be hidden there still, she thinks. And some of the people in the village may know something."

"Was there anything to suggest the suicide theory or was that an afterthought when the police were at a dead end? Was there any letter, for instance? Suicides nearly always leave a letter behind. They feel they've got to defend themselves."

"There was something," Olive admitted. "A sort of letter, only it wasn't addressed to anyone. In French. Mr. Polthwaite had a copy. They wouldn't give him the original."

"Do you know what it said?"

"Lady Markham said it was only a few words: 'J'en ai des écus jusqu'aux yeux, en avoir peur.' I don't see that it means much, do you? 'Avoir des écus' is a sort of idiom —means you've got more money than you know what to do with. One of the French police, an inspector or something, his name was Clauzel, argued it meant she had worked herself into such a state of nerves over her diamonds and things that she went clean off her head and decided to end it. Of course, she was a bit funny, hoarding it up like that instead of using a bank or a safe deposit like everyone else. Lady Markham says she was convinced the first thing when the revolution came would be seizing the banks."

"If the police think it was a case of suicide, why did they talk about this Camion chap?"

"That was largely the gossip in the village. They didn't know about her having valuables by her. Mr. Polthwaite made the Clauzel policeman person admit the note she left might have meant she was afraid not of her money but of someone she thought might be planning to rob her. He had to leave it there. He doesn't talk French very well."

"Could the diamonds and stuff be identified if I did come across them?"

"They have a list of what she bought, numbers, weight, everything."

"Ought to be good enough," Bobby agreed. "Don't see much chance of being able to do anything though. You have to be on the spot at once, not months late. Probably the diamonds and the rest of it have been got rid of already. You can always sell small stuff safely enough if you do it by degrees."

"You might find out enough to clear Miss Polthwaite's name?"

"Perhaps I shouldn't," Bobby said slowly. "Perhaps I should find out the other way. Perhaps it was like that. Perhaps she had fallen for this Camion bloke. Old spinster ladies do go off the rails sometimes."

"I think Lady Markham was facing that. She doesn't believe it, but she knows it's there. She said if you found the diamonds, there would be the reward. If you didn't, but just got at the truth, whatever it is, then they'll try to get you the private secretaryship with the chief constable they know."

"Sporting," agreed Bobby. "If she sticks to it. Do you think she will?"

"Well, she pays cash," said Olive simply.

"Good enough," agreed Bobby. "Sort of a threefold mission—the diamonds, the murderer, the truth. All right, I'll take it on if she can wangle that month's leave she talks about."

CHAPTER II
CITRY-SUR-L'EAU

Lady Markham proved even better than her word. Evidently it is not for nothing that one has attended school with the future wife of a Home Secretary. The leave granted Bobby was not for a month merely. It was for six weeks. The more simple-minded among Bobby's colleagues understood that it had been granted because he had not fully recovered from the effects of a slight concussion received in a recent case during the course of which he had been knocked out by a former amateur boxing champion. His other colleagues—a large majority—looked down their noses and muttered to each other about favouritism. Another sergeant was appointed to the squad formerly in Bobby's charge and Bobby wondered uneasily whether that portended promotion when he returned or banishment to one of the outer suburbs. Or whether there was anything in that vague hope Lady Markham seemed to have held out of her ability to wangle him a job as private secretary to a county chief constable.

All three possibilities were present in his mind as a few days later he sat sipping his after-dinner coffee outside the Hotel de la Belle Alliance, de la Victoire, et des États Unis, in the village of Citry-sur-l'eau in the 'Massif Central' of France, a little to the south of Clermont. Upon his thoughts a voice broke suddenly, startling him, for he had not heard anyone approach. It was a tall, thin man who was speaking, a man with a thin, eager face and eyes that burned but yet that had a trick of veiling themselves behind heavy, slightly swollen lids. His hands were thin and eager, too, almost transparent, and gesticulating easily. He had been standing when he spoke first but now he seated himself at an adjacent table, and Bobby noticed how quick and silent were his movements, how efficient those thin delicate-looking hands of his.

If he walked as silently as he seated himself, no wonder, Bobby thought, that he had not heard anyone approach. He said now:

"Monsieur is an artist? Monsieur then will understand that we of Citry-sur-l'eau are a little proud of our view."

"With reason," Bobby agreed amiably, for there was nothing he desired more than to establish friendly, chatty relations with the local inhabitants.

Indeed the view was magnificent. In front, to the west, where the sun was sinking in a riot of glorious colouring, lay a wide and lovely valley, one of those rich vales by whose soft beauty Nature has seemed to wish to throw into greater relief the bare, tormented splendour of so much of the Auvergne. Through the valley, past the village, ran a small stream, probably the 'eau' from which the village took its name, on its way to join one of those rivers that, fed by the snows and rains of the Massif Central, issue from it to water the wide land of France. North, in the far distance, the great round summit of the Puy de Dôme hung in the evening air as though it floated in the clouds, detached from any earthly base. East and south hill rose behind hill in a series of never-ending rocky ramparts, rock heaved upon rock, here a solitary pillar starting up like a finger thrusting at the sky, there a great bare wall like that of some enormous castle, then again a gigantic crag balancing in apparent insecurity almost as if at any moment it might topple over in dreadful ruin, everywhere such a medley of crag and gorge, of ravine and rock, as though it were here the Titans had started to build their tower wherefrom to storm the heavens and these were the relics of their defeat. Over the whole scene hung a red glow from the setting sun, so that now it seemed all things were seen through a haze of blood. Magnificent indeed, Bobby thought, and yet with about it something of the ominous, of the sinister, as though here lurked dark forces of nature man had not yet conquered, perhaps would never conquer.

"Magnificent," Bobby said, this time aloud. "A little terrifying, too. One would say here Nature had been at war and might one day begin again."

"Not war, but birth," smiled the other. "Yet perhaps they are the same. Here in the Auvergne we have traces of the pangs of

Nature before she gave birth to her child, the earth. Here where we sit, here first the interior fires began to cool and solid land to form itself from fire and steam. Perhaps some day all that will re-commence. Who knows? Quiet without, but fire within. Like the society man has made for himself. All so calm above, so different below—but one must not talk politics. In the meantime, Monsieur, you look with the eye of the artist and see beauty, I with the eye of the scientist and see the story of the earth's formation."

"I'm afraid I'm not much of a scientist," Bobby admitted. "How did you know I was an artist? I've always flattered myself I had not the air."

"Monsieur," said the other, "all the village knows." He got to his feet and bowed. He said: "Permit me to introduce myself. Eudes. Schoolmaster in this village of Citry-sur-l'eau. Jacques Pierre Eudes."

Bobby in his turn rose and bowed.

"Owen," he said. "An artist, yes, but, alas, it would be truer to say—trying to become one."

"Monsieur," said Eudes gravely, "those who try to be, already are."

It was an echo of a famous saying of Pascal's, but Bobby did not recognize it. He said in return and with equal gravity:

"Monsieur, I perceive you are a philosopher."

Eudes was plainly gratified by the remark, and those eager, yet half-hidden eyes of his opened into a smile of appreciation. He went on talking about the village. Bobby was content to listen. He had a feeling that he was being discreetly pumped, but he answered fully all the questions delicately dropped at intervals, even though he was careful to give in reality very little information. Simply an artist, impressed by the austere beauty of the country and anxious to do some sketching, was the impression he wished to leave of himself. Later on, it would be his turn to ask questions. For the present, it would be best to show no more than the casual and natural interest of the newcomer. He did make a smiling remark about the interest his arrival seemed to have caused in a village, where surely tourists, artists, too, for that matter, came frequently enough. But Eudes began at once to talk of something else. Bobby remembered that his welcome at the little inn with the long name had been cordial even beyond the usual cordiality of a welcoming landlord and yet had been touched with a certain quality of reserve and hesitation, as though this welcome had in it some unusual element of doubt. Perhaps it was simply that the villagers had been uneasy lest the tragedy of Miss Polthwaite's death might keep visitors away and he was welcome as a proof to the contrary and yet was feared as possibly bringing fresh trouble. When presently another reference was made to his supposed status as artist, he laughed and said:

"I wonder how that was known so quickly. Disappointing when I always try so hard not to look like one."

"You have not indeed the air," agreed Eudes, and gave Bobby so quick a look from those sharp, restless eyes behind the heavy lids that Bobby wondered uncomfortably if Eudes entertained any suspicions. A bad beginning if that were so. Eudes went on: "But the true artists never do. If nowadays there is someone with sandals and no hat, with a velvet jacket and a tie like a hand-towel; well, then all the world shrugs its shoulders and knows what to think. Monsieur Shields, for example—"

Eudes paused for a moment. Bobby guessed he was watching to see if the name were recognized and connected with the Polthwaite tragedy of which as yet no mention had been made. Bobby gave no sign and Eudes continued: "A lion of a man, Monsieur Shields. A figure of a Goliath. One would say probably a boxer of the first rank, renowned. My faith, how the farmers would jump at him for the harvest field in days when all the young men go off to the towns and farmers are glad of any old crock to help in the harvesting. And dressed always like a real bourgeois. Yet an artist of the first rank, famous indeed, one understands. One can believe it, for his work is superb. At the first glance it can be told what it represents, almost like a photograph in colours."

"But what made you think I was an artist?" Bobby insisted. "I'm not famous by any means, and you haven't seen any of my work, though I hope you will let me show you some presently."

"That indeed will be a privilege I shall value," declared Eudes, "and for the rest, Monsieur, you must make allowances. These are troubled times. Spies. Refugees. Agitators. Conspirators. The police smell a plot everywhere. Before the ink was dry in the hotel register, our good Nicholas David was there, making his inquiries.”

“Who is he?” asked Bobby.

Eudes answered that David was the 'garde-champêtre'. Bobby knew the word but had only a vague idea of its significance. Eudes explained that a 'garde-champêtre' was an officer of the judicial police stationed in rural districts. He seemed indeed to be a kind of village watchman, acting chiefly on the instructions of the mayor, used also for making all necessary public announcements, available as well, apparently, for private individuals who wished to make anything known, a sale, the loss of a purse, the arrival of a circus or anything similar. Bobby decided that Nicholas David might be worth cultivating. Presumably he would know the details of the Polthwaite tragedy and it might be possible to get him to talk. Eudes said frowningly and abruptly:

“A tool of our government of bankers and capitalists.”

The phrase seemed to have slipped through the self-control Bobby felt Eudes habitually exercised. He had been cautious before when referring to politics but this time there had been an edge to his voice. Evidently anxious to cover up the words and tone he had used, Eudes went on talking about trivial matters. Bobby began to watch him more closely. A nervous, excitable man, Bobby thought, secretive as well. One of those perhaps who hide their thoughts behind a screen of words. Bobby remembered, too, how quietly, almost secretly, Eudes had come up. Was it possible, Bobby wondered, that behind Eudes's apparent frankness, his readiness to talk, the occasional questions he dropped with so casual an air, there was something more than the natural curiosity and interest it was only natural should be felt towards a stranger in this quiet and somewhat remote village where most likely any such appearance furnished matter for a week's gossip?

Eudes's flow of chatter slackened a little, and Bobby noticed a tall, unusually good-looking lad, black hair, black eyes, dark strongly-marked features with a nose like a great thrusting beak, coming striding up to the door of the hotel. He carried his head a little thrust forward, too, as if to emphasize the dominance latent in that great curved nose, and he had about him an angry and frowning air. He gave them a quick look as he passed, exchanged a half-hostile, half-hesitating salute with Eudes and passed on. A girl came to the door of the hotel as if she had been waiting for him. Bobby had not seen her before and wondered if she were one of the staff. She was dressed simply and wore no hat. Without being strikingly handsome, she had pleasant, well-formed, somewhat large features, with eyes of clear grey below a broad, smooth forehead. Her hair caught Bobby's attention. It was twined in thick masses about her head and was of a rich dark brown that had somehow a reddish tinge to it, so that a stray beam of the setting sun caught in it lay there as if at home. But then Bobby saw that when she spoke to the new-comer, who had quickened his step on seeing her, they both looked at him, and that the young man's expression grew even more dark and angry than before. The girl laid a hand upon his arm and drew him within. They vanished from sight so, and Bobby said carelessly to his companion:

"Two good-looking youngsters. Who are they?"

"The girl is Mademoiselle Simone. Lucille Simone. She has come recently to live with her aunt, Madame Jules Simone. Madame keeps the little shop there." Eudes pointed down the street. "The young man is Charles Camion, the son of the proprietor of the hotel."

The name, Bobby remembered, of the suspected murderer of the unfortunate Miss Polthwaite!

"Oh, indeed," he said indifferently.

He had seen Monsieur and Madame Camion on his arrival, a smiling, comfortable, pudgy pair, like two well-fed, friendly spaniels. Difficult to believe they could have produced this haughty-looking off-spring with his eyes of an eagle and his step of a leopard.

"He hasn't too amiable an air," Bobby added after a pause. "Doesn't he like the hotel or is it just guests he disapproves of?"

"Ah, no, it is probably something else that has displeased him," Eudes answered. "He is perhaps too easily displeased but then he is young. He will change all that presently."

He shrugged his shoulders and got up to go, saying something as he did so about preparing lessons. Bobby asked if he might accompany him part of the way and Eudes expressed his pleasure at the suggestion and added a compliment about the quality of Bobby's French. He wished, he said, he could speak English, but not a word did he know of that admirable language, the language of Shakespeare and George Eliot, a collocation of names that slightly staggered Bobby who had not known before how much George Eliot was still admired and remembered in France. They walked together, the schoolmaster with a word to everyone they met, and a little outside the village passed a field where men were still at work, late as it was. Eudes stopped and pointed to one of the workers whom Bobby had already remarked for his different dress and from the fact that even a glance showed he was having some difficulty in keeping up with the others.

"Our curé," Eudes said, making no effort this time to disguise the contempt and dislike in his voice. "Monsieur, the Curé Georges Granges. He has here a fat living, with his regular salary from the bishop, his fees for the masses fools pay him to say, the christenings, the marriages and the rest of all that flummery. It is well known, too, that he has his little investments, his income in addition. And yet he hires himself out to work in the harvest field where any pair of hands is welcome. A scandal, though the Church takes no notice. Ashamed of it, they admit over there at the diocese headquarters, but they do nothing. Even they understand that a miser who would shave an egg for what he could get from it, does their precious Church little credit."

"I gather you are no great lover of the Church," Bobby observed.

"It is," said the schoolmaster firmly, "the eternal enemy of the people. Remember Voltaire. Wipe out the Infamy! How wise. How true. How necessary. Yet the task has not yet been accomplished. Why? Because," said Eudes, still more firmly and without giving Bobby any chance to answer, "because we have been too high-minded, too scrupulous, too honest to fight the Church with her own weapon."

"What is that?"

"Money," declared Eudes, and for once he forgot to hide those fierce and eager eyes of his and let them blaze with fanatic fervour from behind their heavy, slightly swollen lids, "and it is money we need—money wherewith to establish a journal of liberty and enlightenment. Oh, I know there are those published in Paris, but here in the Auvergne we do not think so much of the Paris gentlemen, we have our own ideas. Let me have money to establish here a journal of the Auvergne for the Auvergnats and very soon you will see the Church upon the run." He paused and apparently recollected himself, looking at Bobby a little uneasily. He went on: "But I am taking it for granted that you do not believe? You are English. You are an artist. In England the Church has not such power as here. And artists—artists are at least free. We others—no." He came to a standstill before the gate of a small and pleasant cottage in a well-kept little garden. It contained an arbour with a table and bench, shaded by a freely-growing vine. With a gesture towards it, Eudes said: "You will enter? You will drink a glass of wine with me?"

The invitation was given with a touch of hesitation and Bobby guessed that Eudes was feeling a little nervous at having spoken so freely to a stranger. On the excuse that he would like to continue his walk before returning to the hotel for bed, Bobby declined the invitation. He bade his new friend good night and then asked, pointing in front and a little to the right:

"Isn't that an old mill over there? I suppose it isn't used now?"

"Oh, the Pépin mill," Eudes answered. "No, it is long since it was used as a mill. Now it is used for summer visitors. The Père Pépin to whom it belongs had it restored and fitted up, and every year he lets it in the holiday season. At present there are two of your compatriots there—a Monsieur and Madame Williams. Very often our little village has had the privilege of welcoming English visitors. Even up there—" Eudes pointed upwards to the bare, desolate expanse of hill and scrub that lay to the north towards Clermont, and, as he did so, a light shone out suddenly, high up on the slope of the hill. There, he said, "the beacon. When our good peasants see it, they cross themselves. Amusing?"

"Why? what is it?"

"Another of the black army, another of the flock of crows," Eudes explained darkly. "But that one up there, he has perhaps some glimmering of enlightenment growing in him. Possibly it comes from his English blood." Seeing that Bobby looked puzzled, Eudes went on: "It is a priest who lives there, the Abbé Taylour. For a year, nearly a year, he came late in the autumn, he has been there, by himself, in a hut he has rented. It is said that he is under excommunication. That, one does not know, but it is seldom he comes to the village and never to mass. It is true his hut is more than three miles from the church. One says, too, that he is an Englishman, but it seems he has his papers, for our good David went up to investigate." Eudes smiled gently. "It is an experience he does not talk of. But since a boy of the village was lost on the hill—he was dying when they found him, he had been lost three days, and to be lost up there, it is as dangerous as to be lost in the desert or on a raft at sea—the Abbé Taylour hangs out always that lamp at night we see from here." Eudes bade Bobby good night again and entered the cottage, and Bobby walked slowly on, his eyes lifted towards the lamp upon the distant, bare hillside that shone out so plainly now the evening shadows had fallen and night had come.

CHAPTER III
BLIND BEGGAR

From the spot where Bobby had left the Citry-sur-l'eau schoolmaster it had seemed as if the Pépin Mill, the scene of the Polthwaite tragedy, stood not far from the road, between it and the stream that ran the length of the valley. In actual fact, as a result of bends both in the road and in the course of the stream, the mill stood on the farther bank, about a quarter of a mile from both it and the road which here nearly met each other. A rough track, little used apparently, so rough indeed as hardly to deserve the name even of path, branched off nearly at right angles from the road, crossed the little stream here only a foot or two deep by a somewhat unsteady plank bridge, and went on to the mill. As the bridge would clearly not carry wheeled traffic, Bobby supposed there must be other means of access. In this he was wrong. The mill had not been used as a mill for at least a century and had been nearly a ruin before its present owner had had the idea of fitting it up to be let to visitors in the holiday season. In former days there had probably been a more substantial bridge, or another road now ploughed up and cultivated, but to-day everything destined for delivery at the mill had to be carried across by hand.

The mill itself was surrounded by trees. A windscreen of poplars sheltered it from the current of wind that often blew down the valley through a gap in the hills to the south-west and that in times past had been the reason for the selection of this site. North of the building again were more trees, chiefly chestnuts and oaks, and to the east lay an orchard, though one that did not look as though it had ever been very fruitful. Through a gap in this sheltering circle of trees, Bobby, from where he stood, had a clear view of the mill. He could see there was a light, so the tenants were evidently at home.

A little strange, he thought, that the mill had been occupied so soon and by English people. Generally there is a tendency to avoid the scene of a recent tragedy. It put an end anyhow to the idea Lady Markham had suggested that he should rent the mill himself. Unless, of course, Mr. and Mrs. Williams were only making a very brief stay. He found himself wondering who they might be as he walked slowly across the rickety little plank bridge. Nearer the mill he halted in the shadow of some trees. He wondered if some time he might venture to call. They were English and visitors, like himself, and he could make the excuse that he wished to sketch the mill. All the time the thought was running in his mind as he stood there watching this aloof and solitary building, half hidden in its encircling trees, where an old woman had met a death still unexplained, that there was something strange in this prompt appearance on the scene of other English people.

Something doubtful, too, and menacing in the long, heavy shadows that lay all around, in the silence and the solitude, as though the mill stood there in the circle of its trees withdrawn and apart from the common healthy intercourse of everyday life, as though it lurked and crouched there in the night for purposes hidden from the day.

He was growing fanciful, he told himself, and then he heard footsteps, firm and confident steps, as of one who knew the way and his purpose and his destination. Bobby drew back into the shadows further still. He did not wish his interest in the mill to be remarked. The footsteps drew nearer. A tall and bulky form became dimly visible. Bobby made out that it was a man, walking fast and swinging a stick in his hand. He aimed blows at the shrubs and plants he passed as though to strike them down gave him a certain pleasure. He swung by at the same brisk pace without noticing Bobby and went on towards the mill. The Mr. Williams who was the new tenant, Bobby supposed, and then he became aware of another figure slipping by, stooping and silent, following the first.

So silently this second figure flitted by, so softly and so quietly, one shadow among others, that Bobby almost doubted if he had really seen it, or if his imagination had not betrayed him. Yet he knew it had not, and he wondered uneasily what this might mean, this silent pursuit through the night.

He wondered, too, whether to wait developments or to take action of some kind. He made up his mind to wait the return of the unknown watcher and then to speak to him. He would say he had strayed from the road and inquire what was the best way back to the village and his hotel.

There came the sound of a door shutting, banged to with unnecessary noise. Nothing silent about Mr. Williams, apparently. Presumably, he had reached the mill and entered and banged the door behind him. Bobby emerged from his shelter and moved cautiously forward, almost unconsciously treading as softly as he could. Abruptly a shot rang out. Bobby began to run. He heard shouting. The light in the mill went out. Someone was running towards him. He called:

"Who's that? Who fired? What's up?"

Instinctively he spoke in English. Whoever it was running towards him swerved quickly and fled away among the trees. The door of the mill opened and from a lamp apparently re-lighted a long beam shot out to illumine the darkness. No one appeared. There was only the open door and the light streaming out. Bobby began to run after the fugitive who had disappeared among the trees. But now he was invisible, swallowed up in the darkness, hidden by the trees. Bobby could hear him running and tried to follow but soon gave up the chase as hopeless. He stood still and heard a splashing that told him his quarry had crossed the stream. Bobby turned and went back towards the mill from which no one had yet emerged though the door still hung open and the beam of light from it still poured into the night. Anyhow, he now had an excuse for presenting himself. He supposed the inmates thought it safer to stay inside since they had not even yet shown themselves. There came a crash of falling glass as from a broken window. Curious, he thought. Why should a window be broken now, long after the intruder had disappeared in such haste? Was it possible that someone in panic had broken a window to escape by? Or was some-thing else happening?

He became aware of a faint movement in the night behind him. He stopped and looked back. He saw nothing, he heard nothing. Yet once again when he moved forward he was aware of that same faint and cautious rustling behind. He stood still and even walked back a step or two. It was all very quiet and still, and stare and peer as he might he could see nothing. A rabbit, perhaps, he thought, if, that is, there were rabbits in the Auvergne, a point on which he was by no means certain. Or it might be the harmless and domestic cat. Only he did not think so. Without quite knowing why he felt there had been something menacing, something hostile, in that stealthy whispering sound he thought that he had heard behind him. It was as though he knew intuitively there was an evil presence lurking there, waiting chance and opportunity to do ill. Almost against his will, he called out:

"Who is there? Who is it?" and then, remembering, he repeated the words in French.

No answer came. Again he walked back a few steps in the direction whence that small and secret rustling had seemed to come. Only a few bushes grew there, hardly enough to give cover to a man. To a boy perhaps but scarcely to a man. He stumbled over one of the bushes in the darkness and then gave it up. Search at night is little use. He walked on briskly towards the mill, trying to throw off the impression he was still aware of that there was something small and secret and evil that followed him. He reached the mill and knocked.

No one came. He could see plainly into the interior. The door admitted directly into a large room, occupying about two-thirds of the ground floor. It was sparsely and not too comfortably furnished. There was a second door, admitting, apparently, to premises behind and to the stairs. Of the two windows one was broken, presumably by a stone thrown from outside, since pieces of glass together with a small jagged pebble, lay on the floor. Why, Bobby wondered, had the stone been thrown after the shot and who had thrown it? Evidently not the fugitive he had attempted to pursue, since whoever that might be was in full flight in the opposite direction when the tinkle of the falling glass had become audible. A little odd, he thought.

He knocked again. The door at the back opened. He had a brief glimpse of a kitchen as a tall, heavily-built man came through. Bobby decided at the first glance that he did not much like the appearance of this new-comer. His features were coarse and heavy, his eyes small and closely set under heavy brows meeting above the squat insensitive nose in a thick straight line that looked as if it had been ruled beneath the low, sloping forehead. The mouth was large and hung a little open, showing broken and discoloured teeth. Although he was clean shaven, except for a heavy straggling moustache, his beard showed already dark beneath his skin, giving an unfair impression that he did not wash very carefully. He did not speak but looked scowlingly at Bobby, and he still held in his hand a heavy stick, the one, Bobby supposed, with which he had amused himself by striking at the plants and flowers he passed. Bobby said:

"Is anything the matter? I heard a shot?"

He spoke in English and the other answered in the same language:

"Shot? What shot? There's been no shot here."

"I heard one," Bobby said, wondering what might be the meaning of this denial. "I heard it plainly."

"Well, we didn't," the other repeated. He turned to the door he had just come through and opened it and shouted: "Ma, did you hear any shooting?" He turned back and saw Bobby looking at the broken window. "Someone's just chucked a stone through there," he said. "That'll be what you heard. One of the village boys. I caught some of them prowling round the other night and chased them off and I expect they're getting their own back."

A small elderly woman sidled nervously into the room.

"What is it, Joe?" she asked. "Supper will be spoilt. Is it those boys again?"

"Gentleman here says he heard a shot. You didn't hear anything, did you? I mean, except the window smashing."

"Oh, no, Joe," she answered, blinking first at him and then at Bobby. She produced spectacles and put them on as if to see Bobby more clearly. "What sort of shot does the gentleman mean?" she asked.

The man guffawed at this.

"Just a shot," he said. "You know—bang! Like that."

"Oh," she said doubtfully.

She was pale, thin, elderly, with a wisp of grey hair lying across her forehead. She wore a loose, not very clean overall and she still held a large kitchen spoon in one hand. She blinked at Bobby from behind the spectacles she had now adjusted and said again:

"I didn't hear anything, Joe. Nothing at all."

"No more did I," Joe said aggressively. "No shot I mean. There wasn't one."

Bobby was quite certain they were lying and he wondered why. The little nervous woman sidled away back to the kitchen, though first with a timid, deprecatory glance at her companion as if to ask his permission.

"I'm sorry," Bobby said. "I was certainly under the impression it was a shot I heard. Apparently I was mistaken."

"That's right," the other grunted. "Something else it was."

No use persisting, Bobby told himself, in the face of these deliberate denials. He said:

"Oh, well, it's all right then. Interesting old place you have here. My name's Owen, by the way. I suppose you are Mr. Williams. I heard your name mentioned in the village. I only got here to-day. I'm staying at the hotel. I'm on a sketching tour. I'm looking out for good bits to do. I wonder if you and Mrs. Williams would mind my having a try here. The mill would make rather a jolly little sketch, I think, if I got it right."

Williams looked slightly taken aback at this request. It seemed as if he did not quite know what to say, and Bobby noticed that he glanced at the door behind him as if wishing to appeal to his wife. To prevent any refusal getting uttered, Bobby went on quickly:

"I'll be off now. Sorry to have disturbed you. Too bad about that window. Kids want talking to. I'll look in some other time if I may. Good night. Jolly to meet English people. Good night again."

Without giving Williams any chance to reply Bobby waved a hand and walked briskly away. He did not look back but he was sure that Williams had come to the door and was standing there, watching him go, and he thought that Mrs. Williams, too, still firmly clasping that large kitchen spoon, was watching meekly from behind her husband's bulky form.

"A queer couple," Bobby said to himself as he walked away. "Don't like 'em myself. Don't think they like me, either. What are they up to? Are they up to anything? Why did they lie about that shot? They can't have helped hearing it. The man looked scared but she didn't, only nervous of hubby as if he bullied her. Perhaps she really didn't hear anything."

The door of the mill closed, closed with a bang. The light that had poured through it was shut off. On a sudden impulse Bobby crouched down and waited. Nothing happened. The silence of the night lay unbroken around and he heard no more of the small secret rustling that before had seemed to follow him. He waited still and then, sure no attempt was being made to watch him, got to his feet and walked on. He was not quite certain of his direction now. Anyhow, he must keep the mill behind him and then he would come to the stream, even if he missed the bridge. He hoped he would find it, though, he did not want to have to wade the stream as had done the unknown fugitive. He noticed an erection on his right and saw that it was a framework above a well; the well, presumably, in which Miss Polthwaite's body had been found.

He went nearer and his thoughts were dark and heavy as the night around. There came a vision to his mind of a woman creeping out on such a still, black night as this to end her life by one desperate, downward plunge. He stooped and lifted the cover by which the mouth of the well was closed. It was heavy and he had to use both hands. There was a small protective wall around and a frame above from which rope and bucket could be let down for drawing water. No one could possibly have fallen in by accident, so small was the aperture and so well protected. He peered down into the blackness he had uncovered. Straight, damp walls of brick and far below a blackness and a void. Difficult to imagine any one deliberately ending life in such a way, by leaping down into that dreadful and attentive darkness. He found himself shuddering at the thought, and now he seemed to have a vision more horrid still, that of an unconscious body, the helpless unconscious body of a woman carried here and thrust down, down into that pit of darkness. He seemed to hear the sullen splash echoing slowly upwards, to see figures slinking hurriedly away. Or, perhaps, still more horrible, the victim had not been unconscious but had known her fate, had sent upwards from the black pit a cry that none but murderers had heard.

Bobby replaced the cover. If it had been like that, then such a crime must not go unpunished, the cry that had issued from those sullen depths must yet be heard. For a sudden conviction had come into his mind that here cruel murder on an old and defenceless woman had been done and that the call had come to him to see that it did not pass unavenged.

"Please God," he said aloud and walked away.

He found himself trembling a little. That long look he had taken down the dark descent of the well to the sullen gleam of the water so far below, had moved him more profoundly than he knew. He came to the stream, he found the little rickety bridge that crossed it, he walked quickly to shake off the impression still sharp in his mind. He turned from the track he had been following into the main road and from the roadside came a low chuckle and a voice that said:

"This time it seems one is not in such a hurry."

"What's that? What? Who's there? What do you mean?" Bobby asked sharply.

He moved to the spot by the roadside whence the voice had seemed to come. He made out there was some one sitting there, huddled up so as to make form and feature indistinguishable. The voice had been that of a man, though, and it went on now:

"Not one of us others, I think, not of the Auvergne, not of France elsewhere. No, not German either. Russian perhaps? No, English, isn't it? A voice of a soldier, too, of one who knows how to command. An officer without doubt?"

"I am English but not a soldier," Bobby answered. "Do you mean some one went by just now?"

"Some one who ran," the voice answered, "who fled indeed, as if pursued, yet none followed after."

"Did you see who it was?" Bobby asked eagerly.

"I saw nothing," came the reply. "Who ever it was, he passed so close I could have touched him. But I saw nothing."

"You must have," Bobby said sternly. "It's dark, but if he passed as close as that, you must have seen something."

From the huddled form by the roadside came another weird chuckle but no other response.

"You must have seen something," Bobby insisted.

"But no, monsieur, no," the other replied. "No, for I am blind, I who speak, I, the Père Trouché, the blind beggar of Citry-sur-l'eau." Changing his tone to a professional whine, he added: "Of your charity, sir, of your charity, and God will reward you."

CHAPTER IV
THE BLACK VIRGIN

Bobby gave the old man a small coin and passed on. He had noticed before a café that stood nearly in the centre of the village, not far from his hotel. Late as was the hour, it seemed to have plenty of customers still, and in pursuance of his plan to make himself as friendly and familiar with the local inhabitants as possible, Bobby went in and took a seat at a vacant table.

His entry was followed by a kind of general pause and break in all the busy noise and chatter that had been going on. A game of dominoes over which excited shouting had been till now continuous came to a standstill. A furious discussion on market prices ceased abruptly. A roaring argument on something that M. le Maire had either done or not done, sank into whispers. All eyes were turned in Bobby's direction as a stout man in an apron, apparently the 'patron', proprietor of the café, came bustling up.

Bobby began to ask him about the merits of the local 'cru'. He was aware that almost everywhere in France there is a local wine of distinctive nature, not always of the best quality, perhaps, but often well worth getting acquainted with and at any rate always moderate in price. As it happened the proprietor had an interest in the vineyard from which that of Citry-sur-l'eau came, and he waxed enthusiastic in its praise. Bobby listened gravely, pleased to have found a subject on which he guessed it would always be easy to start a conversation, and yet still acutely conscious of the fact that he remained the centre of attention, to a degree far beyond anything that natural curiosity might account for. He had the impression that there was not only curiosity but an element of hostility and doubt he did not understand.

"They are suspicious," he thought. "What of? Can Miss Polthwaite's murder have been a communal affair and are they all guilty and afraid together?"

He dismissed the suggestion as impossible, and he noticed more especially one tall, well-built young fellow, a small head set upon tremendous shoulders, who was seated at a table by himself and who was watching him even more intently than were the rest of the company. Bobby, still talking to the proprietor, or rather still listening to a discourse on the merits of the local 'cru', felt he would know this youngster again anywhere, if only from the contrast between his unusually large ears standing out nearly at right angles and the smallness of the rest of the rather indeterminate features of his small round face. It was as if Nature, in forming him, had forgotten his ears, and then, aware at the last moment of this oversight, had snatched a pair belonging to some one else, twice the appropriate size, and hurriedly stuck them on. Bobby wondered why this youngster was watching him so closely, with an hostility and a suspicion, too, even more marked. The question of the local 'cru' having been settled by now he said to the proprietor who had talked himself into an excellent humour:

"Who is that youngster sitting there by himself? Is he a visitor here, too?"

The proprietor turned to stare.

"Henri Volny?" he said. "The young Volny? A stranger, my faith, no, his father owns the best farm in all the commune. But evidently he is in a bad temper to-night and when he is in a bad temper and wishes to sit alone—well, it is best so."

Evidently the young Volny guessed that they spoke of him. He looked angry, very angry indeed, and yet, Bobby thought, frightened, too. He got to his feet. The proprietor took sudden alarm and bustled away, muttering something about fetching the wine he had praised so abundantly. Volny began to move towards Bobby's table. Bobby took no notice. Producing a cigarette, he lighted it. He thought Volny was about to speak, but the young man seemed to change his mind and left the café. As he went by Bobby noticed that the boots he wore were quite clean, though those of every one in the place were thick with dirt and dust.

Bobby found himself wondering if that was because Volny had changed them after getting those he had worn before soaked through by wading across a running stream? The proprietor returned with the wine and Bobby said: "A fine, strong-looking young fellow, the young Volny. He had the air of an athlete."

"He is a boxer," the proprietor explained. "Renowned. He wished even to adopt it as a profession but his father forbade it. He was disappointed, but when one's father is rich, a farm, vineyards, property—well, he has a right to expect obedience, hasn't he?"

"Yes, indeed," agreed Bobby. "In such a case obedience is only prudence. I suppose, then, young Monsieur Volny doesn't often do much work in the fields himself?"

The proprietor stared.

"But why not?" he asked, "seeing the fields will one day be his own? All this day he has worked at the harvesting like two, like three, like—" said the proprietor, drawing a deep breath, "like four."

Fortunately at this moment he was called away, much to Bobby's relief, thus putting an end to an enumeration that seemed as if it might have gone on indefinitely. At any rate, it seemed fairly certain young Volny had changed his shoes, and was that because he had got them wet?

Thoughtfully Bobby sipped his wine, and, though he was no great judge, decided that it deserved at least a proportion of the praise given it by the patron. He observed, too, not without some relief, that the interest taken in him seemed to be lessening. The game of dominoes broke out once more into a spate of protest and argument. The discussion on market prices resumed its stormy way. The merits or de-merits, whichever it was, of Monsieur le Maire once more occupied the attention of the group by the window, all talking at once at the top of their voices. People drifted in and out. Bobby began to hope that his presence was now going to be accepted as normal. Fortunately he felt sure it would be easy to start conversations when he wished to do so, though it would be better, perhaps, not to try to-night. All he would have to do would be to get out his sketch book and begin to make a drawing of some one present. He knew from experience that that would soon result in his being the centre of an interested group. Then a little tact, the purchase of a bottle or two of wine for general consumption, would be enough to break down most barriers. He was wondering, however, whether to-night it would not be better just to drift away back to his hotel and to bed, when the door opened again and there came in that tall youth of the dark and haughty looks, the dominating nose, whom he had seen before and knew to be Charles Camion.

The effect was curious. Of the entry or the exit of no one else, save of Bobby himself, had any notice been taken except for a few conventional shouts of greeting or farewell. But now with this young Camion's appearance, there seemed a sudden change in the general atmosphere of the room. It was not the silence of curiosity and doubt that had greeted Bobby's appearance. The game of dominoes continued, but quietly. The production of a double six produced not a murmur, went almost unremarked. The discussion on market prices continued, but in whispers. The group by the window seemed suddenly to lose interest in the crimes or the virtues, whichever it was, of their mayor. One or two of those at other tables got up and sidled out, and Bobby observed that one man, at least, hurriedly crossed himself as he went. Yet whereas Bobby had been the centre of all eyes, at young Camion no one looked.

He went up to the zinc counter and ordered something and stood there, looking slowly round, and where his dark and proud glance rested, there showed at once uneasiness and doubt, and a shuffling of heavy, uncomfortable feet on the boarded floor.

One man joined Camion, and apparently, though Bobby could not hear what was said, made some sort of advance. The rest of the company seemed to think this was a daring thing to do. Camion took not the least notice and the other slunk away. The game of dominoes broke up. The market discussion died into silence. Yet there seemed no hostility. One or two as they were going even shouted a good night to Camion but seemed to take care to do so from the safety of the door. Bobby could not help thinking that it was all a little like what he had seen happen in certain disreputable haunts in London, when colleagues of his put in an unexpected appearance. Yet it was not quite like that either. All that seemed clear was that in some way young Camion had been set apart, that there was about him something of which they stood in awe, that they dreaded, and yet that invested him with a kind of awful fascination.

Camion himself did not speak. He stood there, his face dark and expressionless, and yet Bobby watching him intently noticed signs of nervousness, of tension. He was only too plainly exercising a strong self-restraint and Bobby found himself wondering what would happen if it broke down. He felt certain, too, that behind Camion's air of pride and aloof indifference there was strong emotion, an even stronger resentment.

People were beginning to drift away now. It was late, certainly, but all the same there was a subtle air of relief about them as they

slipped off, as though they felt safer in departing. Bobby heard
Camion say abruptly to the man behind the zinc counter:

"Has Volny been here?"

"He was here," the other answered, "but he went a little while
ago. That was before you came in."

This last sentence had evidently been added by way of excuse
or reassurance and Bobby thought that Camion winced as if he
realized the underlying implication.

"Then I'll go, too," he said, "or there'll be no one left. I only
came to speak to Volny about to-morrow, so don't be afraid."

"But why? What for? Afraid of what?" asked the patron from
behind, where he was assiduously polishing glasses.

"Afraid that I should come again," Camion answered very
bitterly. "Heap of fools," Bobby heard him mutter as he turned
and left the café.

"The poor lad, now he does not sleep well," said some one
sitting at a table near.

"Who? That young man?" Bobby asked, turning to the speaker.
"I thought it was only in the town that one did not sleep, not you
who live in the country."

"In the country also there are those who do not sleep well," the
other answered and got up and went away.

Bobby followed him soon, the prospect of bed not unwelcome,
for the day had been long and tiring.

It seemed to him plain that in this apparently quiet and
normal little village there were many currents and cross-currents
at work, of which some at least, it was only reasonable to
conclude, resulted from the Polthwaite tragedy. Had they also
anything to do, he wondered, with the missing Polthwaite
diamonds?

Once in bed he slept soundly, untroubled by the problem he
had come here to try to solve. In the morning after coffee and a
roll he went out for a stroll and on the pretext of buying some
picture postcards he entered the little shop Eudes had pointed out
as kept by an aunt of the girl, Lucille Simone. An old lady
appeared. Bobby lingered over his choice. The old lady, apparently
bored, disappeared, and Lucille came instead. Bobby began to ask

questions about the cards and the localities shown. Lucille answered readily enough, but again Bobby had that feeling that he was being watched with suspicion. He thought it time to try to find out the cause. He said abruptly:

"Have you one of that old mill I noticed last night?

"No, monsieur," she answered and it was plain that the question had made her uneasy.

"Is that because of the murder there?" he asked.

"Yes, monsieur," she answered in a low voice.

"But that was months ago," Bobby said.

"It is not forgotten, it will never be forgotten," she answered and in her voice there was a deep and strange passion.

Bobby reflected that though officially Miss Polthwaite's death had been put down as suicide, this girl made no comment on his use of the word murder, 'assassination' he had called it in the French phrase he had used. He said gravely:

"A terrible thing. An old defenceless woman so barbarously, so cruelly killed. Such a thing has never been heard of before in the village?"

"Never," she replied with the same deep passion and emotion in her voice.

Bobby saw that she was twisting her hands together as in some fierce effort of control. She was pale to the lips, too. Bobby said:

"It has never been known who was guilty?"

She made no answer but her small teeth began to close upon her lower lip so that a drop of blood showed. Bobby felt he could question her no more. He began to pay for the postcards he had chosen. When he had done so, he said, and it was in a way in self-defence that he spoke:

"Such a crime should not go unpunished.'"

"Ah, my God," she breathed, "no, that could not be."

She turned and almost ran out of the shop, to hide her tears, Bobby felt sure. The old lady he had seen before came in. She looked at Bobby very indignantly but said nothing. Bobby bade her a polite farewell.

"I shall come back for some more," he told her cheerfully and she made no comment, though he was sure she would have liked to say they had no wish to see him again.

He felt convinced that Lucille Simone either knew or guessed something. He wondered if, perhaps, she had been in some way an accomplice in the commission of the crime. He did not much like to think it of those clear eyes beneath that tranquil brow, but he had seen enough of life to know that fair without is no proof of fair within. Evil itself can put on at times an air of majesty, an aspect of beauty. He walked on towards the church. It stood a little distance outside the village. Close by it was the presbytery, a modest little dwelling standing in a small garden given over entirely to vegetables which, however, did not seem to grow well, since the church had been built on rising ground, on land that was stony and sterile. The garden had, in fact, been made almost entirely by soil carried up in baskets from the foot of the hill, but it was a labour of Sisyphus, for owing to the steepness of the slope of the land here and to the exposed position, the wind was continually blowing away the soil, the rain perpetually washing from it all elements of fertility. Both the house and the church, Bobby noticed, were badly in need of paint and repair.

The church was an old building, but architecturally it was of small interest. At the time of the Revolution it had been partially burnt and the interior entirely cleared. Then it had been roughly restored, used for a time as a stable, and subsequently transformed into a Temple of Reason. Later, it had been returned to the Church. It contained, however, one of those Black Virgins, for which Auvergne is notable. Bobby was examining this image with much interest when a priest came out of the vestry where he had gone to disrobe after celebrating a mass.

It was the curé Bobby had seen the night before working in the harvest field. He was a thin, emaciated man of middle age, with hollow cheeks and deep sunken eyes. His hair was almost white, the long soutane he wore was shabby and patched, his boots looked as if they had been taken from a scarecrow in the field. Not in any way fit, to judge from his appearance, for the heavy toil of the harvest field, and Bobby noticed with disfavour that the grime inseparable from work in the fields, had been only very imperfectly removed from his face and hands. Eudes had described him as a miser who lost no opportunity of picking up a few sous and Bobby thought that evidently he grudged spending them on soap and hot water.

At first he did not seem inclined to take any notice of Bobby's presence, except for the slightest possible movement of the head on seeing he was there, but, in pursuance of his determination to make himself as familiar as possible with the village background, Bobby stopped him and began to talk about the image of the Virgin. It stood by the altar, elevated on a tall wooden pedestal, before it a kind of shelf on which reposed an offering of faded flowers. A trail of grease that had dribbled down showed that candles burnt there occasionally, though there were none at the moment. The image itself, about three feet in height, was carved in wood, black oak, Bobby thought, though he was not sure, and he even wondered if it had been passed through fire. Of incredible antiquity, probably antedating Christianity itself, since quite possibly it represented some goddess of an earlier religion—for the mother and child, symbol and proof of the perpetual miracle of birth and of renewal, are objects of worship in many primitive creeds—it had been so battered through the long passage of the ages that now the face was hardly recognizable as human and the child might almost have passed for a bundle of faggots. But the reverence of the curé for it was plainly intense.

Not just at first did Bobby succeed in breaking down the curé's reserve. He did not, apparently, much want to talk about the image to a stranger who was probably a heretic or worse. Even after he had begun to answer Bobby's questions he still seemed uneasy, giving Bobby odd, sidelong questioning glances, as if wondering what was behind his questions and what he really wanted. He kept, too, putting up a hand to fidget with the dried-up flowers on the shelf at the foot of the image, re-arranging them and pushing them further back, till Bobby began to wonder if he were under suspicion of harbouring some ill design, perhaps of wanting to run away either with the flowers or the image.

Gradually, however, the good man appeared to forget whatever it was that was troubling him. He became more animated, and those deep-set, sunken eyes of his began to brighten and glow. It seemed the image was one that once had enjoyed a widespread fame. In the early middle ages the Black Virgin of Citry-sur-l'eau had drawn pilgrims from all over Europe.

"Even, monsieur," said the curé, "even from your own country which then, of course, was still a faithful daughter of the Church, before you others, English, ceased to believe."

Even in the time of Louis XIV, the Virgin of Citry-sur-l'eau had shown her power by miraculously converting on his deathbed a rather specially wicked nobleman of Auvergne, famous always for having more wicked lords to the square mile than any other province of France. But after that there had been few manifestations, owing, the curé explained earnestly, to the hardness of heart prevalent in the district. Then had come the Revolution and naturally the Black Virgin of Citry had lost power to grant petitions no longer addressed to her. Her image, once so revered, had even been thrown out of the church. Fortunately it had not been chopped up for firewood or burnt in a bonfire as had happened to other images of almost equal sanctity and fame in that dreadful time. It had been pushed away in an outhouse. It had lain there for long years. One did not know what indignities it had not suffered. The story, the almost incredible story, was that finally it had been identified in a stable, as one of the posts supporting a manger. It had been rescued and replaced in the church just before the Franco-Prussian war. Unfortunately the villagers had been much dis-appointed, when, in spite of all prayers and petitions offered, not only had there been failure to stop the advance of the enemy but the men from the village at the war had suffered with unusual severity, the company to which most of them belonged having been annihilated.

"As if," said the curé indignantly, "after so many years of neglect the Virgin of Citry-sur-l'eau could have been expected to manifest her powers the very first moment my misguided parishioners chose to appeal to her. Perhaps it was not even possible, perhaps the heavenly power needs a certain time, as it were, to concentrate itself, to form for itself that channel which must be aided by our prayers."

The disappointment of the people, however, had been vocal and profound. Such a pass had it come to now that many of the faithful, having vows to make or petitions to put forward, neglected their own Virgin and actually took themselves and their offerings to a neighbouring Black Virgin a few miles away and reputed to be of great efficacy and power.

By this time the curé was getting really excited. His words poured out in an indignant torrent, he hammered one fist into another, those hollow, famished-looking eyes of his blazed in his hungry face, he backed poor Bobby into a corner and thundered his denunciations at him.

Then he seemed to grow quieter.

"I do not deny," he said, "that grace may flow more abundantly through other Virgins at other shrines which have not been so long neglected, scorned, as here. But if my people repented and turned again, one would see a different state of things and once more the Black Virgin of Citry-sur-l'eau would show her powers."

He seemed to hesitate and then drew nearer Bobby. He almost whispered.

"I have a dream," he said. "It comes to me often. A great church built here, a shrine for our Virgin so magnificent all the country could not show the like, a shrine blazing with light, a perpetual adoration, a beacon of faith in this forgetful land. It would need much money, much, very much. But perhaps it may come, monsieur, perhaps some day that vision may be fulfilled, when there is the money."

He turned again to the image, and, putting up his hand, began once more to fidget with the flowers that lay on the shelf before the Virgin. He looked at Bobby uneasily.

"Monsieur will forgive me," he said. "I grow a little excited at times with the thought of what I might do if some day, soon perhaps, by chance, the money came; yes, no matter how it came, so that in the end it came."

Now he was gently shepherding Bobby out of the church as if he wished to see him safely away from the vicinity of the Virgin. Once outside he seemed relieved, muttered some words of excuse about affairs to see to, and hurried away. Bobby watched him go till he was out of sight. He never once looked back.

"Half cracked," Bobby muttered. "Queer place this altogether."

He went back into the church. He remembered the way the curé had fidgeted with the dried and fading flowers laid before the Virgin's image. There had been something furtive, something odd in his manner, in the way in which he had kept doing this, in the sidelong glances he had at the same time given Bobby. Probably it did not mean anything but Bobby had learnt to neglect no indication and so, back in the church and getting a chair to stand on, for the shelf before the Virgin was at some distance from the ground, he lifted the flowers. Nothing in them or about them to interest him, but standing on a chair as he was he could now look down on the shelf and he saw where on it, at the foot of the image, in a small crevice or crack in the wood, were five small stones he was able to recognize as uncut diamonds of probably ten or twenty pounds value each.

CHAPTER V
ARTISTIC COINCIDENCE

Bobby descended cautiously from his somewhat uncertain perch and seated himself on another of the rickety straw chairs that occupied in rows the body of the church.

He was a little tempted to take prompt possession of the diamonds in order to hand them over to some one in authority. But this was a foreign country in which he had no official standing whatever. He might well be asked what business it was of his what offerings were made to the statue of the Virgin. There might be some perfectly satisfactory explanation of their presence and though to him it seemed plain enough they must be some of those that had belonged to Miss Polthwaite, of that there was no proof. No identification possible of a few odd stones. Besides, if he took any such action an end would probably be put at once to any hope of the successful accomplishment of his mission. As for what had happened the previous night, it was evidently no good saying anything about an incident which would be at once denied. Bobby perceived ruefully that there are advantages in that subordination against which he had so often inwardly rebelled. At home he would simply have made a report to his superior officers and there his responsibility would have ended. Now he had to decide his course of action for himself.

The curé presumably knew all about the diamonds, who had given them, and why. But that knowledge might have come to him under the seal of confession. Or he might know no more than that the offering had been made. Possibly he did not even realize their value; though the uneasiness he had shown, and that had betrayed to Bobby the presence of something of interest on the shelf at the Virgin's feet, suggested that of that at least he was well aware. Bobby wondered if Miss Polthwaite's assassin could have made the offering with some superstitious idea of placating heaven by sharing the booty. If so, the curé might know his identity, but would he betray the secret?

A more disturbing thought came into Bobby's mind. Was it possible that this priest, with his fierce and sunken eyes, his fanaticism, his strange, burning looks, his dreams of building a great new church to the honour of the Virgin, his need and apparent expectation of money required to carry out his purpose, his evident unease and restlessness that suggested at any rate some degree of mental instability, was in fact in possession of the other missing diamonds, as well as of those that had apparently been offered before the image here? And if so, by what means, in what way, had that come about?

A vision rose before Bobby's eyes of those dark depths, of those straight and damp walls of brick, of the sullen gleam of the water below, of all that he had seen and shuddered at when he lifted the cover of the well by the Pépin Mill.

He tried to put the thought out of his mind, telling himself it was incredible, but none the less it remained there. Abruptly he found himself deciding he would accept it as a possibility to be kept in mind, and he decided, too, that, at any rate for the time being, he would keep his own counsel. That determination come to, he reflected that the light continental breakfast of coffee and rolls lacks the virtue of permanence, and that it was now nearly noon and time for luncheon.

He returned to the hotel accordingly and was soon enjoying an excellent meal, carefully balanced in flavour and substance. In addition to Bobby himself some ten or twelve others were present, some probably local notabilities, the 'big bonnets' of the village as the French say, but most apparently strangers and visitors. The service was presided over by young Camion, and Bobby was struck by the grave dignity with which the young man conducted affairs. Not the Ritz or the Savoy could have shown a more meticulous care in every detail. It was quite plain that Camion took his duties very seriously, as of one who respected himself in the task he was performing, a task to which he attributed all the importance that, after all, good food does possess in human economy. Especially good food, well cooked, and served with the accessories and refinements that make the difference between feeding and dining. Nor did he show any trace of that unpleasant and unnecessary obsequiousness sometimes shown in restaurants. His air of pride was as marked as ever, he dominated the hors-d'oeuvre, the soup, the other courses, a little like a general marshalling his forces. On any question of the choice of wine, he was specially firm.

"No, monsieur," Bobby heard him say to one man seated near, "that would not be suitable, that wine. This requires a—"

Bobby did not catch the name of the wine recommended, but the dictum was accepted meekly as from superior authority. Bobby was indeed quite relieved that his own choice, the local 'cru', was allowed to pass unchallenged. Evidently here dining was an art taken as seriously as the other arts by which man has learnt to express himself in his rise from barbarism to civilization.

All this interested Bobby, for it was new to him to see dining treated thus as an expression of human culture, but what interested him even more was that the some-what strained and uncomfortable attitude shown towards Camion in the café the night before was evident here also. There was a marked tendency to cast uneasy glances at him when his back was turned, to grow silent when he was near. It almost seemed indeed as if some of those Bobby had thought were strangers, had come simply to stare and whisper, and Bobby thought that Camion realized this and resented it bitterly, though his sense of professional duty prevented him from appearing to be aware of it.

Luncheon over, Bobby got out the sketch book with which he had provided himself as with other requisites appertaining to his assumed character of artist, and went out to seek some picturesque spot whereon to exercise his talents. The mill he had decided to leave for the present. Some day he might be glad of an excuse for calling there.

Soon he found a setting of rock and trees he thought not too far beyond the limit of his powers, and set to work accordingly, though, as he worked, his mind was occupied less with what he was doing than with the currents and cross-currents he seemed already to have discovered beneath the placid surface of village life.

It may have been to this absorption, because there is truth in those current theories of the unconscious which teach that all capacities are there, though on them the conscious will acts as a hampering and restraining check, that the result was due. In any case, when Bobby stopped thinking quite so much about the problems troubling him and turned more active attention to what he was doing, he found himself surprised by its excellence.

"Dear me," he said aloud, "I must be going to turn into a real artist."

What with his work and his thoughts the hours had slipped by and now it was time to think of dinner.

Over this meal, too, as over luncheon, Camion presided with the same effective and indeed remarkable mixture of quick competence and grave dignity. One felt that to him dinner was a rite and he the presiding priest. There were a good many more present than there had been in the middle of the day. Among them Bobby noticed a tall, bigly-built, imposing-looking man, wearing plus-fours and obviously English. His large, florid face in which his tiny nose and little twinkling eyes seemed lost, beamed with good humour, he expressed a loud appreciation of the dishes offered him and of the recommended wine, compliments Camion accepted as a tribute rightfully due. He even deigned to ask the stranger's opinion on some question of sauce or flavouring, and Bobby noticed that this new-comer's attitude to Camion had in it none of that half-frightened fascination others here seemed so often to show. Bobby noticed, too, that once or twice this new-comer glanced in his direction and he was not altogether surprised when the coffee stage was reached to see the stranger get to his feet and come across to him. In spite of his bulk he moved easily and lightly. Something of an athlete apparently. He said, speaking in English:

"Camion tells me you're an artist, too. Artists may know each other, mayn't they? especially when a coincidence brings them together in a foreign country. I'm Basil Shields. Very likely you don't know my stuff. In private hands, nearly all of it."

"I'm afraid I'm not as well up in art matters as I ought to be," Bobby admitted. "Do sit down, won't you?" Even had he not wished to, he would have been almost forced to give this invitation, since Shields was already drawing out a chair for himself. "But I do know your name anyhow." This was perfectly true, for he remembered Basil Shields was the name of the artist, to be near whom Miss Polthwaite had settled here and from whom she had been taking occasional informal lessons. "My name's Owen," Bobby continued. "I'm afraid as an artist you'll think me a bit of a fraud. I'm really only trying."

"Not bitten by any of the 'isms, I hope?" Shields asked genially. "I know I'm old-fashioned. Traditional. I'm the scorn of the impressionist and the wash pot of the cubists. As for the surrealists, they're just a little sorry for me. More than I am for them. I call them criminal. It's a base commercial point of view, I suppose, but I do sell two canvasses for every one the whole boiling of them get rid of. But perhaps you're bitten by that bug. If you are, I do apologize."

"No need," Bobby assured him. "I suppose I'm traditional as far as I'm anything."

"Let me have a look at what you've been doing, may I?" asked Shields, and Bobby, who had brought his portfolio down with him from a vague wish not to be separated from work with which he was so pleased, promptly produced the sketch made that afternoon.

Shields took it, raised his eyebrows, looked surprised, even a little relieved, Bobby thought.

"I know that spot," Shields said. "I've done it myself. You've a good eye for the right thing to spot it so quickly." Then he said, almost accusingly: "You've moved that tree."

"Well, yes," Bobby admitted. "I suppose I thought it tied up better there."

"So it does," agreed Shields. "Composes much better, catches the eye at once. Gives the whole thing more significance, unity. You've an eye for composition all right. Gad, it's quite a relief to find a young fellow doing good sound honest-to-goodness work instead of all this modern inner reality stuff." He looked at the sketch again. "Good work," he said briefly.

Bobby beamed. There had been times in his young life when he had dreamed of trying to earn his living by his pencil. Discovery that his eye for colour was defective and that though he had a distinct sense of form and a real ability to draw, his gifts even there were hardly outstanding, had persuaded him that he had small chance of ever being able to 'muscle in', as the Americans say, on an already much overcrowded profession. All the same, this warm appreciation of his afternoon's work by a professional and apparently unusually successful artist gave him a very warm and comforting interior glow.

Shields began to talk about himself. His work, it seemed, was not much appreciated in London. ('Paris won't look at it,' he said in parenthesis, 'and Berlin and Rome are washouts. No money, and if you did get any, you would have to leave it there.') But he had a very useful connection in New York among private friends. Made a baker's dozen of sales last year at an average of four hundred dollars each sale. Not so bad these days. Oh, journeyman's work, it might be called. He never claimed to be a genius, but his stuff gave him pleasure to do and apparently gave pleasure to the people who bought it. At any rate, he knew no other reason why they did buy. God knew it wasn't because it was fashionable. Bobby must come over to Barsac some time and have a look round his studio. He chuckled a good deal over this and admitted that such an invitation to the ordinary tourist sometimes meant a bid for a sale. ('Walk into my studio, said the artist to the tourist', explained Shields, still chuckling.) Well, a fellow had got to live. But a brother artist was safe. Artists didn't buy pictures, they painted 'em.

Bobby said how pleased he would be to accept the invitation and asked:

"Barsac? Is it near here?"

"Well, that depends," Shields answered. "It lies between here and Clermont, about fifteen miles as the crow flies, over there." He pointed north where the land rose into that tangle of hill and rock, ravine and crag, intermixed with long patches of scrub, which Bobby had remarked before. "But it takes three or four hours by train. You have to go round by Clermont and the connection is bad. By road, it is about four or five times as far as it would be direct. The road has to circle right round the Bornay Massif," and he nodded again towards the desolation to the north where the bleak savagery of the land bore witness still to the convulsions of long ago.

"If it's only fifteen miles direct, it would be almost as quick to walk, wouldn't it?" Bobby asked.

"I never heard of any one trying," Shields answered doubtfully. The elder Camion had come into the room now and Shields beckoned to him: "Monsieur Camion," he called, "I suppose one could get across the Bornay Massif on foot, couldn't one?"

The elder Camion came up and again Bobby thought how strange it was that this round, smiling, commonplace little man could have produced that youngster of the fierce and haughty mien who was his son. There was a distinct family likeness though. It was as though Nature had said: 'Just to show you, I'll take this humble, commonplace type, the very image of the "little man", and show how easily I can transform it into the type of the leader and the chieftain.' He looked faintly puzzled now, a familiar expression on his countenance, Bobby thought, and said: "But with what object, monsieur? Why should any one make such an attempt?"

"Well, if they did, would it be possible?"

"It might be done," the elder Camion agreed though somewhat hesitatingly. "It would be difficult, success would be quite a triumph. There is the great crevasse it would be necessary to cross. That alone would require help and ropes. Doubtless it could be accomplished, but hardly in a single day. And if one were alone and met with an accident, even slight, or got lost—finished," declared the hotel-keeper with emphasis. "But why should one try?" he asked and wandered away, evidently puzzled that so mad an idea should ever have occurred to any one.

"One of the village lads did get lost on the Massif a few months ago," Shields remarked. "He was still alive when they found him, but he died from the exposure."

"I heard about that," observed Bobby. "Some one up there always shows a light now after dark, doesn't he? A sort of guide?"

"That's right," said Shields. "Excommunicated priest—and they don't excommunicate priests for nothing. I wonder sometimes what that lantern is really shown for."

"You mean?" asked Bobby, startled.

"Did you know there was a murder here some months ago?" Shields countered.

"I think I've heard of it," Bobby said. "An English woman, wasn't it? A Miss Polthwaite?"

"That's right," Shields said again. "I knew her slightly—old friends in a way though we never got intimate. Fussy old girl but not a bad sort. I used to have to come over here to pay her a visit at times. Bit of a drag, I found it. She liked to play at being an artist and I gave her a few hints sometimes." He smiled faintly. "It was really I who told her about the Pépin Mill. I panicked a bit when I found she was looking for a place round my way so I headed her off here as I happened to know about the Pépin Mill. Had had a look at it myself but decided on Barsac instead. And I definitely didn't want her too near. She would have been on my doorstep all day and every day, wanting to know this and that. Makes me feel a bit responsible sometimes. I don't care about the idea that if I hadn't mentioned the Pépin Mill to her she might be alive still. I mentioned other places too, of course. I really wanted her further away if possible. There was a place at Vienne I thought would suit her down to the ground but she took a great fancy to the mill here. Picturesque sort of place, I know. But I hate to think I ever told her about it. Suicide they say. I wonder?"

"Do you think it's possible it was something else?" Bobby asked gravely.

"Yes, I do. She wasn't a rich woman really. Lived on a small annuity. Told me so herself. But the story got about that she had money. There's an old blind beggar goes about here and he spread the story. He's responsible for half the gossip that goes on and that's plenty."

"The Père Trouché?" Bobby asked.

"Oh, you've heard of him. Mischief-making old scamp. Ought to be drowned or something. He tells spicy bits about their neighbours to people and then he gets handouts. Kind of blackmail to keep his tongue quiet very often, I expect. Anyhow, the story got about that she had what they call a stocking here and next thing she is found at the bottom of the well. Very likely it's all right, but I don't like it. Nothing you can do, of course, but sometimes I lie awake at night and—well, wonder."

"The police?" Bobby asked.

"The French police are about the best in the world," Shields pronounced. "Scotland Yard." He made a slight gesture of contempt. "Dull. Routine. Red Tape. No imagination."

"I've heard that before. I expect it's true," agreed Bobby meekly.

"But even the French police can't do miracles," Shields continued. "They went into the whole thing very thoroughly. I will say that for them. Made up a procès-verbal a mile long and then turned it down with a 'non-lieu' as they call it. Questioned me about our being friends, and how, and why, and what for, and what did I know? which wasn't much. Grilled the young fellow here, young Camion, for half a day over at Clermont."

"Do they think he is guilty?"

Shields shrugged his shoulders.

"Impossible to say what they think, but anyhow there was nothing they could prove. The village still gets a kick out of thinking that perhaps it was him after all. Gives them a thrill to think they may have a murderer in their midst. People come out here just to look at him. Fascinated. Morbid, I suppose. Law-abiding sort of people, these, and murder's a new idea to them. They'll skin you to your last sou in honest bargaining but serious crime's practically unknown."

"Why was Camion suspected?"

"Well, for one thing, immediately after the murder, he visited the évêché—diocese headquarters, you know, where the bishop hangs out. Only a bishop can give absolution for murder and all the village was sure Camion went to confess the murder and get absolution. All rot, I expect. Anyhow he either didn't get absolution or he didn't get much of a penance, for he's been carrying on much the same ever since. But that visit to the bishop's place fairly damned him in the eyes of all the village."

"Was there anything else against him?"

"He was friendly with the old girl. He used to go there. She was trying to paint his portrait—awful bit of work. Naturally as he was often there pretty late, the village was quite sure she was his mistress."

"But wasn't she rather elderly?"

"Oh, yes. But they think she paid him. And they think he got so shocked and fed up he did her in."

Bobby blinked.

"Look here," he said. "Have I got this straight? The idea is she was his mistress though she was old enough to be his mother and after he had taken her money he killed her in an access of moral indignation?"

"A bit complicated," Shields grinned, "but that's about it."

"Sound's a bit topsy-turvy to me," said Bobby.

"Mind you," Shields said earnestly. "To my mind, it's all poppycock. Miss Polthwaite wasn't that sort. She took a fancy to the boy. He's good-looking enough, Lord knows, to take any old maid's fancy. I believe there was some question of her lending him money. She hinted as much to me. I told her not to be a fool. He has ambitions, that youngster. Means to be a great hotelier, a new Ritz. Dreams of the Camion as the leading hotel in every capital.

The Camion in New York, the Camion in London, the Camion in Paris, in Buenos Aires, in Rio de Janeiro, everywhere. And then politics, to put the world straight. Oh, quite a programme. If you can manage a big hotel, you can manage a country. He told me that once. Miss Polthwaite was to give him his big start. But it was all on the Up and Up—on her side. Sort of maternal instinct. The French don't go strong for maternal instinct between an elderly spinster and a handsome boy. Not their line of country. I don't know that it's mine either. Most likely the boy himself expected to pay in the only way he could. Well, there it is. The village half believes he was the murderer and more than half approves. Thinks she got what was coming to her. But they've the wind up, too, for fear he continues. I suppose that happens. You bring it off once and you think you can again. Why not?"

"Well, I hope whoever is guilty will be caught some day," Bobby said. "Not that it would do poor Miss Polthwaite much good."

"No," agreed Shields, "she's not interested. She was a fair age, anyhow. Nothing much to lose, only getting older and lonelier all the time. I daresay she was spared a lot." Perhaps thinking that this sounded callous, he added: "She was a good friend of mine; no one felt it more, what happened, I mean. No one." He shook his head. "Well, these things have to be," he said, "but I don't mind saying it shook me, shook me badly."

Bobby said sympathetically that it was no wonder, and then added:

"I thought of trying to do the Pépin Mill some time. I thought it ought to make rather a good sketch when I was by there last night."

"I've done it myself two or three times," Shields said. "One sunset piece I thought not bad. I'll show it you if you come over to my place some time. There are English people there now. Did you know?"

"Yes, I had a chat with them the other evening. Williams is the name, isn't it?"

Shields nodded. He appeared to hesitate. He leaned across the table and said in a confidential whisper:

"Scotland Yard."

Bobby gasped, for the moment thinking that his own identity had somehow become known.

"Scotland Yard," repeated Shields. "Williams, I mean. He's over here to see if he can find out anything about Miss Polthwaite's death."

"Oh," said Bobby feebly. "Oh—how interesting. Are you sure?"

"Oh, yes, he started asking questions and it came out. Keep it under your hat though."

"Of course," said Bobby, still more feebly.

Shields got to his feet.

"Well, I must be off," he said. "Glad to have met you. Quite a coincidence to run up against another English artist, especially one who isn't a cubist or a squarist or any other of the fashionable ists. Only mind you, don't run away with the idea that I'm an old stick-in-the-mud. Good work. That's my idea. Some of the Victorian stuff was pretty sticky, of course. But look at Holman Hunt now, or Millais. Take some beating still. I agree that Landseer or Gustave Doré were rather awful—I was looking at some of Doré's illustrations the other day. A pain in the neck, that's all you can say. What do you think?"

"I've hardly ever seen anything of Doré's," Bobby answered. "I've always thought that anyhow Landseer knew how to draw."

Shields was looking at his watch.

"I must be off," he repeated. "I'm popping round now to have a word or two with the schoolmaster chap here before I go. I got a bit pally with him when I used to run over to see poor old Miss Polthwaite. He's rather an intelligent chap. No time to lose or I'll be getting stranded at Clermont—the last train Barsac way leaves pretty early."

"Awkward if you miss it," Bobby suggested.

".Oh, if I do, I'll walk," Shield said cheerfully. "Shan't mind that, though. Fifteen miles and I shall enjoy every step. I like a walk at night sometimes, good for the eyes, too. Rests them and trains them at the same time till you can see in the dark nearly as well as by day. A little gift of mine I've cultivated. But when it comes to walking, the curé here has me dead beat. He's got quite a name for the way he marches up and down the roads, walks for miles and no one knows why, unless it's to say his prayers." Therewith he took his departure, leaving Bobby with much to think about.

Over on the hill-side, too, high above the village, shone out that distant light in which Shields seemed inclined to suspect some hidden, sinister significance.

CHAPTER VI

THE SOLITARY

Bobby's intention had been to spend the rest of the evening in the cafe he had visited before, in further pursuance of his plan of making himself as familiar and friendly with the villagers as possible.

His talk with Shields, however, had given him so much to think about, had seemed to make it so necessary to get some kind of order into the confused tangle of his ideas, that instead he went up to his room and sat there at the window, trying to sort out his impressions and to decide what to do next, whether he ought now to report to the authorities his discovery of the diamonds in the church or whether he should still preserve silence about that curious and somewhat disconcerting fact. Then, too, there was the troubling statement that Williams apparently claimed to be a Scotland Yard man.

Could it be, Bobby wondered, that Williams was a private detective employed by some one who knew of Miss Polthwaite's hidden hoard? If so, who was that employer? In that case he might really be a retired police officer. Retired Scotland Yard inspectors and superintendents sometimes take up private detective work. So sometimes do those who have not retired but been dismissed. In some such complication lay, it seemed to Bobby, a possible explanation both of the shot he had heard and of the denial by the Williamses that anything of the kind had happened. Or was this Scotland Yard claim entirely unfounded, and if so why was it made?

It was a clear and lovely night with a young moon near to setting and stars brilliant in the heavens above, numerous and bright as they seldom are in English skies. One or two constellations Bobby could name, and then on the distant hill-side he saw a twinkling, stationary light that he took to be the lantern hung out by the Abbé Taylour, the supposedly excommunicated priest of English birth or extraction, of whom Shields had spoken with so much doubt.

Suddenly Bobby made up his mind. He would take a walk up there and try to form his own judgment. Also he decided it would be a good plan to try to make friends with the Père Trouché, the blind beggar of Citry-sur-l'eau as he called himself. According to Shields he was general gossip-in-chief to the neighbourhood and probably—for adequate remuneration—would be willing enough to tell anything he knew.

These decisions come to, Bobby went to bed, slept soundly, and after a breakfast that seemed less tenuous now since his previous night's dinner was still more than a mere memory, he asked to be provided with a picnic lunch, procured his sketching materials, and sallied forth on what he hoped would be regarded as merely a search for fresh subjects for his pencil.

His way led him past the church. He entered. The little bare building was quite empty. Bobby went to where the black Virgin watched from her high pedestal as she had done through so many centuries, through so many changes. There were fresh flowers on the narrow shelf at her feet. But when Bobby got a chair and stood on it, balancing himself with difficulty, and looked, he saw that the diamonds were no longer there.

Presumably the curé had removed them. Why? Because he was suspicious? Suspicious of what? Of Bobby himself? Of theft? Or of—discovery?

Anyhow, it would be useless now to make to the authorities a report of the truth of which he could offer no proof. He went back to the door of the church. The curé was in the poor and meagre garden of the presbytery, searching through the scant foliage of some pea plants that looked too thin and of too feeble a growth to have produced any pods. However, the curé seemed to find some, for it was with quite a satisfied air that he returned to the house, carrying with him a small basket.

Bobby continued his way. It was still early, the air fresh and cool, and he found the climb up the hill-side pleasant and exhilarating. It was a steep ascent, and as he climbed beech and chestnut gave place to oak and fir, and then there were no more trees but only stunted shrubs and stretches of purple heather and yellow flowering gorse. He came to a bank where the wild thyme grew, and, remembering Shakespeare, decided it would be a good place to rest. The scent was strong and sweet; he thought how nice it would be if he had no other object than to sit here and try to transfer to canvas something of the loveliness of the valley at his feet, its rich and peaceful beauty so strange a contrast to the wild tangle of scrub and rock and ravine on which now his back was turned. But he could see quite plainly, too, the Pépin Mill, cut off by its barrier of chestnut and beech as if it hid behind them, and his face hardened as he thought of the deed done there, such a deed as even this fierce and hostile land had, he supposed, scarcely known before.

He got up and resumed his climb and came presently to a kind of plateau where were still visible what even his inexperienced eye could recognize as traces of ancient fortification. A little distance away, where the land began to rise again, but well sheltered by a high cliff behind, stood a small hut, built of the lava slabs, of which, too, were formed the walls of many of the houses in the village. A man of middle height, thin and gaunt, dressed like any peasant, was standing just outside, leaning on a staff and watching him intently. Skirting the edge of one of the mounds that told how here, too, men had sought for that security no arms or fortresses can give, but only a mutual good will, Bobby found a rough track that led towards the hut. He followed it, and when he was nearer called a cheerful greeting to the man at the door, adding some comment on the view. He spoke in English and explained: "They told me in the village you were English but they never told me it was quite such a stiff climb up here. Good thing I brought my lunch with me so I haven't got to hurry back. You are, monsieur, the Abbé Taylour, aren't you?"

"Yes," Taylour answered, speaking in English, too, though with a faint touch of French accent. "They told you more than my name in the village, I expect."

He had been standing quite close to the partly open door of the hut, with his back to it. He turned and closed it, making sure that the latch was secure. An ordinary garden chair of the hammock variety stood against the hut wall. The abbé took it down, opened it, placed it in position at a little distance and in the shade. Near by, between it and the door of the hut, was a rough block of lava. On this the abbé took his own seat. Bobby watched all this carefully, and wondered if it was fanciful to find a certain meaning or significance in these various movements. With a gesture Taylour invited Bobby to occupy the chair. Thanking him, Bobby complied. Taylour said: "I see you sketch. An artist perhaps? But I think it was not only to make sketches that you climbed up here."

"Well, partly for the view, and anyhow I've enjoyed the climb," Bobby answered.

"I suppose," Taylour continued, "they told you in the village I was excommunicated and in constant close communion with 'Le Vilain?'"

"'Le Vilain'?" Bobby repeated, puzzled.

"The devil," explained Taylour. "The good people about here think it more prudent not to mention him by name. Probably the idea is that if he heard himself spoken of, he might come along. An old superstition common in many forms. Neither tale is true I may explain. I have no more to do with 'Le Vilain' than most other people and I am not excommunicated. At least, if I am, I do not know it, and therefore, by canon law, I am not excommunicated. But I daresay such stories interested you a little?"

"Well, you see," Bobby answered slowly, wondering if all this meant that Taylour regarded his visit with suspicion and was trying to find out if anything lay behind it, "the fact is, I saw a light up here, and I asked about it."

"I hang it out each night," the abbé answered. "I pretend it is meant as a landmark and a guide. I call it the lighthouse of the Bornay Massif—the local name for this neighbourhood. In reality it is, I think, because I feel it a kind of link between myself and the world. But it is true one poor lad did get overtaken by darkness up here—he was looking for some strayed animal, I believe—and lost himself and died from fatigue and exposure. Perhaps if I had been showing my light he might have been saved. They found him not very far from here and a compatriot of yours, a Mr. Shields, who had helped in the search, remarked to me on the tragedy of the poor lad's dying so near the food and shelter I could have given him. So then I made up my mind it must not happen again and I hang up my light now every evening. Not that it is really much use. People don't wander about here at night. No object and no paths for that matter."

"Isn't Clermont just over there?" Bobby asked, pointing to where showed the great round summit of the Puy de Dôme. "Mightn't some one be trying a short cut?"

"No one could get to Clermont that way," answered Taylour smilingly. "Practically impossible. Of course, it's all been surveyed, but by parties properly equipped and supported. No one caught by himself out here at night would stand much chance."

"Well, I had thought of trying," Bobby said, "but if it's like that, I won't. It struck me as looking as if it would make a nice country walk, that's all."

The Abbé Taylour smiled.

"A nice country walk," he repeated. "A townsman's idea," he said. "You are a townsman, I expect? Yes. Ah, well, towns are one thing; and people who live in them and who think of the country as a place all made up of villas and gardens and cultivated fields, don't even dream of what the real country is like, the untamed country, where nature's savage still. But in England, I suppose, there's none left like that. You English conquer Nature as you conquer everything else."

"Do we?" Bobby asked. "I don't know that we feel much like conquerors these days."

He produced his lunch and without too much difficulty persuaded the abbé to share it. He had been provided with one of those small wooden casks in which the workingman of Auvergne carries his day's ration of wine, but in order to get an additional glass, the abbé had to get up and enter the hut to find one. Bobby noticed that he was again careful to close the door behind him, both entering and coming out. The wine, it was the local 'cru' unmixed with water and fairly strong, seemed to loosen the abbé's tongue and he was soon chatting freely, showing himself the possessor of an intelligent and cultivated mind. He told Bobby a good deal about the surrounding country and its history and its customs. He told Bobby, too, that the ancient fortifications, still to be traced on the plateau before them, were relics of a Gallic fortress stormed by the Romans during the war with Vercingetorix.

"You remember his statue in the Place de Jaude at Clermont?" Taylour asked. "He is the national hero in these parts. You would think it must always have been as peaceful and quiet here as it is now, but here, too, has been battle and slaughter, man slaying man and rejoicing in the act, cries of dreadful despair, of still more dreadful victory, all those things that God still permits upon the earth—if God there be," he added under his breath.

His quiet voice, for he had spoken without emotion, sank into silence. Bobby was silent too. He did not know what to say. After a pause, the abbé continued in the same quiet, almost indifferent manner:

"Sometimes at night I think I hear them still, those cries, those groans. It may be that when the human soul has fled in such anguish and such terror, the memory remains even in things that seem to us inanimate."

"If so, there can't be many spots in the world," Bobby said, "where such memories don't remain." He pointed towards the valley so far below. "There was another tragedy down there only a little while ago," he said. "An old, defenceless woman."

"Yes," agreed the abbé. "You are interested?"

"She was English," Bobby said. "Perhaps that doesn't matter. But she was old and weak and defenceless and alone. And that does matter. I do not much like to think of it—not even if it was suicide and still less if it was murder."

"You have been told that she was murdered?" Taylour asked.

"Well, hardly that. But there does seem a pretty strong suspicion that's what it was, even though the official idea is suicide. What do you think?"

Taylour shook his head.

"I know so little about it," he said after a pause. "I was ill at the time—an attack of fever. Luckily a good man who sometimes brings me my letters happened to find me and I am afraid got a bad scare. You see, I was delirious, and unluckily it appears I made some reference to the devil. He was quite persuaded the devil was there in proper person waiting to carry me off. Luckily, he talked about it down in the village and the doctor heard and very kindly came up to see for himself. The fever had left me by then but I was so weak I believe I might have died for sheer lack of strength to get my own food."

"It was certainly fortunate," Bobby agreed, and he could not help thinking that, whether consciously or unconsciously, the Abbé Taylour had provided himself with an alibi. If he were so ill and feeble as he said he had been, he could certainly have had no hand or part in the Polthwaite tragedy. But was his story true? Delirium is easily assumed. An ignorant peasant could as easily be scared. By the time the doctor arrived, the fever had gone, if it had ever existed. No need, therefore, to pretend the existence of symptoms the falsity of which a medical man might detect. The suggested alibi is always so much stronger than the one supposed to be impregnable and therefore challenging investigation. Bobby told himself that he did not much like either it or the apparently casual but possibly intended manner in which it had been put forward. He said: "I wonder if the truth will ever be known. You are English, too?" he added abruptly.

"Of English descent. My parents were English but I was born in France. I am a French citizen, I have done my army service. Then I entered the Church. You wonder why I live up here by myself, in such solitude?"

"Well," Bobby answered, "it's a grand view and lovely air and all that, but it does seem a bit out of the way."

"A typically British way of putting it," observed the other with a faint smile. "It is undoubtedly a bit out of the way. But I wanted peace and quiet, I wanted to be for a time alone with my own thoughts."

"I wonder how you manage for provisions?" Bobby remarked.

"I fetch what I need from the village or sometimes I arrange for it to be brought here. For water, there is a stream about a hundred metres away. At times I have visitors. Once or twice artists like yourself, seeking good subjects. Then it is known I am a priest and occasionally even I hear confessions. I cannot refuse, though I am afraid it vexes my good friend, the Abbé Granges."

"The curé of Citry-sur-l'eau?"

"Yes. You have met him? He is sure I am excommunicated. He is still more sure when he hears of his parishioners visiting me. It seems he has the name of being too severe towards the sins of the flesh and because of that, perhaps, he gets criticized himself in other ways. A good man, I think, but limited in experience. It is not his fault. The Church puts down a man in a parish and then forgets all about him—at least, unless he has friends in high places or he proves a saint or makes a scandal."

Bobby noticed that he spoke of the Church with bitterness and he remembered, too, that earlier, half-whispered, 'if God there be'. It began to seem to Bobby that if the Abbé Taylour were not excommunicated, it was probably not for lack of having given sound cause, in theology and discipline, at least. Bobby said:

"Speaking of confession, is it true that only a bishop can give absolution for murder?"

The Abbé Taylour looked gravely at Bobby and for some moments did not answer. Then he said:

"Why do you ask that? You spoke just now of what happened at the Pépin Mill. English people are there, a Mr. and Mrs. Williams. Are they friends of yours?"

"I never saw or heard of them before," Bobby answered. "I know nothing about them."

The abbé made no answer and did not seem inclined to chat so freely now. He took to replying only in monosyllables or not at all and soon Bobby departed. But when he had gone some distance and was well out of sight of the hut he sat down and, getting out his sketch book, set to work. He had chosen a spot where a tall pillar of stone, like the last remaining column of some vast palace that otherwise had vanished utterly, hid him from view. Quite near was a deep crack or small crevasse in the ground, twelve or fifteen feet deep, and so hidden by a growth of gorse along its edge and climbing down its precipitous sides that it was nearly invisible. Bobby, indeed, had been close upon it before he was aware of its presence, and he reflected that if there were many of such traps for the careless walker, no wonder every one said there would be small chance of survival for any overtaken up here by the fall of night.

He did not make very good progress with his sketching. If it was his unconscious that had helped him the day before to do such good work, now it did not seem disposed to give him any assistance. But then it was not primarily to sketch that he had settled himself in this snug and hidden corner, and presently his patience was rewarded, for he heard approaching steps. He got to his feet and looked round his sheltering column of rock. Coming down the hill at a swinging pace was that tall youngster of the small head set upon the tremendous shoulders whom now he knew to be Henri Volny, son, he had been told, of the richest farmer of the district but kept, apparently, on short allowance. Bobby came further out. Volny saw him and stopped and stared. Bobby waved a greeting.

"Hullo," he called. "I've just been paying a visit to the Abbé Taylour. Jolly up there, isn't it?"

Volny began to walk towards him, his small features, the little eyes under their heavy overhanging brows, the tiny nose, the small pursed-up mouth over the round, slightly-receding chin, all touched now with a new significance given to them by a passionate and fierce emotion.

"What do you mean? What do you want?" he said slowly and menacingly. "Meddle with your own affairs." He paused, stood still—he was quite close now—and shot out the one word: "Spy."

"Oh, come," Bobby protested. "Nothing to get excited about and don't call honest folk by ugly names."

"Spy," was Volny's retort, snarled out with even more intense vigour. "What's it to do with you where I've been?"

"I didn't say anything about where you had been," retorted Bobby. "I said where I had been—visiting the Abbé Taylour. One thing, there's not so much risk of getting your feet wet up here, is there?"

Volny's instant reply was to make a wild rush, his clenched fists raised. Bobby had been more than half prepared. He was holding that small round barrel of wine the hotel had provided him with for his lunch. He flung it on the ground before Volny. Volny tripped over it and went headlong. He was a heavy man and he fell heavily.

"There now," said Bobby gently. "Why aren't you more careful? Hurt yourself?" he asked sympathetically.

That was too much for Volny, and, with what can only be described as a scream of rage, he pulled a small revolver from his pocket. And that was too much for Bobby, who, with a sudden leap, the leap a man makes when he feels his life may hang upon his speed, sprang forward, caught Volny, as he was struggling to his feet, a heavy blow between the eyes that sent him sprawling again, snatched the revolver away and hurled it into the crevasse.

"Nasty things. I've always hated them," Bobby remarked. He turned to Volny: "Evens now," he said.

Volny, a little dazed, for the blow had been a severe one, was slowly regaining his feet. He said:

"You hit me when I wasn't looking, when I was down."

"I know I did. Your own fault," Bobby answered. "Revolvers are outside the rules of the game so I went outside, too."

"Give it me back," Volny said.

"I never liked the things," Bobby explained again. "I chucked it away. You can look for it if you want to."

"Spy," said Volny once more but with less spirit this time. "You can tell your friends so, the Williamses."

"Not my friends," Bobby interposed. "I know nothing about them."

Volny waved this aside, as unworthy the trouble of a contradiction.

"Tell her from me," he said, "tell her to be a little careful. Tell her to take a walk and look at the well of the Pépin Mill. Where one has gone, another can follow; yes, and you, too. Spies deserve what they get. Give me back my revolver. I won't shoot you."

You jolly well won't get the chance," Bobby answered amiably. "Look here, Volny, don't be a fool. Tell me what you mean. About the Pépin Mill and the well there. Look here. Why not be friends? I may be able to help you."

"If you hadn't stolen my pistol, if I didn't know you might shoot me and hide my body where no one would ever find it, then I would knock your head off," said Volny and turned and strode away, ignoring utterly Bobby's exhortation to wait a moment and not make such an utter ass of himself.

CHAPTER VII
BLIND MAN PHILOSOPHY

Bobby had a good deal to think about as he went slowly down the hill in the track of the slowly-receding form of young Volny, past oak and fir, by birch and chestnut, down to the cultivated valley levels. That he had been right in his guess that Taylour's care to keep closed the door of his hut, indicated the presence of something or some one he wished to keep concealed, was now sufficiently evident. Only what reason could Volny have for wishing to hide his presence from Bobby, and why the mingled fear and suspicion he had displayed—somewhat forcibly? The one thing that seemed certain was that in some way there was some kind of connection between this solitary priest of whom the artist, Shields, had expressed his doubts, and young Volny. Yet what could that connection be?

It was a question to which Bobby could find no answer as he continued slowly and thoughtfully on his way. By the time he reached the village it was after four and he thought longingly of tea. In the hope that the café he had visited before might be able to provide some, he turned in and asked. He was assured with some pride that tea was always ready and presently a cup was placed before him, a battered coffee-pot in which tea was apparently kept perpetually brewing was produced, his cup was filled, a triumphant eye watching all the time for the signs of that appreciation so confidently expected. A loud 'Voila' of mingled relief and triumph announced the end of the operation, and the operator retired, taking the battered coffee-pot with him and leaving Bobby facing with resignation a cup full of a lukewarm liquid in which even long brewing had failed to produce anything more than a faint and unpleasant discolouration.

Bobby sighed and sipped. The 'patron' came up to receive congratulations. Bobby launched into a description of the way tea is made in England. The patron was interested but puzzled. He asserted that his English visitors were always pleased. One could tell that from the way they laughed to each other with glee while they were being served. True, there had been sadly few English visitors this summer, but he had kept tea ready for them all the time. Whether, said the patron proudly, one asked at his establishment for tea, for coffee, or for wine, it was always ready, it required but to be poured out. Truly, tea was not a beverage he himself greatly appreciated, but each to his taste. For himself, frankly, he preferred a glass of the good wine of the district. Bobby agreed that he himself preferred a glass of wine to the concoction now before him and so he and the patron parted on good terms and Bobby went on to his hotel.

On the way he had to pass the little shop kept by Lucille Simone's aunt. He turned in, ostensibly to buy more postcards. Lucille did not appear. He was served by the old lady who in spite of all his efforts to make himself agreeable, preserved an attitude of cold suspicion. He asked her again if she had any postcards showing the Pépin Mill and received once more a brief and emphatic negative.

"A picturesque old place," Bobby explained. "I should like to do it—make a sketch, I mean."

The old lady regarded him with renewed and even more intense suspicion.

"To-morrow, is it?" she asked. "It is to-morrow afternoon you make your sketch? Then Lucille does not go."

"Go where?" Bobby asked and when the old lady made no answer, he added: "I don't know when I shall be having a try. I haven't asked for permission yet. But why not to-morrow afternoon?"

Madame Simone looked more unfriendly still and still made no answer beyond an indistinct muttering. Bobby told himself it would be better not to press the old dame at the moment. Anxious as he was to get on friendly terms with her, he felt it would be better to proceed cautiously. He paid for his cards accordingly and departed with a cheerful promise to return presently to make some more purchases, a promise received with little apparent gratitude.

"Lots of puzzling things in this village," he told himself as he sought his room. "Why doesn't old Madame Simone like me and what's up to-morrow afternoon and where is Lucille not to go and why?"

Bobby was quite ready for his dinner when the time came. Over the service Charles Camion presided with the same air of proud efficiency. He made Bobby think of a general performing a sergeant's task of drilling recruits. So far Bobby had not tried to do more than exchange a casual word with him. Not, Bobby had made up his mind, until he knew more of the village background would he take any active steps, but to-night he noticed that young Camion was showing in him a more direct interest. He even asked Bobby if he had had a profitable day and found suitable subjects for his sketch book, and Bobby said he had hardly put pencil to paper all day.

"Even the one sketch I began I hardly did more than start," he said. "But it was very pleasant up there on the hill-side. Beautiful air, lovely scenery. Everything quiet and peaceful and open— nothing dark or hidden or secret up there."

Camion looked at Bobby doubtfully as if by no means sure what to make of this, but he said nothing and went away. Dinner over, Bobby decided to pay another visit to the neighbouring café. He had discovered by now that there were small social and political distinctions between the café and the hotel, the hotel being slightly superior in status while about the café there was a faint, very faint, communistic flavour. To-night Eudes was there, holding forth in earnest whisperings and mutterings to an attentive group at one table. Volny was there, too, his bruised face conspicuous; before him a bottle he was rapidly emptying. He greeted Bobby with a furious glare to which Bobby responded with a friendly wave. He was glad to see that this time his appearance seemed to excite less interest than it had done before. He hoped that meant he was coming to be accepted as a normal visitor interested only in his sketching, and presently, to a neighbour with whom he had managed to get into casual conversation, he made a remark about the young man near who had managed to bruise himself so severely. For indeed one of Volny's eyes was nearly closed and his nose was badly swollen.

"You mean the young Volny?" answered the other, smiling. "Yes, it seems he stepped on the teeth of a rake and the handle leaped up and hit him between the eyes. That happens."

"Yes, I know," agreed Bobby. "Nasty when it does."

"Carelessness unheard of," said his new friend severely. "No rake, no fork, should ever be left lying on the ground for others to tread on. It is unforgivable."

"So it is," agreed Bobby. "Gave Monsieur Volny a nasty knock. Too bad altogether. He is a great friend of young Camion's at the hotel where I'm staying, isn't he?"

The other stared at him.

"You think so?" he asked with evident caution and still more evident surprise.

"Well, two young men, neighbours, living in the same village, natural, is it not?"

"There is also," said the other gravely—perhaps he would not have said it had he not been drinking a little freely of the local 'cru' Bobby had been very pressing with, "there is also Mademoiselle Lucille Simone."

"Oh, yes, of course," said Bobby, "ah, the young ladies, always there, aren't they? Then it wasn't Volny and Camion I saw chatting together this evening in such an interested way?"

This was strictly true. He had not seen it, nor anything of the kind. He had only said it by way of making conversation. But the remark seemed greatly to disturb his new friend, even a little to alarm him. He put down untasted the glass of wine he was just raising to his lips.

"Oh, la, la," he muttered, "that bruise, too. The handle of a rake could make it but scarcely like that. And what'll happen now?" he added still more uneasily, twisting round in his chair as he did so to stare at Volny.

Volny stared back with an evidently mounting rage. Bobby guessed suddenly that Volny thought he had been talking about their adventure of the afternoon and boasting of being the author of that damaged eye and swollen nose. Volny got to his feet. He was pale with rage and the look he threw towards Bobby was murderous. Bobby almost thought he was going to be attacked then and there, but instead Volny walked straight out of the café, leaving his bottle of wine unfinished. This last detail evidently surprised every one very much. Bobby heard some one say:

"Look then, he has not drunk all his wine."

To himself, Bobby thought:

'Well, I've made an enemy all right. No tact, they would tell me at the Yard. Volny will never believe I wasn't boasting about what I did to him.'

Bobby's neighbour muttered a word of excuse and went to join in the talk at another table. Bobby thought that was mischief enough for one night and, in a somewhat worried and dispirited mood, returned to the hotel and bed, for which his long day in the fresh, clean, keen air on the hills had made him more than ready. He had a feeling that his remark, so carelessly made, had started something of which it was difficult to see the outcome. Probably it would soon be all over the village that he had seen Volny and Camion quarrelling bitterly, that they had fought, and that Volny had evidently got the worst of it since he showed a bruise but Camion none. In fact, the story of the stepping on the rake and the blow received from the upspringing handle had not been very well invented. A blow can easily be received in that way, but hardly one producing quite the sort of bruise Volny showed. Bobby felt uneasily that the version now probably spreading through the village would be more widely believed and might lead to developments.

Interesting, too, to know that the young men were rivals for Lucille's favour. Was that, Bobby wondered, with the approval of their respective families? He reflected sleepily as he prepared for bed that Charles Camion almost certainly dominated his mild-looking parents. But Volny's father apparently exercised at any rate a certain amount of parental control since he seemed to have laid a firm veto on his son's desire to take up boxing professionally, and would the richest farmer of the district, as the senior Volny was said to be, approve of a marriage with the niece of a small shop-keeper, a girl who probably had little or no money of her own?

'Another complication,' Bobby thought yawning, and remembered, too, that though it was harvest time, and urgent work necessarily waiting for every pair of hands, Volny had spent that day up on the hills, visiting the Abbé Taylour.

"Perhaps the elder Volny would not be pleased by that, either," Bobby murmured as he drifted away into sound slumber; "doesn't look as though the young man were awfully keen on farm work."

He was up early the next morning. A few inquiries he had made from a sympathetic chambermaid about the poor old blind beggar he had noticed in the neighbourhood, had brought him the information that the old man was quite methodical in his rounds. He made a point of visiting his 'clients', as he called them, at regular intervals, and he expected to be suitably received. It was still remembered how when one good housewife told him she had nothing for him that day, he must wait till next time, he had asked sternly what she supposed would be the result if everyone made that excuse? To-day, for example, said the chambermaid, he would probably be on the Nosière road. She knew that because her uncle lived that way and would be expecting Père Trouché.

Along the Nosière road Bobby accordingly took his way, making an early start. By eight, he was already a mile or more beyond the village, keeping as he walked a sharp look out. All the same he would have passed Père Trouché unknowingly, but for a chuckle he heard coming from the road-side, from the shelter of a clump of trees and bushes. Bobby stopped and made his way Père

Trouché, stretched out at full length on the warm turf as he basked in the morning sunshine.

"He, the little Englishman once more," he greeted Bobby. "Yet not so little either."

"How did you know who it was?" Bobby asked.

The blind beggar chuckled again.

"I have ears, have I not?" he asked. "When one sees nothing, one hears all."

He relapsed into silence. Bobby sat down beside him and produced his cigarettes. He lighted one himself and offered one to the blind beggar who accepted it with dignity. After they had both been smoking for a little, Bobby remarked:

"You heard me going by?"

"But naturally," Père Trouché answered. "Why not? Ah, the poor deaf ones, unhappy that they are. To lose the hearing, it is to lose everything. It must be insupportable, to be shut out from all the sounds that make up the world. Consider, monsieur, from here, where we sit, could you see who came along the road?"

"No, you couldn't," agreed Bobby, for in fact the trees behind cut off entirely all view of the road.

"But one can hear," Père Trouché said. "I heard a step. Ah, the steps, all a man's mood, all his character, all his past, one had almost said, all his future, too, it is there in his steps. I, who speak, I know, have I not been listening to them all my life?"

"You mean you knew me by my step?" Bobby asked.

"Naturally. I know the steps of all or else I know it is a stranger. Your step, it is one to remember. It is distinctive. Your shoes also. They are excellent quality, of the best leather, new, for they have not been mended. Is it so?"

"Why, yes," agreed Bobby.

"It means then," Père Trouché went on, "that you understand that the feet must be taken care of. You are then of a profession that requires you should spend much time upon your feet? Not a soldier, you say, and yet a man of action, of movement. That gives furiously to think. Certainly not the step of an artist."

"What is the step of an artist like?" asked Bobby, a little disconcerted by the old man's remarks that seemed to be getting near a truth he did not wish revealed.

The Père Trouché shrugged his shoulders.

"It is difficult to describe," he said. "A step of wonderment, perhaps, of one who marvels at all around. The step of monsieur, it is the step of one who searches. For what does monsieur search? Is it the same thing that he sought on the hill-side yesterday?"

"You know about that, too?"

"Monsieur," replied the blind man with dignity, "the good God and I, we know all that happens in the village of Citry-sur-l'eau."

"Do you though?" said Bobby thoughtfully. "That must be useful sometimes."

"Very useful," agreed the other. Then he gave again his harsh, unmirthful chuckle. "For example," he said, "I know the name of the rake that sprang up when it was trodden on and hit young Henri Volny in the eye."

"Really?" Bobby said. "Well, then, in that case, and since you know people by their step, you know who it was went by you so close the other night near the Pépin Mill when you told me you were blind but not that you could hear so well?"

For a little the Père Trouché seemed a trifle disconcerted and it was a moment or two before he replied. Then he said slowly:

"The question of an examining magistrate. Perhaps monsieur, too, is of the police?"

Bobby ignored this. He said:

"You do not answer my question."

"Ah, monsieur, a blind beggar, what does it matter what he knows or thinks he knows?"

"It might matter a good deal," Bobby said.

He took out his wallet and began to finger some of the bank notes it held. Purposely he made them rustle between his fingers. The blind man chuckled once more and Bobby had the impression that for some reason he felt now less disturbed, less uneasy.

"Money," he said. "Money. All men's price. What would it not mean to me? For example: leisure? Freedom from work? From worry?" He stretched himself lazily. "Ah, well," he said, "but then I never work. As for worry, why should I when I possess nothing? Worry only comes with possessions. The good sunshine and the air? Alas! They are not for sale and when they are there I have them, I, who sit within no four walls, toiling for no master. Freedom? Who has money has a master. Respect? Bah, the respect of fools for folly. Health? Why, when one has money one visits the doctor and then one has neither money nor health. Power?" He chuckled again. "I have it," he said. "Half the neighbourhood trembles for fear I may tell what I know. Safety? Only the poor are safe, only on the ground are you sure you won't fall from the ladder. What does money mean except work, worry, responsibility, more work, all that I have fled from all my life as the devil flies from holy water. Monsieur, money is man's supreme stupidity."

"I see you have ideas," Bobby said.

"Monsieur," replied the old man, "in seventy years on the road, one has time for ideas. But that reminds me, time passes. It is time I got to my work."

"I thought you did none," Bobby said.

"It would be good for no man," answered the Père Trouché severely, "to be entirely idle. I, too, should deteriorate like others, if I had nothing to do but sit under a tree and wait for food to come. No, I recognize that it is better for me that I should have to go and ask for it and I do not complain. Fortunately, none refuse the poor blind beggar. They have pity for him and they know well that if they had not, then the good God would punish them. Their poultry would die, their beasts would stray, their secrets become known. Why, I even heard of a man who had no pity for the blind and somehow a goat got loose in his garden one night and ate all the young lettuce, all the young peas, till none were left. The justice of heaven!"

"I wonder how the goat got loose," observed Bobby.

"Probably an angel from heaven freed it."

"A blind angel," Bobby suggested.

The old man chuckled once more.

"That, only the good God knows," he said.

"But not, for instance, the garde-champêtre?"

"The garde-champêtre," the old man repeated disdainfully. "He, he knows nothing, that one. Bah!"

"There was an English lady died here a little while ago," Bobby said slowly. "In a well. A cruel death."

There was silence for a little. The old man got to his feet. He said, and now his voice was different:

"A cruel death. Yes. I would not wish to die like that I, who have lived in the sunshine and the open air. A cruel death."

"Will you tell me what you know about it?" Bobby asked. "You, who know everything."

The Père Trouché answered slowly:

"I have blasphemed. I said that I and the good God, we knew all that passed in Citry-sur-l'eau. What happened at the Pépin Mill that night, He knows but not I."

"Are you sure there is nothing you could tell me?"

"Ask rather Monsieur and Madame Williams who have gone to live where some would not much care to be." With that, with no form of farewell, the blind beggar went quickly away, feeling his path with marvellous accuracy and speed, so that it was difficult to believe he could not see.

Bobby made no attempt to follow him. If he could be got to talk some day, it would be in his own time. It was nearly the lunch hour now and Bobby went back slowly to the hotel. After that, sketch book in hand, he took a walk in the Pépin Mill direction, for he was curious to know what Madame Simone had meant by the remark she had let drop the night before.

CHAPTER VIII
GOLD PENCIL CASE

It was in a spot well hidden among the trees around the Pépin Mill, and yet commanding a clear view of the path that led across the plank bridge to the mill door, that Bobby established himself with his sketching materials. Artistic pursuits, he reflected, provide useful cover, and as he worked away busily he kept a sharp look out.

Near the mill itself no sign of life appeared. Lazily it drowsed in the warm afternoon sunshine. On the road there was an occasional passer-by, and now and then a vehicle, either a farm wagon or a motor car. About three o'clock he saw Lucille Simone approaching. She turned from the road towards the little plank bridge and when she reached it stood there for a time in the full glare of the sun, apparently hesitating. Then as if suddenly making up her mind she came on briskly.

Her arrival had evidently been expected, for as she came to the door of the mill it opened to her before she had time to knock. No one appeared. It was just that the door swung back. Perhaps some one called to her to enter but Bobby was too far away to hear any such summons. For a moment or two she stood still, staring at the open door; and then, again with that air of abruptly and resolutely making up her mind, she went forward. The door closed immediately behind her, nor could Bobby tell why there seemed to him something ominous, something of a strange and deadly significance in this quiet, as it were, unseen, reception.

He began to put away his sketching materials. It was, he supposed, impossible to imagine for a moment that real harm threatened the girl. Her aunt, for instance, would know she contemplated making this visit. Yet what could be its meaning? Why had she had that air of hesitation? Conscious of a distinct uneasiness, certain that Lucille's presence here must have some significance, Bobby began to draw nearer to the mill. Trees and shrubs afforded shelter of which he took full advantage, and he hoped, too, that those within would be too busy with their own affairs to be on the look out.

When he was as near as he judged it prudent to attempt to approach, he crouched down behind some bushes and set himself to the old familiar, tedious task of the detective, that of watching and waiting. He would look an awful fool, he supposed, if some one found him there and wanted to know what on earth he was doing, squatting there on the ground behind a clump of bushes. One has to take one's risks, though, and fortunately artists are supposed to be eccentric. He reflected ruefully that here he had no official standing, no warrant card to produce with a flourish, that here the magic words 'Scotland Yard' had no efficacy. Nor any superiors in the background to whom he could go for instruction when he wanted to dodge responsibility.

For almost the first time in his life he realized, with a touch of astonishment, that after all senior officers really have their uses. A chastening thought!

It was nearly an hour that he waited there when suddenly the door opened and Lucille appeared. Bobby was conscious of a touch of relief. He had not actually believed she was in any real danger, but all the same one could never tell. Then he saw that her arm was being firmly held in a grip that might be friendly or might not. It was Williams who held her thus, with his huge hand grasping her arm, but even as Bobby watched, on the point of showing himself but anxious, too, to see if anything more definite happened, the girl turned sharply, snatching her arm from Williams's grip and standing still to face him. She said something. Bobby could not catch the words, though he could see that her attitude was defiant and even challenging, her head held back, her slender form drawn to its full height.

Williams seemed to mutter some response and then they both began to move down the path, his bulky form towering above her, his long strides keeping pace easily with her hurried walk. When she tried to go straight on towards the bridge, he interposed a huge arm and seemed to make some remark. She shrugged her shoulders and together they turned aside towards the well.

Bobby was watching them closely, ready to spring and run should the need arise. They reached the well and stood there, the girl erect and quiet and still, Williams appearing to watch her intently. He stooped and lifted the cover, exposing that dark shaft which went down and down to where the dull gleam of the water showed so far below. He seemed to invite the girl to look, but she shrank away. Bobby thought it time to show himself. Williams could hardly contemplate murder—and such a murder—in broad daylight, and yet how easy for that huge man with his powerful muscles to seize the girl and thrust her into those black and horrid depths and then to replace the cover, leaving no sign of what had happened, no possibility of any cry reaching the upper earth.

Of an incredible audacity, if such a deed were contemplated. Yet something of the sort had already happened here and the possibility of a repetition could not be ignored. It had to be remembered, too, that once the thing was done, and it could be quickly done, once the cover replaced, then rescue in time would be impossible.

On his feet now, Bobby hurried towards where they stood together by the well, its black chill narrow mouth gaping and grim in the sunlight. They did not at first hear him. Lucille had moved a step or two aside, turning her face away as she did so, and Bobby could see how pale she looked, how terrified. Williams took her by the arm again and pulled her nearer. Bobby began to run.

They heard him then, as indeed he meant them to. They both turned, Lucille evidently astonished by his sudden appearance, but with an air of great relief as well; Williams equally surprised, angry and scowling, too, though hardly, Bobby thought, looking like a man surprised in the act of attempting to commit a murder. Yet what else had he intended and why was relief even plainer than surprise in Lucille's expression?

"Oh, how do you do?" Bobby said amiably.

Lucille began to giggle as if she thought this greeting funny. Williams glared and scowled more formidably still, but said nothing. Bobby heard the door of the mill open, and, looking round, saw the meek little form of Mrs. Williams appear. Apparently she had been watching. Bobby wondered why? Had she also been afraid of what might be going to happen? She began to walk towards them. Lucille said:

"I must go. My aunt will be expecting me. Good day."

She hurried off. Williams did not make any attempt to stop her. It was quite plain that he was controlling his anger with difficulty as he muttered to Bobby:

"Well, what do you want? Hey? What the devil, snooping round. What's the game? Heh?"

"What were you saying to that girl?" Bobby asked.

"For two pins I would knock your head off," Williams told him. "For two pins I would give you a sound thrashing, you interfering, meddling fool."

He made a threatening movement forward, but Bobby was so obviously unalarmed, so plainly prepared, that he hesitated. Bobby said:

"What was it I interfered with? What is it I meddle in?" He paused and repeated: "What were you saying to that girl?"

"Mind your own business," Williams snarled and then added: "She wanted to see the well where they say some old woman or another drowned herself a while back. Got scared when I took the cover off and told her to look. I thought at first she was going to faint."

"Well, I should put the cover back now if I were you," Bobby suggested. "Once is once too often. We don't want it to happen again."

Mrs. Williams had joined them now. She said:

"I told you so, I told you not to, Joe. I knew she would get frightened if you let her peep. Morbid, I call it, the way people come and ask if they can see where it happened." She looked at Bobby. "Did this gentleman want to see the well, too? Morbid, I call it," she repeated severely. "Morbid."

"Curiously enough," Bobby said, "I've been asked to give you a message. About this well. I didn't mean to, but now I may as well. The message was to ask you to remember that where one had gone, another might follow." The Williams looked at each other. Then the man spoke, Bobby thought in response to a sign his wife made. He said:

"Who was it?"

"I wasn't asked to give you the name and so I don't think I will," answered Bobby. "The message is enough. I never meant to give it you but now I have. I wonder what it means?"

Williams did not answer. He began to put back the well cover. It was heavy and he seemed to have some difficulty in adjusting it. His wife went to help him and Bobby saw that they exchanged whispers. Williams straightened himself and said once more:

"What's your game, hanging about here the way you do?"

"When I do hang about," Bobby said slowly, "things seem to happen, don't they? The other night I thought I heard a shot fired. A mistake, you told me, though there was certainly a window broken. Just now I thought—well, never mind that. Another mistake. They tell me in the village you are from Scotland Yard?"

"What about it?"

"Is it true?"

"What's it to do with you if it is?"

"Oh, I was just wondering. Odd, though, if British police are trying to investigate something that happened in another country. No jurisdiction. The French police say what happened here was suicide. Perhaps they are right. Perhaps they are waiting to see if anything else happens. You can never tell with police."

Williams was looking now even more puzzled than angry. Mrs. Williams pulled at his sleeve and whispered something. Then she said:

"Joe, ask the gentleman to come in and have a cup of tea with us. It's just a misunderstanding, I'm sure the gentleman didn't mean to trespass. We've been so bothered with trespassers, stealing fruit and vegetables and things and peeping in at the windows," she explained to Bobby, "Mr. Williams wants to complain to the police, only I asked him not to, because it would make such a lot of bother, and then it's foreign police, so you can't ever tell, can you? Do come in and have a cup of tea with us."

"Please don't trouble about tea," Bobby said, "but I should like to have a bit of a talk."

They went back to the mill together. Mrs. Williams disappeared into the kitchen. Williams pushed a chair towards Bobby and sat down himself. Bobby noticed that the broken window had not yet been repaired. A piece of paper had been pasted over the hole to keep the wind out. He could see nothing in the barely-furnished room in any way personal, nothing to throw any light on the aims, pursuits, or characters of these two people. Williams was evidently feeling very worried and disturbed. He began to fill his pipe and then laid it aside. He took out a small gold pencil case and began to scribble something on a piece of paper and then changed his mind and tore it up. The gold pencil case attracted Bobby's attention.

It was a pretty, dainty thing, incongruous between Williams's thick, hairy fingers, and the incongruous always interested Bobby.

There were initials on it, a monogram, but Bobby could not see what they were. Williams noticed his interest and scowled and pushed back the pencil case into his pocket, somewhat hastily, almost as if he regretted having let Bobby see it.

"What are you staring at?" he demanded angrily. "What's the game? I mean to say, you had better look out or you'll be getting hurt."

"You haven't told me yet," Bobby said, ignoring this—he had always found it best to ignore threats, "if it is the fact that you are from Scotland Yard."

"No, it isn't," Williams admitted sulkily, "and what's more, I never said I was. What I did say in the café one night when I was having a drink there, was that Scotland Yard would have found out fast enough what happened to Miss Polthwaite. When we took this place for a quiet holiday—saw it advertised in the Paris papers—we didn't know an old girl had been done in here. If we had known, we shouldn't have come. Not that it matters a lot, only you don't choose where there's been a murder for a holiday stay. That goes for us. What about you? You a private detective?"

"No," said Bobby, promptly and emphatically, for he did not like private detectives.

"Well, then," said Williams. "I take it you can't be one of the regulars—they couldn't very well shove in their noses in France. Get told off if they did. So what's the idea, you hanging round here all the time?"

"I didn't know I was," Bobby said. "I knew about Miss Polthwaite's death. I read about it at the time. The night I got here I was out for a stroll and just thought I would have a look at the place where it happened. I thought I heard a shot. You say I was mistaken. To-day I came to ask if you had any objection to my making a few sketches here."

"Well, we have," interposed Williams, "a lot of objection."

Unheeding this, Bobby went on:

"I saw you and a girl standing by the well. I thought she looked afraid—upset."

"What about it?" interrupted Williams again. "So she did. So she was. Wanted to have a peep where it happened and then got the wind up. Like a girl, little fools, all of them."

"There has been one death there already," Bobby said. "Enough to frighten any girl, fool or not."

He noticed a sudden change in Williams's expression. The truculence went out of it. All at once he seemed uneasy as if for some reason he felt no longer so sure of himself. He began to laugh loudly but not very naturally. Bobby, puzzled, wondered what had brought about this change. Mrs. Williams, tray in hand, was standing just behind him now. He had not heard her come in. She must have entered, have moved, with extraordinary quietness, and a memory stirred vaguely in Bobby's mind of how on his first visit to this mill, on the night when he heard a shot fired, he had seemed to be aware of something small and silent and secret creeping softly behind him. Williams stopped laughing and said boisterously:

"Why, of course, do all the sketching you want to. Why not? All day if you like, all night, too, for that matter. At least, as long as you don't want us to buy your stuff."

He began to laugh again as if he thought this an excellent joke. Mrs. Williams moved forward with her soft prowling step, put down her tray, and began to pour out the tea, chatting amiably as she did so. The conversation grew general, almost genial indeed. Williams appeared to be trying his best now to be friendly. Bobby presently took his leave, receiving again a fresh invitation to return as often and do as much sketching as he liked.

He felt a good deal puzzled by this sudden change to geniality and very little inclined to believe the plausible stories he had been told. Yet he had no real reason to doubt their declaration that their presence here was entirely accidental and the interest they showed in the Polthwaite case merely a natural result of their chance tenancy of the mill. All the same he was little inclined to dismiss the possibility of some connection existing between their presence and the Polthwaite murder. But surely they themselves could not be guilty, since even the most callous murderers would hardly choose for residence the scene of their secret crime? Or would they? hoping so perhaps to watch or hinder any investigation. Or was it the store of diamonds Miss Polthwaite was believed to have had in her possession, that they had heard of and hoped possibly to secure for themselves? It might be the diamonds were still concealed somewhere about the mill and they hoped to find them?

But then again, if Miss Polthwaite had been murdered, as Bobby now felt was certain, must not the crime have been committed for the sake of the diamonds and was it not certain they would be now in the possession of the assassin?

Bobby sighed and shook his head at himself, vexed to think he could find no way through the tangle of doubt and hesitation in which he felt himself ensnared. One thing alone stood out clearly in his mind: that he disliked and mistrusted both Mr. and Mrs. Williams. Nor was he sure now that Mrs. Williams was quite so colourless and insignificant as she had at first seemed to be.

When he reached his hotel again he went in for a few minutes and then on to the little postcard shop near, where, when Madame Simone appeared, he asked if he could have a word or two with her niece. The old lady looked very doubtful and grumbled inaudibly to herself, but this time seemed a trifle less unfriendly. Finally she took him into the small living-room behind the shop. Lucille was there and Bobby said to her:

"Mademoiselle, I have come to ask if you will tell me exactly what happened this afternoon."

"Oh, no," she answered quickly, looking terrified at the suggestion.

"It was Mr. Williams and his wife who asked you to go to see them, wasn't it?" he asked.

"Why? How do you know?" she retorted.

He let that pass, not bothering to explain that the guess had been an easy one. He said instead:

"I wish I could persuade you to trust me. I know I am a stranger. I don't like Mr. and Mrs. Williams. I think they have some reason for being here and I don't think it is a very creditable reason."

She still shook her head and then after a time she said suddenly:

"I was glad when I saw you this afternoon. I was terrified before but not then." She added when he did not speak: "Please do not think I am ungrateful."

Bobby took a photograph of Olive from his pocket. "That is the girl I am going to marry," he said. "If some one was trying to bully her, I hope any one who saw what was happening would try to interfere."

She took the photograph from him and looked at it and then at him and then back again at it. He thought she looked doubtful and he said:

"I will give you her address if you like and you can write and ask her if you can trust me. Because I think it is important you should tell me about this afternoon."

"If she loves you, then of course she will say you can be trusted," Lucille answered. "If you love a man, you trust him, too. It is the same thing." She looked at Bobby: "Do you love her?" she asked.

He did not answer, suddenly shy and embarrassed. She gave him the photo back and smiled:

"You need not say it," she told him. "It is in your eyes."

"Oh, well, now then," he muttered, scarlet now. With an effort he recovered himself. He said: "A woman died in that well. You were afraid when Williams lifted the cover."

An almost imperceptible nod answered him.

"He was threatening you?"

She hesitated again. It was a moment or two before she gave another almost imperceptible nod. Then she said:

"But not in the way you mean."

"Well, then. How?"

"He said—" the words came slowly, hesitatingly, with long pauses between. "He said—there was proof—down there— somehow—proof—something dropped—proof who was—guilty."

"Proof? What sort of proof?"

"He did not say. I think perhaps it was not true. But he made me afraid. I think he is a bad man."

"Proof against whom?"

"He did not say."

"If he knows anything, it is his duty to tell the police. It is serious if he does not."

"Yes, he said that," she almost whispered.

Madame Simone had gone back into the shop, but she was watching them from behind the counter. She came to the door now and said to Bobby:

"That's enough, you'll make the child ill."

That Lucille was very distressed was in fact plain enough and Bobby felt he could not press her further. "Can I see you again some other time?" he asked.

A customer appeared in the shop and knocked for attention. Madame Simone went to answer the summons. Lucille said:

"Perhaps. Another day. Please go now."

"Very well, thank you," Bobby said, and was in the act of retiring when she called him back and asked if she could see again Olive's photograph. Flattered, he produced it. She took it and studied it carefully and gravely for some moments before she gave it him back.

"I was wondering," she explained, "if that style she has of doing her hair, would suit me."

CHAPTER IX
STILL LIFE COMPOSITION

It was not yet the dinner hour, but feeling a need to be alone for a little to try to think out the implications of all that he had seen and heard during the day, Bobby returned to the hotel. Since the evening of his arrival, he had seen nothing of Eudes, the village schoolmaster, but now as he entered the hotel he saw him in the background, talking earnestly and quickly to young Camion. They heard Bobby come in and both looked round, and, when they saw him they moved away. Bobby wondered if it was self-consciousness that gave him the impression it was of him they were talking.

He shook his head gloomily at himself. It had been his hope and his intention to avoid in every way attracting the notice of the inhabitants of the village and he could not help feeling that in that respect he had not succeeded very brilliantly. This man, Eudes, for instance. On the very first day of his arrival Eudes had made an excuse to talk to him. Then there had been that visit by the artist, Shields, who afterwards had gone on to call on Eudes. Bobby found himself suspecting that Eudes had asked Shields to come over on purpose to test Bobby's claim to be an artist. If so, Bobby hoped that the unexpected excellence of the sketch he had made that day had satisfied Shields and, through him, Eudes. At any rate, since then he had not seen Eudes again till now.

Thoughtfully Bobby asked himself what reason Eudes could have for showing such an interest in him and he remembered the touch of fanaticism with which Eudes had spoken of the journal of 'enlightenment' he hoped to found and of his need of money for that purpose. Now here was Eudes again, talking privately to young Camion, and appearing anxious to keep out of Bobby's sight. Curious, Bobby thought, and he was not much surprised when, the meal over, Camion, instead of disappearing as usual, came to the table in a quiet corner where Bobby had chosen to sit. Seeing him coming, Bobby pushed out a chair.

"Nice evening, isn't it?" he said. "Do sit down." Camion, whose expression had not been amiable, scowled even more heavily. Nor did he accept the invitation. Leaning over the back of the chair, he said: "Monsieur, I trust I am right in believing you do not contemplate making a long stay?"

Bobby did not answer at first. He looked thoughtfully at Camion, wondering what this new move meant and if he owed the making of it to Eudes. But then why should Eudes be anxious to get rid of him? Camion said:

"It would in fact be a convenience if monsieur would vacate his room."

"I took it for two weeks," Bobby said. "I even got a reduction in terms as it was for that long certain. I may stay longer. I am not sure yet. What's the idea?"

"Monsieur," said Camion, looking more haughty and dominating than ever, "if you by any chance prefer to leave to-morrow, no charge will be made for the time you have already stayed here."

"My dear friend," said Bobby in his most amiable tones, "it is evident that we are neither of us good business men. If you were, you would not make such a suggestion. If I were, I should accept it. Let us sympathize with each other on our common misfortune."

"You mean you refuse?"

"Guessed it in one," said Bobby approvingly.

"You force me then," said Camion, "to inform you that I am well acquainted with your identity, your profession, your purpose in wishing to stay here."

Bobby felt slightly ill. If Camion knew, all the village knew. The authorities would soon know, too, and then he would be asked to explain his errand here and that would certainly mean an end to all his hopes of success. Very likely he would receive a polite hint that there are many other districts of France equally attractive to the tourist. It might even get back to Scotland Yard that he had been indiscreet.

"Oh, well," he said moodily, "no use asking you to hold your tongue, I suppose?"

Camion's gesture might have been that of one of the Borgian guests refusing the customary parting cup of poison.

"Who told you?" Bobby asked.

"I am not at liberty to say."

"Oh, aren't you? Well, then, run away and amuse yourself."

"It is understood that you leave in the morning?"

"No, it isn't," snapped Bobby, who had no intention of quitting till he was actually booted out—and only then if the boot was too big to resist.

Camion drew himself to his full height. His glance was fiery, his nose was as that one of which it is said that once British soldiers thought a glimpse of it worth ten thousand men. He flung out one hand.

"Monsieur," he announced, "I shall give instructions to the hotel porter to bring down your baggage in the morning. I shall see that the door of your room is locked."

"Monsieur," responded Bobby, "if the hotel porter tries to remove my baggage from my room I have taken for two weeks certain, I shall throw the hotel porter out of the window. If I find my door locked against me, I shall break it open. Understand? Hang it all, this is an hotel, isn't it? And I'm paying for my room, aren't I?"

"Very well," said Camion. "Very good. I had wished to keep your secret, but now all the world shall know it. Ah," he added triumphantly, seeing Bobby wince, "you do not like that? Naturally. Very well. You go or all the world shall know you are a married man, that in Nice last year you persuaded an unhappy girl at the hotel where you stayed to accompany you to San Remo, where you deserted her in a foreign and unfriendly country without a penny."

Bobby fairly gasped. He struggled for speech but none came.

"We are simple here, in our village, but we know the morality of the artist," Camion went on. "You did not, I imagine, dream that all this was known?"

"I shouldn't have dreamed it," said Bobby earnestly, "even if I had been living for a month on nothing but lobster salad and cold boiled rice. Who on earth has been telling you all these fairy tales?"

"Yes, I was warned you would deny it," Camion said darkly. "I warn you, here in Citry-sur-l'eau, we have ideas, we others. When our honour is touched, we—kill."

"The dickens you do," murmured Bobby thoughtfully, for Camion looked as if he meant what he said.

"Question of honour; question of life; question of death," said Camion.

"It's a sentiment worth remembering," Bobby said, still more thoughtfully.

"Useless to deny," said Camion. "I have proof."

"So have I," said Bobby cheerfully. "Proof that while you want to manage a chain of big hotels in all countries of the world—"

"What's that?" interrupted Camion, gasping in his turn, "Who... what... I never..."

"You haven't enough sense or knowledge or experience," swept on Bobby relentlessly, unheeding Camion's dismay at this exposure of ambitions that he probably thought were locked deep in his own breast, "to manage a—" Bobby had been going to say 'peanut stall' but not being sure of the French for 'peanut' altered it to "—a gingerbread stall in a country fair. Some one's been stuffing you."

But here Bobby rather spoilt the effect by using the word 'farcir', which is chiefly employed in a culinary sense, instead of some equivalent French colloquial term for our slang 'stuffing'—se payer la tête, for example. Camion looked bewildered at this sudden reference to the kitchen and its operations, of which he could make nothing. He let it pass and said:

"It happens that I have a photograph of your children, their names and yours written on the back."

"Children?" said Bobby, growing interested now. "How many?"

"Three. The twins and another."

"Twins?" Bobby almost shouted. "Twins, did you say? Oh, well, thank God, it's not triplets."

Camion produced a photograph. It showed three small children. On the back was written: 'John, Henry and Mary Owen, children of Robert Owen, artist.'

Bobby studied it with great interest. Then he put it in his pocket.

"Can't deprive a loving father of his own offspring," he said. "Listen, I said just now you hadn't sense enough to run a gingerbread stall at a country fair. Optimistic, that was. I expect when it comes on to rain, they have to send some one to tell you to come in out of the wet?"

"I don't know what you are talking about," Camion said, but beginning to look a little uneasy.

"About your intelligence," explained Bobby, "or rather your total, complete and absolute lack of it. I suppose Williams told this pretty yarn to Eudes and Eudes told you?"

"How did you know?" Camion asked.

"By using my brains," Bobby told him. "Probably you've never heard such things exist. They are used for thinking but if you can't think, I suppose you don't need them." He paused and looked again at Camion: "Is all this because I've been buying postcards at the shop where Mademoiselle Lucille Simone—"

Camion started to interrupt but Bobby checked him.

"Probably her aunt began it," Bobby went on, "she looks a bit like that, looks like an old body with a tongue she can't help using. And then I daresay you heard I had been in the shop before dinner and that mademoiselle seemed disturbed afterwards. You know it's silly but it has its interesting side. Williams wants to get me out of here and Eudes is willing to help. Why? It was your jealousy they thought they could work on."

"I am not jealous, I have no right to be, it is nothing to do with Mademoiselle Simone, her name should not have been mentioned, it is insufferable," Camion cried angrily.

"I expect she'll say that and a bit more if she gets to know," agreed Bobby. "Has she any friends or relations about here?"

"No, she only came to live here a year ago, there is only her aunt she lives with."

"So you thought you had to take her under your protection," Bobby observed. "Well, I hope she will be grateful, but I doubt it. She might want to know why you were butting in?"

"If anything happens to me," Camion muttered, "there would be for her no one even to notice, no one to know, to protest."

"Perhaps the young lady may prefer to look after herself rather than trust to a silly, meddling, thick-headed, conceited, ignorant prize imbecile from the last house in imbecile town. And you," said Bobby, "who want to establish a chain of hotels in all the capitals of the world! You mean perhaps a chain of cat's-meat barrows?"

Camion wilted under this version of a commination service, Bobby pronounced very slowly and thoughtfully, pausing every now and again for reflection in his search for the 'mot juste'. Camion tried to interrupt once or twice but Bobby's upraised hand checked him. Bobby said: "Another thing, what do you mean? 'If anything happened' to you? Why should it?"

"That at least," Camion answered, "is my affair. They are not true, then, the things I was told about you?"

"Silly rubbish," Bobby answered. "Only a boy like you, without sense or experience, would have paid any attention to such a tale. I don't suppose you would either, in a general way, only you're a bit rattled; upset, I mean. Not quite yourself just now, are you? what with murders happening round here and general excitement and jealousy. Do you good if you put your head in a bucket of water and kept it there every night for an hour or two. Williams would like to clear me out. So he thought he would have a try. Clumsy. The fellow's a fool. Look here, what's this about something happening to you? Has Williams asked you to pay a visit to the mill for a talk?"

"How do you know?" asked Camion bewilderedly. "You know then everything?"

"I've a few brains," Bobby explained. "You know. Brains. I mentioned them before. First time you knew such things existed? Not that I mean I've got so many myself. At least, I know that's what they think where I work over in London. See here, you keep an eye on Williams."

"I am not afraid."

"It's always wise to be afraid," Bobby said quietly.

Camion began to look scornful and haughty again.

"That is not our idea here," he said. "If anything happens to me, it will not be through Williams."

"Through whom, then?" Bobby asked, but Camion only shrugged his shoulders and then after a pause walked away.

"Now, I wonder," Bobby said to himself, "what the young fool means. Something upsetting him so badly he can't think straight. Only what?"

Useless though to try to guess with so little to go upon, since even a guess must have some starting point.

It was a warm fine evening, and, having nothing else to do, Bobby went for a short stroll. Coming back, he turned in again at the café he had visited before. The first person he saw was Williams sitting alone at a table, before him an empty glass and a bottle nearly empty. Bobby at once went towards him. Williams scowled and, pouring out what was left in the bottle, drank it off. Bobby said with his most amiable smile:

"Oh, about that photo. I just wanted to thank you for not making it quins. You know I really could not have endured quins."

"Think you're funny, don't you?" snarled Williams.

"More a faint and far-off hope than an actual thought," explained Bobby. "But people I have to do with often laugh—only sometimes it is on the wrong side of their mouths."

Williams scowled again and went angrily away. Bobby watched him leave the café and then sat down at the same table, took out his sketch book and began to make a drawing of the bottle and the glass.

"It is a most superb composition," he explained to the waiter. "Whatever you do, don't move them. A superb still life. Ah, they could only have been arranged like that either by genius or by happy chance. Ask the patron if I can have them—the bottle and glass. I'll give you twenty francs for them—the composition. It is perfect."

The waiter smiled tolerantly and told the patron. The patron came himself to see if it were really true that such an easy twenty francs was coming his way. Finding that Bobby seemed to be in earnest, he asked twenty-five francs, which Bobby paid on the spot and was only just in time to prevent the waiter from seizing his purchases and taking them away to wrap them up.

"No, no," protested Bobby earnestly. "They must not be touched." He explained gravely: "Only an artist, a real artist, can understand how perfect a composition in still life they make together."

He looked at it admiringly, and then, picking up bottle and glass with great care, went off with them in triumph, promising though to return shortly for a glass of wine in which to drink to his good luck in having discovered so superb a subject for his pencil. When he reached the hotel he noticed that old Madame Camion, at the reception desk, was sound asleep. His arrival broke her slumbers though she did no more than open one eye, see who it was, and fall again to slumber. Bobby, instead of going straight to his room, wandered into the back premises, found them deserted, collected another bottle and another glass, as closely resembling those already in his possession as possible, and ascended to his room. There he put the bottle and glass he had taken possession of very carefully away in a drawer. The other bottle and glass, those from the café, he packed with even greater care, and addressed to

Olive in London. He took the package downstairs and woke Madame Camion, sleeping more soundly than ever, and asked her to put it in the hotel safe. Much experience of the whims, the fancies, and the eccentricities of hotel guests, whom she had come to look upon as a race apart, had long ago exhausted all the good lady's curiosity anent their doings, and she complied with Bobby's request as just another item in the day's work. Then she resumed her slumbers, and he went back to the café where by this time every one had heard of this fresh proof of the general, all-pervading eccentricity of artists.

Bobby stayed till late, pleased to find he had now won for himself an amused tolerance and a firm footing as beyond all doubt a genuine artist. He won even greater popularity by making a sketch of the patron that every one said was so good you could almost see him overcharging a client, but all through his sketching, all through the general chatter and laughter in which he joined, his mind was busy with the interpretation of the new facts and new questions that every moment seemed to thrust themselves upon his attention.

Camion was evidently so fiercely in love with Lucille that in his jealousy he was ready to believe any story told him and to suspect any one going near the girl of being a possible rival. But was Lucille inclined to accept these attentions or did she share in the general attitude of, as it were, awe-stricken dread which his fellow villagers seemed inclined to adopt towards the young man and that must surely imply some knowledge of, or at least a strong belief in, his guilt. There was Henri Volny, too, said to be a suitor for Lucille's favour, and jealous of Camion both on that account and because of what had seemed Camion's good luck in winning the favour of a rich and elderly spinster. Another detail came to Bobby's knowledge during the idle café chatter. Once or twice he turned the conversation towards the Pépin Mill, speaking of its picturesqueness and his wish to sketch it. He made a reference to the owner's good luck in letting it again so soon after it had been the scene of such a tragedy, and this produced a casual comment by some one sitting near, to the effect that the other's good luck had been bad luck for their schoolmaster, Monsieur Eudes, who had had the idea of taking over the mill garden to grow vegetables for the Dijon market.

"He is always passionate to make money, that one," somebody else remarked, and there was some laughter about the schoolmaster's schemes and his various attempts to get hold of enough money, by hook or by crook, to enable him to start his famous 'journal of enlightenment'.

It was a piece of information Bobby tucked away in his mind for possible future reference. Not till nearly midnight did the café begin to empty, and when Bobby returned to his hotel, he was not much surprised to find that his room showed signs of having been very thoroughly and efficiently searched. To a casual glance there was little to show, but Bobby had had his expectations, and he could see at once that everything in the room had been examined, his clothing, the drawers, even the bed had not escaped, for an exploring hand had certainly been thrust under the mattress and the pillows. Fortunately he kept both his money and his papers on his person and he soon assured himself that nothing was missing except that bottle and glass he had so carefully secured from the back regions of the hotel.

"Oh, well, one mustn't grudge them that," he said to himself. "My loss and their gain, only not quite the gain they think: I wonder who did the job?"

On that point though he thought he could make a good guess, since he had seen hurrying away from the hotel a form of which he had caught only a glimpse but which he was much inclined to believe was that of Mrs. Williams, a lady whose soft and silent step and secret manner of approach he had already had occasion to admire. Contentedly he retired to rest, and was soon in a deep slumber wherefrom he was aroused, just as daylight was beginning to appear, by the faint rattle of earth and gravel tossed from below against his window pane.

CHAPTER X
DUEL

Bobby was a sound sleeper, as is befitting in the young and healthy, but also he slept lightly, and that sound of earth and gravel on his window pane brought him instantly to his feet, as alert as at the ringing of his 'phone by his bedside at home. He crossed quickly to the wide open window. Beneath was Père Trouché, his face upturned. The moment Bobby was at the window he knew it and called softly:

"Come down quickly. Disturb no one. Lose no time."

Bobby asked no questions. Hurriedly he dressed, and carrying his shoes in his hand, slipped out of his room and along the passage to the stairs and down them to the entrance lobby. He had expected to have some difficulty in opening the front door, but it was unlocked and unbolted. Did they leave it so all night, he wondered. Not likely, he decided, so some one had been before him. He opened it cautiously and went out. At a little distance he saw the blind beggar waiting for him. Stopping only to put on his shoes, Bobby joined him.

"What is it? what's happened?" Bobby asked as, impatiently beckoning him to follow, the blind man began to hurry away.

"There's been one murder in the village this year," Père Trouché answered over his shoulder. "We do not want another—it is through you, so it is for you to stop it. Hurry. There is no time to lose."

"Through me?" repeated Bobby. "Why? How? What have I done?"

"Hurry, hurry," the old man insisted. "It was you who quarrelled with the young Volny, was it not? His face gives proof of what happened. But all the village believes it was Camion, for all the village knows they hate each other on account of the Demoiselle Simone, and more bitterly still in recent days, since at first Camion was favoured, but now it is different, and Camion believes it is because Volny has drawn an advantage from his misfortune."

"What misfortune?" Bobby asked, but the other did not answer.

"It seems," he continued, "that something you said has made people think Volny's bruises were given him by Camion. Volny would not explain for he did not wish it to be known that it was you with whom he had fought. That would have made more talk still. But Camion has a reputation among us. There is a fear of him. It is believed that once already he has killed. Children peep and run when he passes, the mothers cross themselves. From other parts people come to look at him. It is a wonder that he endures it so patiently. But always one knows that inside he is on the boil and that at any moment he may bubble over. Is it then a fresh beginning, one asks, this quarrel with Volny, of which Volny shows the marks? It is hinted to him then that while for an old English spinster, of ill-conduct—"

"What ill-conduct?" Bobby interrupted sharply.

"Eh, monsieur," Père Trouché answered, "we have our ideas— we do not approve the elderly rich woman who tempts a boy with money to be her gigolo. Well, that is one thing, but another lad of the village—there we draw the line. That must not be. But when this is said to Camion, not plainly, for one dare not, but for him to understand, then he is furious. He seeks out Volny and demands that Volny should say who it was with whom he fought. Volny is sulky and angry. Eh, Mr. Englishman, you can guess what happens when there meet two young men, sulky, resentful, with no amiable feelings for each other. It is all quite natural. In the end, it seems they agree to meet each other out by the Nozière road early this morning, there to fight it out."

"Well, let 'em," said Bobby. "Is that all you've knocked me out of bed for at this unearthly hour? Perhaps, after they've finished with each other, they'll have a bit more sense. Though I don't think Camion will stand much chance. Volny is taller, got a longer reach, and I should think he is twenty or thirty pounds heavier. Besides, he knows a bit about boxing. Any one can see that. Does Camion?"

"Monsieur," said the old beggar gravely, "he has never boxed in his life. He has laughed at Volny because of his boxing. He has said that only savages fight so. Men of honour have different ideas. In his idea, they use the pistol or the sword."

"Eh?" said Bobby, startled. "Oh, lord, you don't mean—?"

"Charles Camion is proud—proud as Lucifer. It almost consoles him, when people hold him for an assassin, that then they fear him. His mind has become a tumult. Anger that people should dread him for an assassin, pride that they should start and tremble when he passes by. To be thrashed by Volny would make him ridiculous. It is a risk he would never run. Therefore he has made another choice."

"You think they've got weapons?"

"He and the young Volny, too. Revolvers. It is not a boxing match we are concerned with but a veritable duel."

"The blighted young fools," said Bobby uneasily. "You don't really think that?"

By now they had left the village some considerable distance behind. Père Trouché was walking with as much speed and firmness as if in full possession of his sight. He held his staff a little in advance but apparently he made small use of it. It was as though every inch of the road they followed was pictured in his mind as intimately and as clearly as it showed itself to Bobby's physical sight. No doubt the old man had been up and down it many hundreds of times, and Bobby noticed, too, how he turned his face from side to side, listening intensely to all the sounds that reached them and seeming to know instinctively their correct interpretation. Now, before he had time to speak again, they heard the report of a shot, clear and distinct in the calm morning air. They stood still. They heard no more. Yet the peaceful, gentle morning, still drowsy in the quiet air, seemed all at once to have become charged with a dark and dreadful meaning; and warm as was the sunshine now encompassing all the earth as in a universal mantle, Bobby felt a coldness at his heart. He heard Père Trouché mutter:

"Are we then too late?"

"There was only one shot," Bobby said.

"One, it is sometimes enough," answered the old man.

"Well, come along," Bobby said irritably. "Most likely it's all right. Why did you come to me? Why didn't you go to the maire, or the police or some one?"

"The maire," answered the blind man, "is an old fool, and when a man is old and yet has remained a fool, he is altogether beyond hope. The maire would have believed nothing, done nothing, chattered like a wet hen, that is all. As for the garde-champêtre, monsieur," said the old man, so far forgetting their errand in his indignation that he stood still to give greater emphasis to his speech, "monsieur, it is inconceivable but once he arrested me, me. It is a thing that never before happened in our family, though for three generations, my grandfather, my father, myself, we have earned our living honestly, begging day by day in the sight of all men. Apparently some chickens, some hens, what know I? were missing, and the fool chose to suspect me. Am I also a fool that I should steal where I collect my gifts?" He paused and then added: "Also, it is not necessary that all the village, all the country for miles, should know about these two foolish boys. There has been enough talk as it is and it is better that none should know, if it can be prevented."

His voice had grown uneasy and Bobby knew he was thinking of that solitary shot which a moment or two before had broken upon the freshness of the summer dawn.

"Duels are allowed in France, aren't they?" Bobby asked.

"On occasion, under regulation," answered the other, "but a duel such as this, that would be considered murder. Is there anything you can see? To hear, that tells, I think, more than to see, for often I understand better what is happening than those who because they see, think there is no need also to hear. But the eyes have in some ways no doubt an advantage." The old man's voice sounded reluctant as if he made this admission unwillingly. "It is that they have a longer range. You others, you can see a man before I can hear him, even though my hearing tells me more than all your seeing. Is there any one visible beyond the reach of sound?"

"No," answered Bobby. "It is early. I suppose few are up yet."

"Foolish of them," Père Trouché muttered. "It is natural to sleep at noon, but the morning is the time to get about. If people slept more in the afternoons, they would be brisker in the mornings. Yet it is perhaps better as it is. In the evening when you others, you, are tired out—too tired to refuse an honest beggar and happy and content because work is over, then is the time to collect one's gifts. If ever, monsieur, you wish to beg"—he used the French expression, 'faire la route' which was new to Bobby but of which he guessed the significance—"beg in the evening when work is over, not in the morning when work is before one and therefore one is depressed and ill-tempered."

"I'll remember," said Bobby gravely, "and now I think I saw some one move by a grove of trees on our left, a few hundred yards away."

"Chestnut trees, chiefly? and to the south a dead oak the lightning has struck?"

"Yes," agreed Bobby. "You know the spot?"

"I might have guessed it is where they would arrange to meet," the old man muttered. "Let us go there, but keep well to the north. To the south the ground is rough and broken, and there is one spot where it is marshy."

Leaving the road they had been following, they reached soon the chestnut grove where Bobby thought he had seen a movement. It seemed deserted but Père Trouché listened intently and then stood for a moment, sniffing the air with distended nostrils. As though these senses of sound and scent told him more than Bobby's eyes conveyed to him, he called Camion's name several times. When no answer came, he frowned and said crossly:

"He is sulking, he will not show himself. Very well, we go to him."

Therewith he moved forward among the trees, feeling his way with his staff but all the same moving fully as quickly and confidently as did Bobby, following behind and picking his way through the undergrowth.

"Ah, there you are, my little Camion," the blind man exclaimed suddenly. To Bobby, who saw nothing, he explained: "A cigarette, you smell it?" He sniffed. "On the left. Not far. Behind that big tree in front of us, the papa of the grove, it is so big."

"How can you tell that?" Bobby asked.

"Eh, one feels it. When one is near anything, one can always feel the change in the air; there is a difference at once," answered Père Trouché, and Bobby remembered having read of modern theories which teach that there is necessarily a modification of space in the vicinity of matter.

Odd, Bobby thought, that abstruse scientific theories should be confirmed by the testimony of a blind beggar, for, though he had not touched the tree or been nearer to it than they both now stood, it was certainly much the biggest in the whole grove.

They picked their way through some bushes and on the further side, comfortably seated on a protruding root that made a kind of chair, was Camion, by his side the stump of a cigarette he had just thrown away, and a revolver.

"Good morning, Monsieur Camion," the old man greeted him. "It seems you are an early riser."

"What has that to do with you?" Camion retorted. "You are too fond of poking your nose in other people's affairs, my friend. Why have you brought the Englishman with you?" He looked challengingly at Bobby. "What are you here for?" he asked.

The old beggar was turning his head from side to side. One could almost see his ears twitching as he tried to catch any sound the soft air might bring. He said:

"Where is Volny?"

"Concern yourself with your own affairs, not other people's," Camion answered angrily.

"Young man," said Père Trouché severely, "all my life, and I have no longer my first youth, all my life I have concerned myself with the affairs of others. It is necessary if one is to know how to beg wisely and well, and if one does not know that, one should seek some other way of living. I ask you again: Where is Volny?"

"That is his business, not mine. He isn't here, anyhow."

"That I can hear for myself," said the old beggar, still more severely. "You are not being wise, my little Camion, when you answer me like that. You had arranged here a meeting with Volny?"

"At any rate, if I did, he has not kept it."

"There was a pistol shot we heard not many minutes since."

"You hear too much, too often," retorted Camion. "That is known."

"You have a revolver," Bobby said, speaking for the first time. "Do you usually take pistols with you when you go out for walks in the morning? Was it you who fired the shot we heard?"

Bobby, as he spoke, made a movement towards picking the pistol up, but Camion was too quick for him and in a moment had it in his hand. He looked at it a moment and put it in his pocket.

"It would serve you right if I did fire a shot or two with you for targets," he said with a formidable scowl.

He got to his feet and for a moment or two stood staring at them in that darkly prideful manner of his, in which however now there mingled with the arrogance and the defiance a touch of unease as well. Then abruptly he turned on his heel and strode away. Père Trouché said:

"That, I do not like. No."

"You don't think anything's been happening, do you?" Bobby asked anxiously.

"I do not know as yet but presently I shall," answered the blind beggar. "We know all that goes on in Citry-sur-l'eau, God and I, but God, He knows it as it happens, and I, I only when I have found out. There I am at a disadvantage." He shook his head, as if making the admission only under pressure and a little as if afraid that he had gone too far. Then he said: "Once again, it seems there is a real advantage in possessing sight. Watch, monsieur, and tell me if when he is out of hearing he turns aside or if he goes straight on."

"He is going straight back home so far," Bobby said, watching Camion's figure swiftly receding towards the village.

"It would be possible for him to turn again when he is beyond sight as well as hearing," muttered Père Trouché.

"He is keeping straight on, walking fast, too," Bobby repeated. Then he said doubtfully and uneasily: "We heard a shot. I wonder if we ought to have a look round?"

"Useless," answered the blind man with decision.

"Camion's voice was angry, sulky, furious, uncertain, what you will—but not excited, not the voice of one who has just been concerned in violence. I listened carefully. Nothing of serious in that voice."

"Yet serious things have happened in this village and not so long ago," Bobby remarked.

"It is true. The shadow is upon the village. Sometimes I think there is more to happen before that shadow lifts."

"You say you know all that goes on here," Bobby said slowly. "Are you sure you don't know something about that, too?"

"Hé, Mr. Englishman, did not the police conduct a full inquiry? True, they asked little of the old blind beggar, but that was because they felt there was nothing an old blind beggar could tell them. But every one else in all the village they questioned—eh, how they questioned. It is the only way they know how to find things out."

"Not a bad way, either," Bobby suggested. "Did they question also your schoolmaster, Monsieur Eudes?"

"Why do you ask that?" Père Trouché asked in his turn and his voice sounded a little troubled. "There was no need, since, as it happened he was away all that week —a conference of the parties of the Left at Dijon. He was a delegate, he spoke. So they knew where he was, the good police. It was a question they never thought of asking the blind old beggar, where he was?"

"Where were you?" Bobby asked sharply and again the old man gave that weird, unnatural chuckle of his.

"Hé, hé, you ask questions, too? But, you understand, to ask is one thing, to be answered is another—the good God and I, we know, but no others, at least, none that are alive."

He spoke with a sudden gravity as he added these last words. Bobby looked at him doubtfully, wondering what he meant, wondering if really he knew something.

"What do you mean?" he asked. "None that are alive," he repeated, wondering if this referred to one who was dead recently, to Miss Polthwaite herself. Had she known? If so, how, in what way? Père Trouché, not answering Bobby's question, said:

"There will be no need, monsieur, to say anything of this morning's happenings in the village. You agree?"

"I suppose not, if nothing's happened," Bobby said. "All the same, I think I'll take a look round."

"As you will," answered the old man indifferently. "For me, I can trust my ears and I think there is nothing of interest for you to find—except perhaps a good appetite for your early breakfast."

"How did you find out about all this business?" Bobby asked.

"Eh, I know, always I know, even if I do not always tell. One hears this. One hears that. Did not the young Camion say to you yourself that something might happen to him?"

"Why, yes, so he did," agreed Bobby, a little taken aback. "You heard that, too, did you? I never dreamed he meant this sort of thing, though."

"I kept it in my mind. I wondered. I did not think it was grave; for the young Volny, he is not so full of courage as all that. With the fists, yes, for there his strength gives him confidence, his fists are his big battalions and he knows God is on their side. But when it comes to pistols, eh, Mr. Englishman, there is a difference. I have noticed it before, the big man, he is very brave with his strength, but often when it is a question of guns and bullets, the big man loses his confidence, the little man is readier. It may be that he feels now he has the advantage, being a smaller target. It is not always so, but I think that it is true of the young Volny. All the same, I was not very happy, for with the young pride and folly often take the place of courage, and Volny has the youth, not of his twenty years but of his ten. So when I found that he was not sleeping at home, I was uneasy. When I threw a little earth against the window of Camion's room and again there was no answer, I was more uneasy still. If they were both out, these young men with their hot heads and their folly, at such an hour of the morning, well, one drew one's conclusions. So it seemed to me the best thing I could do was to waken you. My faith, you responded on the instant. You have then the habitude?"

Bobby ignored this last question. He certainly had 'the habitude', for at home he always slept, knowing that at any moment the 'phone might go, bringing an urgent summons. But that he was not anxious to explain. He said instead:

"How did you know which was my window?"

"But that was simple. I could hear your breathing."

"Do you want to tell me," asked Bobby incredulously, "that you could recognize my breathing?"

"I did not say so. I said I heard breathing. Therefore the room was occupied, and, since I could hear anything at all, the window must be wide open. Therefore the occupant must be an Englishman, and since I knew that only one Englishman was staying in the hotel, I knew that Englishman must be you. That is all. The simple logic."

"So it is," agreed Bobby admiringly.

Therewith they parted, Père Trouché returning to the village by way of a farm where he expected to be regaled with a drink of fresh milk and some bread, and Bobby to walk up and down for a time, making sure there was no sign of any untoward happening.

"One shot needn't mean anything serious," he told himself. "A try to see if the thing was in good order, a practice shot, anything."

Presently he returned to the village, now fully astir. Lucille was at the door of her aunt's shop as he passed, but when she saw him she retired within, barely acknowledging his salute. At the hotel where his absence had just been discovered, he explained he had been for an early morning stroll, and that presently he meant to see what he could do towards getting these glorious Auvergne sunrises down on canvas.

Later on, after breakfast, he went out again to do some sketching, taking care, however, not to go too far away in case of any further developments. Nothing happened, except that various small children came to look on, and that he won the heart of one, a pretty little thing, by making a sketch of her and presenting her with the finished result.

Not till much later in the day, after dinner in fact, did a remark he overheard inform him that young Volny was missing and that his father was furious, since this was the second time recently on which the young man had absented himself for a whole day, in spite of all the work that at this season of the year cried out for attention.

CHAPTER XI
THE CURÉ'S SOAP

The next day, too, Bobby spent quietly sketching. He saw no more of Père Trouché, he noticed once or twice Williams hovering at a distance, black and scowling, and almost expected he was about to receive from him some new threat or warning. But Williams wandered away again with anything he had wished to say still unuttered. Perhaps, Bobby thought, he had been merely watching, though for what purpose Bobby found it difficult to guess. From some of the passers-by who occasionally stopped to look at his work—often with intelligent interest, not merely with the amusement English people feel on seeing a grown man occupy himself with brush or pencil —he learnt that the elder Volny was fulminating threats against his absent son, who was, it appeared, to be disinherited, forbidden the house, married to some strong-minded, sensible, not-too-young woman, who would know how to keep him in order, and generally to suffer various other pains and penalties as soon as he reappeared, which so far he had shown no sign of doing. Also it seemed that Monsieur Volny had visited Lucille, accused her in a stormy scene of being privy to his son's disappearance, and announced that if she tried to follow him, unpleasant consequences would follow. This last threat no doubt was vague, but it had greater force than Bobby realized, for he did not quite understand how formidable parental authority can still be in France, especially in rural France. All the same the final upshot had been Monsieur Volny retreating from the shop before a flourished broom wielded by the Tante Simone, while all the village watched and wondered.

Bitterly did Bobby regret that he had missed this scene which he felt would be historic in the village annals. Not that he felt much inclined to be unduly concerned by Volny's disappearance. His own little encounter with the young man on the hill-side had left him with a strong impression that Henri Volny had a considerable respect for the safety of Henri Volny's skin. Perhaps, too, he had realized that Camion was of a different type, utterly heedless of every consequence once his emotions were deeply aroused, certain to take a duel 'au grand sérieux'.

Two youngsters deeply interesting in their contrasting types of character, Bobby thought: Volny with a dogged determination on ends and yet a shrinking from risk in the means for achieving those ends; Camion with his readiness to face the immediate issue but hesitation in seeking his final ends. A young man with such ambitions towards conquering the hotel world should, Bobby thought, be already seeking the larger fields offered by the great towns. Quite possibly that was what Volny had now done.

All the same Bobby's mind was busy enough, as he sketched and gossipped with his occasional visitors and ate his lunch he had brought with him, and stretched himself out to bask in the warm, scented sunshine of Auvergne. Late in the afternoon he packed up his sketching materials and made his way back to the village for the dinner for which his long day in the open air had given him good appetite. When he reached the church he went inside and looked again at the little shelf before the black Virgin. It was quite bare now, without either flowers or diamonds, and Bobby made up his mind that the time had come to ask the curé a few questions.

He left the church accordingly and went across to the presbytery. One of the village women was coming out of the house. She said to him:

"Monsieur the curé is not there but he always leaves his door open so that one may enter and wait or write a message for him if they will."

"He is not afraid of thieves, then?" Bobby said.

The woman smiled contemptuously.

"They say he would shave an egg," she remarked, "but a thief would have to shave closer than that to get anything here worth the taking."

She went on and Bobby, finding that in fact the door was open, crossed the threshold, though not without some hesitation. The room in which he found himself did in fact present a markedly poverty-stricken, uncared- for appearance. A table, in bad repair; two or three chairs, all a trifle unsteady on their rickety legs; a shelf with a few old and worn devotional books; a clock with one hand broken; a buffet, very old, but in better repair than most of the other things in the room, provided the chief furniture. There were one or two religious objects as well, a crucifix, a picture of the Sacred Heart, two or three small statuettes, but the general impression was of poverty and neglect. The rough wooden boards of the flooring had no covering, for instance, and though they had been recently swept they showed many stains and marks, as though it were long since they had been scrubbed. Bobby strongly disapproved. He had heard that the curé lived alone, his housekeeper having recently left him on the ground that she was not prepared to face another winter without sufficient firing, but all the same Bobby felt that the use of scrubbing brush, soap, and hot water is open to any man, nor are such things hard to procure.

He went on into the kitchen. It was as bare, as neglected-looking, as the room he had just left. A scrubbing brush hanging up in one place had no bristles left. Bobby supposed that it had been worn out by the housekeeper and the curé had refused to supply her with another. No wonder she had departed. In the fireplace stood a brazier in which smouldered a little charcoal. On it was an iron pot containing, Bobby thought, dish water for washing up. A pea pod or two floated on the surface and Bobby wondered a little why it was being so carefully kept warm.

So far he had not seen any place in which either diamonds or anything else of value could be hidden. He went back into the sitting-room and tried the buffet. It was unlocked and its shelves contained only a few odds and ends even a rag and bone dealer would hardly have been willing to take the trouble to remove. At least that was Bobby's first impression till he looked again and a glint of metal caught his eye. It was a revolver lying there, and, though Bobby could not be sure, it looked to him very like the one that he had taken from Volny and thrown away.

Doubtfully, Bobby stood and looked at it. How had it come here, he wondered. An odd thing to find in the possession of a priest. Looking again he saw there was a cap near by, a cloth cap resembling, though again he could not be sure, the one Volny had been wearing. He took it out to look at it more closely and saw on the lining a dull stain that looked to him like blood, that in fact he felt sure was blood.

Troubled and uncertain, for these were discoveries of which he could make nothing, he went to the door of the house. There was no one in sight. He went back into the house, closed the door behind him, ran quickly up the stairs. The first room he went into was empty of all furnishing. The second contained only a wooden bed, nothing else. The third room was a little better furnished, but nevertheless had the same neglected and desolate look the rest of the house showed. The bedclothes looked so old and worn they resembled a heap of rags more than anything else, and Bobby noticed that here, too, the bare boards of the floor, though they had been swept, though they showed a little damp in places as if water had recently been applied, were yet so marked and stained that certainly they had known no touch of soap or scrubbing brush for a long time.

But Bobby experienced now a certain relief; and then smiled at himself for the absurdity of the vague half-fear that had come into his mind when that pistol and bloodstained cap had suggested to him the possibility that Volny had been either killed by Camion in their duel or else seriously wounded, and had sought refuge here. A ridiculous and far-fetched fancy, no doubt, and be-sides in a duel two shots, he supposed, would be fired, that is, at least, if the rules are observed in loyalty and good faith. Bobby found himself, however, reflecting again that pride and self-will can lead a young man into strange paths, and that Camion was already under suspicion of having killed once. Now he dismissed such thoughts with a sigh of relief as he reflected that here there was no sign of Volny, either dead or wounded, and no other suggestion than pistol and bloodstained cap that he had ever been near the place. And of the presence of cap and pistol a dozen explanations could easily be imagined.

Bobby gave another quick glance round the room. The economical and somewhat slovenly habits of the curé, his apparent ignorance of the use and value of soap—Bobby had noted that in the kitchen no morsel of soap was visible—were no business of his, and anyhow there did not appear to be any place here where valuables could be kept. It did not much look, Bobby thought, as if the diamonds removed from the shelf before the black Virgin could be hidden in the presbytery.

He went downstairs again and settled himself to wait, nor had he had time to do more than smoke a cigarette when he saw the curé coming briskly up the steep ascent on which stood church and presbytery. He came in quickly, and looked a little surprised and not too pleased to see Bobby, who for his part thought the curé looked flushed and excited. The suspicion even came into his mind that the curé had been drinking, a suspicion that was strengthened when, after the briefest possible salute to Bobby, he put down on the rough wooden table a package he had been carrying with great care.

"There!" he said, "there is something that goes a little to the head."

In his apparently excited state he had forgotten on his safe arrival home to be as careful with his parcel as before, and he put it down on the edge of a not-too-steady table. It slipped and, falling to the floor, burst open. Bobby had subconsciously been prepared for a crash of breaking bottles. Instead, to his utter amazement, he saw some dozen or so cakes of a well-known brand of soap manufactured in England go rolling about the floor.

The curé stooped and picked them up with caressing, tender fingers.

"Eh, eh, my little ones," he said as if addressing them, "it is not time yet, one is not ready yet, but presently you shall have your introduction to the floor, only not yet, my little ones, not till we have also the hot water and a scrubbing brush, since it is difficult to scrub well without a brush."

For the moment he appeared to have forgotten Bobby's presence. Not until he finished collecting his scattered soap and piling the pieces up on the table in a heap from which he seemed unable to keep his eyes did he speak to him.

"Monsieur will excuse me," he said then. "One gets into the way of talking to oneself when one lives much alone. It is a way of hearing a human voice. Also one is a little apt to lose the head when one receives without warning enough of soap to last a year with care. All one needs now is hot water."

"Well, there's some in the kitchen," Bobby remarked.

The curé looked surprised.

"In the kitchen? Hot water? But no, that, how can that be?" He went quickly to the kitchen door. Bobby followed and pointed to the pot on the brazier of charcoal. The curé said: "Monsieur, that is my soup, my dinner."

"Oh, no," Bobby told him. "Some one must have been playing tricks. That's only hot water, a bit greasy."

Looking alarmed, the curé crossed the floor, lifted the lid of the pot, peered anxiously within, seemed relieved.

"It is my good soup for my dinner," he said. He looked doubtfully and with some suspicion at Bobby: "I do not fully understand why you speak so," he remarked, "but if you mean that you wish for a share, you are welcome. Such as are my meals," he added simply, "I share them always with those who desire it and are hungry. Yet unless there is some trouble at your hotel, you will receive there perhaps more varied nourishment."

"You don't mean that greasy water is your dinner?" Bobby asked.

"Monsieur," said the curé, "it is better to thank God for food than to call it by such names as greasy water. My soup is not rich, perhaps, but it stays the stomach."

He went back into the front room. Somewhat at a loss, Bobby followed him. The curé said:

"You were waiting to see me, monsieur? You do not believe, however? You others, English, you are not believers, you deny Holy Church? You do not believe?" he repeated questioningly.

"Oh, yes, why not?" Bobby said.

The curé looked doubtful and shook his head.

"I have never noticed it," he said. "The English tourists, they come sometimes to the church to stare at the black Virgin, but only as at a curiosity in a museum. It is difficult perhaps to be sure, since they are not able to speak so as to make themselves understood." He turned back to his soap. "I must put it away," he said, "but where will it be safe? for I have no place to keep valuables." He gave a little apologetic laugh. "When one has had no soap for so long," he said, "it is exciting to have all at once so much."

"But surely," protested Bobby, more puzzled than ever, "there's no shortage of soap, is there? You can buy as much as you like, can't you?"

"Without doubt," answered the curé, "if, that is to say, you have the money."

"Well, soap's not as dear as all that," declared Bobby, still very puzzled, more especially as by now it was quite clear that drink had nothing to do with the curé's show of excitement, and surely, Bobby thought, a few cakes of soap were not sufficient cause.

The curé had put his soap away now on a shelf in the buffet and, sitting down, he looked up thoughtfully at Bobby.

"I regret," he said. "I was a little beyond myself. One would not think soap could be so exciting? Ah, well, if for so long you had had to make shift with crumbled lava, you would understand better. You say it is cheap to buy? Monsieur, an ingot of gold at a sou would be dear if you had no sou." He smiled again as Bobby still continued to look very bewildered. "You thought that I was mad or I had been drinking too much wine?" he said. "It was not that. Listen. You are a foreigner. I will tell you things I never tell my own people. Among them one has one's pride, hein? See now. I have from the bishop—" he named a sum amounting, Bobby calculated rapidly, to just about the forty pounds a year on which once in England another parish priest thought himself passing rich. "I have also what my parishioners pay me for a mass, for this or that. But they do not always pay, they economize on their duties to the Church. This soap that I have received, it is for dues owing me for years. The Church, they delay, they neglect, they refuse.

Monsieur Eudes, he receives more each month to establish his
paper of revolution and infidelity than I in a year. Also out of what
I receive the Citry church must come first, the priest may starve
but his church must be cared for, the mass must be said, the
repairs must be made. In winter there must be a little warmth
though the presbytery has none. But all that does not interest you
who do not believe. There was a matter on which you wished
perhaps to speak to me since you were waiting my return? "

"On the contrary, what you say interests me very greatly,"
Bobby said. "Didn't you tell me once you had hopes of rebuilding
your church here?"

"It was a dream," the curé answered. "It is a dream I had.
There was an uncle in America. He used to write sometimes of the
great things he was doing there. But now he is dead and it seems
that he left no money at all so that he was buried as a pauper. It
appears he had misfortunes in business, but that he did not say, he
preferred to write as though he were rich still. Then there arrived
Mile. Polthwaite. She came to look at the black Virgin. She said to
me things. Perhaps I misunderstood. It appeared that she was
very rich. It would have been for the repose of her soul if she had
done what she spoke of. Is it not a good thing to give your fortune
to the Church and die and be received in Paradise?" The curé was
growing excited again. He was on his feet now and in his eyes
shone once more that fanatical gleam Bobby had seen in them
before. "But she is dead; she has received her call, and I, no matter
what black guilt I must confess to, at least I say each day a mass
for the repose of her soul."

"Guilt? Black guilt? What do you mean?" Bobby asked,
startled, but the curé only shook his head and made no other
answer even when Bobby pressed him again.

"Monsieur, I have nothing to say to you on this subject," he
answered firmly. "Neither do I know why you ask these questions.
It is that that is beginning to interest me."

"I will tell you one reason," Bobby said. "When I was in your
church a day or two ago, I saw there, at the feet of the image of the
Virgin, what I think were diamonds —seven of them. They are not
there now."

"Monsieur," said the curé quietly, "you are not the custodian of the possessions of the church."

"There is a story," Bobby said, "that Miss Polthwaite possessed many such diamonds."

"Ah, you know that, you have heard that?" the curé said. He was facing Bobby now and looking at him very closely. "I will tell you then. I removed them. I noticed that you were looking, that you seemed interested. You stood upon a chair, I think, to look more closely. My own people, they do not rob; above all, not the Holy Virgin. But I do not know you, monsieur. You are a stranger. You are not of ours. You are of a country where they do not believe. Therefore I took my precautions."

"Oh, well," muttered Bobby, slightly disconcerted to hear he had himself been an object of suspicion.

"Also," continued the curé, "it was plain you thought the stones of value. Of that, I was not sure before. Mademoiselle Polthwaite insisted that for those few pebbles I could receive many thousands of francs. No doubt she exaggerated, for the diamonds one knows, they sparkle and shine, as these did not, so that evidently even if they are diamonds at all, they are diamonds of an inferior quality, just as to-day there are pearl necklaces all our young girls wear that in former days a duchess or a countess would have been proud to own. But if they were of real value—well, our villagers are honest, yet when politics come in—well, there are some I would not trust. Eudes, for example," said the curé, looking a good deal less Christian than should a good Christian priest, "though I might trust him not to rob me, yet he would rob the Church and boast of it. There is nothing he would not do, treason, murder, anything, to establish his newspaper of blasphemy and revolution that he talks of continuously." He paused, a little breathlessly, for his words had come tumbling out in his excitement, one on top of another as fast as he could get them uttered. Bobby said:

"Was Miss Polthwaite murdered?"

"Ah, you are thinking of Eudes," the curé said. "About that, I know nothing. Yet I will say this, that I believe, I know, there is nothing that unhappy misguided victim of communist teaching would not do in order to secure the means to mislead, to deceive, to entrap honest folk in a net of ignorance and destruction and of folly and so to destroy all that stands for righteousness and peace and the salvation of the human soul."

CHAPTER XII
ARTIST NOT AT HOME

Bobby left the presbytery then and returned to the hotel in a mood of considerable doubt and bewilderment. He did not at all know what to make of this appearance of poverty so extreme that even soap became a luxury of which an unexpected supply produced such excitement. Nor did he much like to remember how at times the curé's eyes had seemed to shine with the fires of fanaticism. Then, too, he found more than a little disturbing the curé's tale of gifts and promises of future gifts made by Miss Polthwaite. Was it a confirmation of this story that the curé was certainly in possession of diamonds formerly her property—or was a darker, more dreadful explanation to be sought?

Was it possible, Bobby asked himself, that the curé, brooding in his solitude on what he believed had been promised, and then abruptly disappointed, had been pushed beyond the bounds of sanity? Not but that he seemed perfectly sane and normal now, even though he was certainly a little excitable and not altogether unaffected by his lonely existence.

Very strongly did Bobby realize how much his difficulties were increased by his comparative ignorance of the environment and psychology of these people. At home, in England, in London especially, he would have been able to place them all much more easily and to form on them a judgment much more likely to be accurate.

He ate that evening an excellent dinner that might have been boiled cabbage and tapioca pudding for all he knew to the contrary. But he did notice that young Camion was not there to supervise the service and that in consequence things did not go as smoothly as usual.

Later on, Bobby went for a short stroll that ended, as he was making it his habit, in the café he had visited before.

It was as busy as usual, and when Bobby had found a table at which to seat himself he was both pleased and surprised when Eudes came to join him. By a lucky chance the child of whom Bobby had made a sketch, and then presented it to her, was one of the schoolmaster's favourite pupils, and one who, in his opinion, showed promise of genuine artistic ability. Probably this nascent talent of hers explained the interest she had shown in Bobby's work that had first attracted his attention to her.

Eudes seemed in an expansive, genial mood, in no way diminished by the fact that Bobby's hospitality took the form of asking him to share in a bottle of the most generous and expensive wine the patron could produce. Would Bobby, asked Eudes, an artist of such high merit, one of whom Monsieur Shields had spoken with respect, and Monsieur Shields was a man who was known, who had arrived, would Bobby look at some of the child's drawings and give an opinion on them? It seemed Eudes wished her talent to be seriously cultivated. Her family disapproved, considering that any girl who knew how to cook knew all that was either necessary or desirable. Bobby expressed his willingness to do as desired, but suggested that seeking the opinion of the director of the nearest school of art and design would be more valuable. He himself, he pointed out, was neither critic nor teacher. It appeared, however, that the director in question was, in Monsieur Eudes's considered opinion, a reactionary of the blackest hue. A strongly-supported rumour declared that he had been known to attend mass. The attention of the local deputy had been drawn to this dread suspicion, but he, a Laodicean, had done nothing, and there was reason to believe that the Sous-préfet, a man far worse than merely Laodicean, had even suppressed in the waste-paper basket certain reports on the subject that had been forwarded to him.

"An intrigue, monsieur," said Eudes darkly, permitting himself, however, the consolation of allowing his glass to be refilled. "It is the curse of France, these currents below the surface by which the people are influenced without their knowledge."

"But surely on a question of a child's ability, no one would bother about politics?" suggested Bobby.

"When one is stone deaf," declared Eudes, whose glass was empty again and who displayed no reluctance to its being filled once more, "one's judgment of all music is affected—whether of a Beethoven symphony or of jazz on a tin whistle."

Bobby did not quite see the analogy, though he thought it would probably be interesting to hear jazz played on a tin whistle. However, he did his best to look impressed and Eudes went on:

"It is the gold of the Church, the enormous wealth she and her agents dispose of that gives them their power, that enables them to live in such unheard-of luxury."

"I had a chat with your curé to-day," Bobby remarked. "I can't say he seemed to me to be living in any kind of luxury."

"It is their cunning," said Eudes earnestly, "they put on an appearance of poverty in order to deceive."

"Oh, I see," said Bobby.

Perhaps his tone showed a certain incredulity, for Eudes continued:

"Oh, I do not deny that some of these black crows are forced to exist in a squalor that shows plainly what fate the rest of us would suffer if the Church secured the absolute dominion it aims at. Also there is a reward in view. If our curé ever succeeded in carrying out his cunning schemes to rebuild here his church in magnificence, so that that absurd block of wood he cherishes so much could become a fresh centre of degradation and superstition—"

He paused, apparently unable to find words with which to express the fear and horror he felt at this prospect.

"You mean the black Virgin?" Bobby asked.

Eudes nodded, gloomily emptied his glass, put it down again firmly.

"That shall never be," he said, but there was uneasiness in his voice. "Never."

"You think," Bobby asked, "that if a new church were built, enshrining the black Virgin, it would have a great influence here?"

"It would give such fresh strength to old superstitions," said Eudes with slow gravity, "as would undo all our work of enlightenment. A little time ago I admit I had a fear, a great fear.

There threatened a danger, more formidable than I can tell. For there is nothing that these misguided, miserable tools of superstition and reaction will hesitate at, no crime at which they will draw back if it will give them and their masters the means to plunge honest folk further into morasses of ignorance and slavery and so destroy all hope of peace and progress and the liberation of the human mind."

His eyes were blazing now with much those same fires of fanaticism which only a little time before Bobby had seen shining in the eyes of the curé. Bobby watched uneasily. With two such fanatics, it seemed many things might have been possible. Eudes lowered his voice and spoke confidentially.

"Happily that danger passed," he said. "The money our curé hoped to get into his claws with which to enslave the population, it eluded him. Ah, what a triumph, how truly superb, for the cause of truth, of reason, of justice, if—"

"Yes?" said Bobby as Eudes paused and once more he filled the schoolmaster's glass.

"If that very money," Eudes continued, "escaped the claws of the church and came to be used for the establishment of a journal of true enlightenment, to achieve the final victory of truth and reason?"

"How could that be?" Bobby asked, as indifferently and as carelessly as he could.

But his hope that, as sometimes happens, a simple question asked naturally and with apparent indifference, might lead to fresh confidences, was disappointed. Eudes changed abruptly. He waved aside the bottle Bobby pushed towards him. He seemed to feel he had said too much, more than he would have dreamed of saying to any one in the village, more than it would have been prudent to say to any compatriot, more indeed than it was wise to have said even to a foreigner little concerned with the conflict of ideas in another country. It even occurred to him that perhaps this rich and generous wine might have been loosening his tongue a trifle too much. All that showed plainly enough in his expression and Bobby tried again—shock tactics this time.

"Was Mademoiselle Polthwaite murdered for her money, do you think?" he asked.

Eudes leaned across the table and spoke in an undertone—a slightly thick undertone.

"Monsieur," he murmured, "of that I know nothing, I suspect nothing, yet I have my own thoughts I breathe to no one for it would be disloyal to say things of which there is no proof. Yet this I do say, that there are fanatics of the Church who would hesitate at nothing, who would persuade themselves that in its service all is permissible. All," he repeated. "But of that we will say no more. Nothing. One's lips are sealed. It is understood? Now we talk of other things."

"Let me fill your glass," Bobby said. "It is empty."

"I thank you. No," Eudes answered firmly. "You understand that I must set an example to the village? It is for that reason I push temperance to the verge of abstinence."

"Admirable," murmured Bobby, surveying a bottle more than half empty, his share having been just one glass.

But now he set an example he hoped might be followed by filling his own glass again. Eudes remained firm. He repeated:

"We talk of other things, hein?"

Occasion was provided almost immediately when from a table near by came some loud argumentative reference to the disappearance of the still missing Volny.

"You hear?" Eudes asked. "How they talk! He has his admirers here, that lad, and there are those who think he has taken a ticket to America and that soon we shall hear of him as a new Carpentier, fighting for the world championship of the box. Ah, bah, he is not so good as all that, our little Volny, he is not even so fond of fighting as all that, not at least against those as big and strong as himself, or even bigger and stronger. Nor would he very willingly leave Citry-sur-l'eau at this moment—would you, monsieur, would any young man in love with a girl, depart and leave her to the attentions of his rival? But perhaps you do not understand that, for you are English, and you others, English, you do not understand love very well."

"Don't we?" said Bobby meekly. "But what's become of Volny then?"

"I could make a guess," Eudes told him gravely. "Up there, up on the hill-side, with that other old black crow who sits there, watching and waiting and hatching mischief. I saw him ride off that way on his bicycle."

"You mean he is staying with the Abbé Taylour?"

"You have visited the Abbé Taylour? Yes, up there, for it is there he went once before, when he quarrelled with his father and wished by his absence to reduce his mother to despair and by that his father to submission, as indeed soon happened. Few know where he was then, but it happens that Monsieur Shields, your countryman and my friend, met him there that night."

"Shields?" repeated Bobby very surprised for he could not think for what reason Shields could have been wandering about late at night near the Abbé Taylour's hut when he himself lived on the other side of the Bornay Massif. "What was Shields doing there?" he asked.

"It was on one of his visits to Mademoiselle Polthwaite," Eudes explained. "He used to come sometimes; he would stay a night or two at the hotel, visit Miss Polthwaite, talk about her work, take little excursions to make sketches and his paintings. On one of them he stayed too long and had to take refuge with the Abbé Taylour."

"Must have been crowded in that little hut with three of them," observed Bobby. "I suppose if it was summer, one of them could sleep outside."

"It was in the winter, before Christmas," Eudes said, "early, before the snow came. It was late that year. No doubt they kept each other warm."

Eudes laughed very much at this idea and then appeared suddenly to realize that he had taken rather more than usual of a rather stronger wine than he was accustomed to. He announced firmly that much as he regretted leaving so dear, so good, so amiable a friend as Bobby, it was time for him to return home.

He went off accordingly, walking very steadily but somehow giving the impression that he was being careful to walk steadily, and Bobby, whose own head was buzzing from the effects of a wine richer than he also was accustomed to, was not sorry to seek his own bed.

The next day was a Sunday, and Bobby thought it would be a good opportunity to visit Shields as that gentleman had invited him to do. That the missing Volny was not, as Eudes had suggested, with the Abbé Taylour in his isolated hut up in the hills, Bobby felt fairly certain. Volny had gone off on his bicycle, and one does not as a rule attempt to go hill-climbing on a bicycle. Eudes's story, though, of a previous meeting with Shields, had struck Bobby as possibly significant. Very probably the meeting of these three men, Volny, Taylour, Shields, in that lonely hut had been entirely accidental, but just possibly it had not. And if Volny, disappearing on his bicycle and without apparently much money in his pocket, since his father was said to keep him on a short allowance and he had none of his own, had taken refuge with Shields, as was at any rate a possibility, then there would be a proof of continued connection that would bear further investigation.

Bobby departed therefore by the first train available next day. At Clermont he had to wait for a train to Barsac and he remembered Shields had told him the connections were always bad. He filled in the time by taking a stroll round the town, admired the Puy de Dome from a new point of view, decided that if ever he had the time to spare he would make the ascent, admired, too, the famous statue of Vercingetorex and the less famous one of Pascal— naturally philosophers have smaller, less noble statues than have warriors—found the church where Peter the Hermit preached the first Crusade, and caught his train to land him in Barsac before eleven.

He knew roughly from the directions Shields had given him where the house lay. So first he treated himself to a light meal at a café, then smoked a reflective cigarette or two and finally reached his destination at what he hoped was the tactful hour of half-past one when he thought lunch would probably be over and yet the business or the repose of the afternoon not yet begun.

The house was situated a little distance outside the small town and did not look in very good repair. The fairly large garden surrounding it had a somewhat neglected air, too, as though Mr. Shields, though more fortunate than most artists in these days, since he seemed to possess a faithful clientele in the United States, was yet by no means inclined to spend money on his place of habitation. Nor did Bobby much like the position of the house. It lay in a hollow, it looked damp, it was cut off on the south by close-growing trees, on the north it was exposed to wind sweeping down from the high ground behind, the Bornay Massif on the other side of which lay Citry-sur-l'eau.

Rusty, unpainted iron gates admitted to the garden. Bobby passed through them and went on up a weed-grown gravel path to the house. He knocked once or twice and rang the jangling and ancient bell whose echoes he could hear resounding from the interior. But no one came, and after a time he gave up the effort. Annoying, he thought, to have come so far, only to find Shields out. Sketching, perhaps, though Bobby had hoped Sunday would be a good day to catch him at home. Thinking that just possibly some one might be at the back or in the garden, Bobby strolled round. Here there were more signs of care and cultivation, most of the space being given up to vegetables. There were two or three outhouses, too. Bobby walked round the garden, noticed there was a back gate that led straight on to the waste ground of the Massif that came right down to the garden fence, and then wandering back and noticing that one of the outhouses was open he went inside to sit down, out of the sun, smoke a cigarette and wait a little in the hope that some one would appear.

The shed was evidently chiefly used as a receptacle for garden and other odds and ends. Dust was everywhere and cobwebs hung in festoons. Not an inviting place, Bobby thought, but it did offer shade and the sun was hot. Various tools, broken, damaged, rusting, lay about. In one corner was a heap of flower pots and in another some of the small glass frames used for forcing early vegetables. Close by stood the remnants of a bale of binder twine, used presumably for tying up plants, and piled against one wall was a great heap of sacks of artificial manure. Bobby regarded this with mild interest, wondering if Shields was an agent for the sale of the stuff or was taking care of it for some neighbouring farmer, since there seemed to be more of it than a garden of this size would require in half a century or so. He noticed, too, a broken-down bicycle in one place, and then observed that there was another, in better repair, pushed away behind the sacks of artificial manure and so well hidden that only because one sack had slipped had it become visible.

Bobby went across to look at it and noticed that it showed no such 'plaque' as French regulations demand. But then regulations in France are not always very closely obeyed, and Bobby, noticing that some of the artificial manure sacks seemed much cleaner and freer from dust than most of the surrounding articles, as though they had not been there long, or been recently moved, made himself a seat on them and was enjoying a cigarette when a gruff voice from the door wanted to know who he was and what he was doing there.

The speaker appeared to be a working man in his Sunday clothes. Bobby explained that he had come to visit Mr. Shields, who had promised to show him his paintings, but there was no one at home and so he had decided to wait for a little. He asked if it were known when Mr. Shields would be back, learned that he was probably out painting somewhere, offered the new-comer a cigarette, and was soon on friendly terms. It appeared that his name was Ducane, that he cultivated the garden on a sharing arrangement, Mr. Shields being entitled to such of the produce as he chose to claim for his own use, and Ducane taking the rest, for sale or use, as payment for his work. Ducane explained, too, that he had heard some one was inquiring for Monsieur Shields's house, and as he knew the artist was out and there had been occasional mysterious and mischievous intruders in the garden who had done a certain amount of damage, he had come along to see what was happening.

"Quite right, too," agreed Bobby. "Your duty both to yourself and to Mr. Shields. But what kind of mischief and what sort of mysterious intruder?"

Ducane shook his head. That, he explained, was a question, a veritable question. Bobby waited patiently. He had soon decided that Ducane was of those whom it is best not to hurry.

"Truly, monsieur," Ducane said finally, "if we knew that, then there would be much that we should understand better. But as it is, it is beyond comprehension, and so indeed Monsieur the Commissaire of Police said himself, for I, I who am now speaking, I heard him say it aloud."

CHAPTER XIII
ARTIST AT HOME

Startled as he was by this sudden reference to so important an official as a commissaire of police having been interested in whatever it might be that had happened here, Bobby was careful to show no special sign of interest.

"Bit of mischief by some boys, was it?" he asked, offering Ducane another cigarette. "I daresay your kids here are just as full of devilry as ours are in England. I'm English, you know, but I expect you spotted that from my accent."

"Monsieur speaks our language admirably," Ducane assured him. "Like Monsieur Shields almost, one could take him for a true Frenchman."

Bobby expressed proper appreciation of the compliment and then remarked:

"Probably you sit for Monsieur Shields, don't you? As a model, I mean."

Ducane looked rather surprised.

"No," he said, "no, that has never been suggested."

Bobby looked very surprised.

"I should have thought any artist would have been glad of the chance of getting you to sit," he remarked. "A countenance so interesting, so—how shall I say it? so different. One can see you have suffered, you have wept, you have understood."

Ducane smirked, purred, behaved as ninety-nine point nine per cent of us would behave on being told that we looked 'different'—dearest praise of all in this standardized civilization of ours—and that we had 'suffered' and had 'understood'. An Englishman might not quite have liked being told he had wept, but for a Frenchman that was an additional proof of insight and of sympathy.

"Got him eating out of my hand now," said Bobby to himself with Anglo-Saxon brutality. Aloud he said: "But without doubt Monsieur Shields has found another model. It is remarkable, it is fortunate. Some one in the village?"

"There is young Pierre," Ducane admitted, somewhat reluctantly. "A youngster, a boy, a child." He paused there, and Bobby thought it just as well or else probably the young Pierre would have been denied even birth. Ducane continued: "Once or twice he has been up there in the studio. But seldom. In general Monsieur Shields paints in the open air, for his models trees and rocks that cost him nothing. As for me, I have no time to waste sitting still doing nothing."

"But one pays?" Bobby pointed out.

"Not so much as all that," retorted Ducane. "It is why the young Pierre would come no longer. All very well to have one's portrait shown the world over but one must gain one's bread as well."

"That is understood," agreed Bobby, "and when one has work, one must attend to it. Cabbages and cauliflowers do not grow by accident. But to-day is a Sunday. See now. Suppose you gave me a sitting? For an hour or two merely." He produced his sketching materials he had fortunately brought with him. "That is all. We talk. We discuss. There are many things two intelligent men can converse upon. You speak to me of your life, of your work, of the village, of what you will. You tell me, for example, of the mischief those boys did in your garden. As for me I work as I listen. At the end there is twenty francs for you. What do you say? Only, remember, I am not an artist of the first rank, like Monsieur Shields, though indeed it is difficult to understand why he has resisted the challenge there is in your features to even the most skilled brush. I shall do my best, but, remember, it is part of the bargain that you are not disappointed if it is a failure. Perhaps then I shall wish to try again."

Ducane promised gravely to control any disappointment he felt but was evidently determined to be critical.

"Good," said Bobby cheerfully as he set to work. "Now let us talk. About anything. Go ahead. I am waiting. I listen." This, of course, as Bobby had expected, reduced Ducane to an embarrassed silence. His mind became blank, which was indeed its normal state, save as regarded growing vegetables, the only subject on which his mental processes had ever troubled to exercise themselves. But then a demand to begin to talk about anything would by the general working of the law of opposites reduce most people to silence.

"For instance," said Bobby, when he judged the silence had lasted long enough, "about—what was it? Oh, yes, boys doing damage in the garden here."

"Ah, no," answered Ducane, finding his tongue now, "it was not boys. The footprints were of a man—enormous. Seven feet high at the least, declared Monsieur the Commissaire, "all over the garden they were and then they vanished—like that—pouf—as if he who made them had turned into thin air."

"Was that all?" asked Bobby.

"It was enough," Ducane retorted in a slightly offended tone. "Would monsieur not be disturbed if he found enormous and mysterious footsteps all around his house? But there was worse. It was as though a deliberate purpose had been to walk on my seed beds I had so carefully prepared. Tools had been thrown about. Some I did not find for days. A ladder had been put up against the house near the window. Monsieur Shields did not like that. My seed beds, my tools, all that was nothing. A ladder near a window, that was something to think about."

"Odd," said Bobby. "When was all this?"

"Early in March, when the snow had gone and one was beginning one's work."

"Nothing else happened?" asked Bobby.

"Nothing. That was what puzzled. Yet it was disconcerting, it was bewildering. As indeed admitted Monsieur the Commissaire of Police himself."

"You reported it to him?"

"It was hardly an affair for him," explained Ducane. "These big bonnets, they would not trouble themselves about the destruction of my seed beds or a ladder against a wall. They had indeed the inconceivable stupidity to suggest that I, I myself, had left it there. It was the brigadier to whom I spoke."

"What did he think?" asked Bobby, who knew that 'brigadier' corresponded roughly to our local sergeant of police. "I suppose he reported it to Monsieur the Commissaire?"

"It was not altogether that," Ducane answered. "An old foreign woman had committed suicide and as she was English also and a friend of Monsieur Shields, the commissaire came to ask Monsieur Shields what he knew about her and if he could tell why she had drowned herself. For me, I should choose a more pleasant end than jumping down a well. But everyone to his own taste. As for those gigantic footsteps, the commissaire made nothing of them. He would have sung a different tune if they had been in his garden, on his seedbeds. Monsieur Shields was angry about that, for he, he feared burglary. He arranged that for a time the brigadier should pass by regularly during the night. After that, the footsteps ceased and my seed beds were not again destroyed. That, it was a relief."

A curious tale, Bobby thought. Was it merely some piece of village spite or mischief or was there some deeper significance? If so, what could it be?

"It was really in connection with poor Miss Polthwaite's death that the commissaire came to make his inquiries?" Bobby remarked. "But what had Monsieur Shields to do with Miss Polthwaite's suicide?"

"It was not altogether plain at first that there had not been an assassination," Ducane explained. "It was only the inquiry that gave proof of suicide. Before that there had been talk. Nor has it altogether ceased even yet. Naturally at first one thought of Monsieur Shields. He, too, was English. They were friends. It was very possible there had been an affair and that he had grown tired, she had remained persistent, and the affair had ended as such affairs sometimes end when the woman chooses not to understand. But it was clear there had been no affair —when he visited Citry-sur-l'eau he stayed always in the hotel, never with her, and also there was another who was her friend. Besides, he had not visited Citry, or indeed left here, all that week. Also, since he was not her lover, he had no reason to kill."

"No, I see that," agreed Bobby, "but one kills sometimes for other reasons than love."

"Seldom," pronounced Ducane. "One loves. One kills. That is to be understood. For love, it goes to a young man's head. Inconceivable, incredible, when one is married, that one ever felt like that, but so it is. For money also one kills, or for hate. But who could hate an old foreigner like Miss Polthwaite—name of names, what a word to wrap one's tongue round—and there was no sign of robbery, nothing missing, nothing seemed to have been taken. Certainly there was no quarrel between Monsieur Shields and Mademoiselle Polthwaite and also as Monsieur the Commissaire said himself, as Monsieur Shields was here, he could not have been there."

"I suppose not," agreed Bobby, "but how do they know he was here? I was in Citry this morning and now I'm here. It's not so far."

"But undoubtedly you came by train—in the daytime that is possible but not at night, and that Monsieur Shields was here during the day, all the world knows and I also, for I, I who speak to you, I saw him myself."

"Well, there are motors, bicycles, one has legs even," Bobby pointed out. "Look here," he added, "I'm only talking, you know, I'm not making suggestions. I don t mean I suspect Monsieur Shields of anything. I can't because I don't know anything. So don't go saying things to him."

"It is understood, my discretion can be perfectly relied on," answered Ducane gravely. "But all that was carefully considered. In such affairs, Monsieur the Commissaire said to us all, everything must be considered, even the impossible. As for motor-cars, Monsieur Shields has none, none was hired—every garage was asked—and, moreover, it happened that the roads were under special supervision by the gendarmerie because of thefts of cars in Clermont. As for a bicycle, again Monsieur Shields had none for a day or two before his had been broken in an accident and he had not then a new one."

"He has now?" Bobby asked, "Without doubt," and Bobby remembered that he had seen in the shed, two bicycles, one a wreck and one pushed out of sight behind the sacks of artificial manure, possibly because it had not yet been provided with the necessary registration 'plaque'. Ducane continued: "Moreover he could not possibly have cycled all the night there and back without being seen by some one. As for his legs, none on foot could cover the distance in the time. In addition, he was in the garden during the evening, his light was burning in the studio till midnight, his hour for bed, as the brigadier himself testified. In the morning he was there to open the door when arrived Mère Potain who comes each day to do for him."

"He couldn't cross the Massif at night, I suppose?" said Bobby. "Every one seems to think it so difficult, I think I shall have to try some day to show it isn't."

Ducane laughed very much and hoped monsieur would at any rate not make the attempt in the dark. By daylight, it might be possible perhaps, though barely so. For himself he would not care to try. But in the dark—he waved the suggestion away as altogether unreasonable. Indeed Bobby was inclined to agree that so it was, remembering what he himself had seen of that wild and rugged terrain, so little different to-day from the state in which the last thundering roar of now extinct volcanoes had left it.

The conversation passed to other subjects. Bobby asked questions about gardening and for what vegetables the soil was most suitable. Ducane responded at length. He believed, it appeared, in deep digging and in hoeing.

"To dig and to hoe, all is there," he said.

It appeared that he disliked in especial artificial manure. Natural manure perhaps, but tight-fisted farmers would only part with that at the cost of the eyes in your head. As for chemical manures, they burnt up the good in the land. In that case, inquired Bobby, mildly puzzled, why was there such a huge stock of artificial manure stored up here? Ducane explained that there was an excellent joke about that. Monsieur Shields spoke French well enough but with an accent that was really extraordinary. Bobby noted in passing that this contradicted Ducane's earlier praise of his employer's French, but supposed that had been politeness and now the true verdict was being rendered. When, however, he had telephoned to Paris for certain garden requisites he had got his figures and weights all wrong. As a result he received, for instance, a penny packet of lettuce seed, but enough of this artificial manure to stock a large farm, and an enormous bale of binder twine instead of the handful or two of raffia needed for tying up plants. Unfortunately he paid the bill before realizing that anything was wrong and though he had been trying—was still trying—to get the Paris firm to take back the binder twine and the sacks of artificial manure, and refund the money paid, he had not as yet succeeded. Ducane did not hide his own belief that Monsieur Shields would never succeed. Probably the Parisians had seen a chance to get rid of the stuff, especially of all that binder twine which is not in much demand early in the spring. In his, Ducane's, considered opinion, Parisians were a tough lot when it came to business, and any one having affair with them, had to keep a good look-out, or he would lose the shirt off his back before he knew more than that he was feeling a bit chilly. Ducane hoped it would be a lesson to Monsieur Shields. If he, Monsieur Shields, had placed the order through him, Jules Ducane, why, then, all would have been well and there wouldn't still be sacks and sacks of artificial manure it was very certain those Parisians, once they had got rid of it, would never consent to take back. The binder twine had apparently, one way or another, got used, but the artificial manure was just as it had been dumped down by the carriers. It was a history of an artist, declared Ducane; children all of them in the ordinary affairs of life.

Bobby sighed and said it was only too true. He himself, but he would not trouble Monsieur Ducane with the history of some of his own misadventures. Instead perhaps Monsieur Ducane would give his opinion on the now completed portrait. For his part, Bobby admitted, he was not too well satisfied. It was not the sort of thing he would like to show Monsieur Shields, for example. Monsieur Ducane must let him try again, and, in the meantime, would Monsieur Ducane please remember he had promised to say nothing about it.

"He'll want to do you himself as soon as he knows what I've been up to," Bobby explained, "and I want first try. And he won't be pleased to think I noticed at once such an interesting model that he had had under his nose and never seen."

Ducane promised once more, accepted the payment due, and departed. Bobby went round to the front of the house and as there was still some time to spare before there left the last train he had to catch if he was to get back to Citry that night he settled down to wait a little longer in the hope that Shields might yet return. Nor in fact had he had time to do more than smoke another cigarette before Shields appeared, coming up the garden path, looking very surprised to see Bobby there and very apologetic for having so nearly missed him. He had cycled over to Clermont, he explained, but had returned a little earlier than he had expected because an acquaintance, one of his neighbours, had offered to bring him, and the cycle, too, back in his car.

"Rather thought I might make a sale," he explained confidentially, "but it didn't come off. In these hard times, when you make a sale about once a year if you're lucky, and when you're luckier still if you got much more than you've paid for paint and canvas, you jolly well can't afford to miss even the smell of a chance."

He took Bobby into the house, apologizing for an untidiness, due to the absence for the last day or two of the woman who cooked and cleaned for him. As a result of this defection there was nothing fit to eat in the house so he couldn't ask Bobby to stay to dinner. He would probably have to make his own evening meal off dry bread.

Bobby reflected that besides the café where he had lunched, he had noticed one or two quite promising- looking restaurants in the town and was inclined to gather, from this and other considerations, a general idea that either Shields had very little spare cash or else very little inclination to spend it. He sympathized, however, with his host on the difficulties of bachelor housekeeping and then in the studio, whither they had now proceeded, he did his best to wax enthusiastic over the paintings and drawings he was shown. He tried to salve his conscience by reminding himself that he was not a trained student of art, but all the same, with the best will in the world, he could not overcome his conviction that the drawing was only second-rate, that the composition was worse, that there was very little sense of atmosphere, and, though he knew his own colour sense was not first-rate, it seemed to him that that of Mr. Shields was, to say the least, eccentric. The only merit he could see was the kind of pedantic and careful accuracy much of Shields's work seemed to show, so that it would often be easy to recognize the places and scenes reproduced—reproduced was, Bobby thought, the exact word required. He noticed, too, that, as if in some sub-conscious way Shields was aware of a lack of interest, of poignancy, in his work, he tried hard nearly always to introduce some dramatic or human incident. One picture of a landscape under a storm cloud, for example, had a child painted in the foreground, and was entitled 'Lost Baby'. Another, a striking little scene, showing a high isolated rock in the form of a sugar loaf and a curiously-shaped, stunted oak displayed against a gloomy background of precipitous cliff in which appeared what seemed the entrance to a cave—all rendered with such care in detail that Bobby was reminded of a coloured photograph—was called 'The Duel', and showed in the foreground two men with levelled pistols facing each other. It was an instance, Bobby thought, of Shields's careless and inefficient drawing that the pistols were pointed in such a manner that the lines of fire were almost at right angles, crossing somewhere by or behind the stunted oak. Shields, however, must have thought it a good example of his work, for he had it framed and hanging on the studio wall in a conspicuous position, so that it would catch the eye of any visitor. Bobby duly admired it, and indeed its evident accuracy of detail gave it some claim to excellence, and then managed to turn the conversation to young

Volny. But Shields did not seem much interested, supposed the young fellow had got fed up with paternal discipline, and would reappear again when he wanted to. Then he produced some drawings he said were the work of Miss Polthwaite.

"She had no talent, of course," he said. "Rather weak amateur stuff. But it amused her, poor soul."

To Bobby, though he kept reminding himself he was no expert, these drawings seemed to have more vitality than any of Shields's own work. He could see they had faults, but all the same they seemed to him to have more of that indefinable something perhaps best described as 'atmosphere'. They did manage to convey an impression of having been not only 'seen' but 'felt' as well, not merely recorded as the camera records. Shields said suddenly and abruptly:

"You've heard about it? She was found in a well. Suicide. It was pretty clear what it was but some of these French police would have liked to pitch on me."

A little startled, not quite knowing what to say, Bobby murmured:

"You don't mean... not really...?"

"They got it into their heads we were lovers. Shock for the poor old soul if she had known. They heard we were friends and that was enough for them—they don't understand friendship between a man and a woman. 'L'amour'—all they can think of. I'm not a boy and she was no chicken, but that made no difference—'toujours l'amour'. Oh, well, luckily I was here snug in bed at the time. Just as well. Or they might have landed it on me." He laughed but not too comfortably. "Don't like the idea of the guillotine," he said. "I much prefer my head where it is. It might have gone if I hadn't had a fool-proof alibi. Most likely it really was suicide."

"I thought that was what was decided," Bobby said.

"Yes. Officially. Sometimes I think they are still watching me. I don't know. I'm going to America soon. I expect I shall have my luggage searched with extra care to make sure there's nothing incriminating. Well, there won't be."

"Do you think it was suicide?" Bobby asked.

"I don't know," Shields answered. "She was moody. Had ideas. Got herself into a bit of a jam with a French boy. You can never tell. Elderly spinsters go a bit dotty sometimes. Anyhow, the police weren't going to have it that it was any of their people killed her. They would have fixed it on me if they could, but as they couldn't they fell back on suicide. Quite likely, too. What do you think of this?"

It was an abrupt change of subject as Shields held up a large canvas which he evidently thought especially good and that Bobby was inclined to think especially bad. It took all his tact to avoid offending Shields and yet remain moderately near the limits of the truth. But Bobby had already discovered that the very modest, deprecatory terms in which Shields, on their first meeting, had spoken of his own work, in no way represented his real opinion of it. In his own eyes it was evident his work was of the highest quality and presently he began to hint that only the jealousy of other artists had prevented him from winning the recognition that was his due.

"Dinners," he said abruptly.

"Dinners?" repeated Bobby, vaguely wondering if now he were going to be invited to share that meal.

"Dinners," repeated Shields firmly. "If I had had the money to give a few smart dinners I should soon have been an R.A. Once there, I should have been one of the gang, they would have had to recognize me—they'll never recognize an outsider, die first—and once recognized, I should soon have been President. And all that missed for lack of a little coin to make a splash. Dining out, that's how an artist wins recognition in England. Oh, well, perhaps I'll come into my own yet. With a bit of money to back me, a little smart entertaining, a few cocktails for the critics, a big one-man show in a swell gallery, that's all there's to it. Only you have to have the money first."

"I see," said Bobby thoughtfully.

Shields showed some more of his work, and Bobby, suppressing his conscience, praised a good deal more freely than he had done before.

"A touch of genius there," he said unblushingly before one of the worst things shown him, and Shields's look grew almost ecstatic.

"I have sometimes thought so myself," he admitted.

He was reluctant now to let Bobby go, but the hour for the last train was near and Bobby protested that he must take himself off, though he did hope he might be allowed to come again another time. Shields insisted he must have a drink before he went, and Bobby begged to be excused on the score of lack of time. He had noticed standing on a tray, apparently waiting for removal and washing up, two glasses in which dregs of wine still stood, as though another and a recent visitor had been treated to refreshment. In turning now he managed to knock over the tray and smash both glasses. In a moment he was on his knees, full of apologies, collecting the broken pieces of glass in a clean handkerchief, wrapping them up with the greatest care, protesting that he would have them matched and two exactly similar glasses provided in their place, no matter if he had to search Clermont, Dijon, Paris itself, all the world, to find replicas. Shields tried to protest against this torrent of words that it was quite unnecessary, they were two of the most ordinary glasses in the world, but Bobby cried out in dismay as he saw the time and fled at full speed for his train, carrying with him the broken bits of the glasses he had so carelessly broken.

Soon another parcel was on its way to England, addressed to Olive with fresh, careful, and detailed instructions within.

CHAPTER XIV

MR. WILLIAMS HAS SUSPICIONS

Early the next morning a heavy thunderstorm broke, and Bobby, having finished looking at the French papers, his own English paper not yet arrived, and having nothing else to read, proceeded to investigate a pile of books he had noticed, most of them probably left behind by previous visitors. He found little to interest him and the elder Camion, passing by, paused to comment on the unfortunate weather—such rain was rare, he protested, in that favoured land of gentle breeze and almost ceaseless sunshine, for indeed he thought of the local weather as hotel-keepers often do think of it when talking to their guests. Discovering that Bobby wanted something to read but could find nothing to his taste, he took him into the private sitting-room of the family and showed him a book-case in which were better-bound books he was plainly a little proud of. There was the inevitable La Fontaine, the edition with the Doré illustrations. It was a prize, the inscription said, won by Charles Camion, for recitation at some local competition. There were a number of French dramatic works, ranging from Racine and Corneille to more modern days, and various other classics of French literature; and if many of the books—this did not apply to the theatrical works—looked as if they had been but little read, they did at least show a recognition of literary values it would have been rare to find in any similar hotel in any small English town. Monsieur Camion also showed with especial pride a large classical dictionary, also with illustrations by Gustave Doré.

"That," he said, "it was the first prize ever won by

Charles. Afterwards, it became a habit with the boy, but this was the first, for before then he had seemed but half awake, the poor child. But one day he was heard declaiming poetry to himself and after that—oh, many triumphs. This book, as the first, was especially dear to my wife, and never, never, has she forgiven Monsieur Shields."

"Why, what did he do?" Bobby asked.

"It was the illustrations, the Doré illustrations. It is understood that to-day, the poor Doré, he is no longer approved. One asks oneself why. But Monsieur Shields, when my wife showed him this first of all Charles's many prizes, asked that he might take it to his room. He wished, it seemed, to copy a drawing that had appealed to him, of Dido waving her farewell, the poor deserted one." Here Bobby wondered for a moment how many small hotel-keepers in England would either know or care anything about the sorrows of Dido. "But my wife," continued Monsieur Camion, "was uneasy, and when the book was returned, she was desolated—the burn of a cigarette, Monsieur, truly not on the picture itself but plain to see in the margin."

"Lucky poor Dido escaped," observed Bobby sympathetically.

"Ah, that, no, it was Ariadne—another of the deserted ones, was she not? See!"

He opened the book at the article telling the story of the exploits of Theseus, including the slaying of the Minotaur by the aid of Ariadne. There was a very small burn at the edge of the margin and also several smudges which Bobby thought could easily have been cleaned away, though the tiny burn was past remedy. Bobby sympathized politely, small as the damage seemed, but kept the book so long in his hands—it was so heavy a work it required the use of both to hold it—that Monsieur Camion grew a trifle uneasy and remarked that Monsieur Owen seemed as interested as had been Monsieur Shields himself.

"They are indeed drawings of a high value," he declared, "even though not in the present mode. Yet never shall I dare lend the book again, for what would my wife say if another misfortune happened to it?"

Bobby smiled, promised that he would not ask for its loan, but all the same continued to regard with great interest the illustration that had caught his eye, that of Ariadne handing to a very magnificent and war-like Theseus the ball of thread by which he was to guide himself through the labyrinth.

"Extremely interesting," Bobby remarked, closed the book, handed it back to its owner much to that gentleman's relief, decided instead of reading to sit with a cigarette in the entrance hall that did duty for a lounge, and there employ his thoughts with the many problems pressing for a solution.

After déjeuner, the rain having stopped but everything being still drenched and dripping so that sketching was out of the question, he went for a stroll, and took his way towards the Pépin Mill. As he had hoped might be the case, both Mr. and Mrs. Williams were in the garden, but as soon as they saw him approaching, Mrs. Williams scurried away into the mill, and Williams, after giving the approaching Bobby a long stare deliberately turned his back and walked off to the bottom of the garden, where it was bounded by the close growth of beech and chestnut trees Bobby had noticed before.

"Meant for a hint," Bobby thought as he crossed the tiny plank bridge over the mill stream, "but then I was never good at taking hints."

He went on and hailed Williams with a cheery good afternoon. Williams turned round with his back to the screen of chestnut and beech, but made no answer. Bobby said:

"I thought I would come along now the rain's stopped. There's a question I wanted to ask you."

"Coming yourself this time instead of sending your pal?"

"My pal?"

"Working in with Volny, aren't you?"

"Volny?" repeated Bobby, a good deal surprised. "You mean the young chap who has just cleared out?"

"Yes. What have you done with him? What's the game? What was he snooping round here for the other morning?"

"Was he?" asked Bobby, still more surprised.

"Yes, was he?" snarled Williams. "My missus heard him, not much she misses," he said with a sort of sombre pride. "Looked out of the window and saw him. Just after dawn it was. Called me, she did, and then he caught sight of us at the window and bunked. Off and out of sight before I had a chance to dress and get after him."

"Curious," said Bobby. "How do you mean, snooping around? Was he trying to get in or anything like that?"

"Don't know anything about it, do you?" retorted Williams. "Oh no. Wouldn't guess he had the cover off the well and staring down it, though what good that would do him, I don't know."

"Nor I," said Bobby, very puzzled, wondering indeed if the whole odd story could be an invention and yet thinking that even more improbable and purposeless.

"Now he's turned up missing," Williams said. "Well, what's the game? What have you done with him?"

"You mean you think Volny and I have been working together for some unknown reason?" Bobby asked.

"Don't know so much about the unknown reason," growled Williams, "but the working together's pretty plain. I'm here. You want us out of it, you and Volny."

"Curious," said Bobby. "I thought it was you wanted me out of it, and in fact that's what I came to see you about."

Williams made no comment. He was looking thoughtfully not at Bobby but past him, at the trees behind, as though seeking counsel from them. Bobby, waiting and watching, became aware of a faint rustling sound close behind, amidst the trees, as though some small cautious animal were lurking there. He remembered that once before he had had that same impression in this garden. He made no attempt to turn. He knew that if he did he would see nothing nor did he wish to let Williams suspect that he was so much on the alert. None the less he was aware of a feeling that he was in peril, and there came into his mind a swift memory of the damp, narrow, brick-lined wall of the well, of that blackness into which once he had peered, of the sullen gleam of the waiting water far beneath. A quick blow on the head from behind, a hurried removal of the well cover, a dull echoing splash below, and what would remain to show a living breathing human creature had once been there?

Fanciful, perhaps. He told himself his imagination was running away with him, none the less he knew well in every nerve and fibre of his being that there was need of caution.

"Was it you pinched my gold pencil?" Williams asked abruptly. "It's gone and I saw you looking at it."

Bobby remembered how once he had noticed Williams fidgeting with such a pencil, but he had seen then, and saw now, no importance in the fact. He supposed that Williams was trying to be offensive and so he took no notice. He said instead:

"You seem to have been telling rather wild fairy tales about me. Apparently you wanted to get me thrown out of the hotel. Well, what's the idea?"

Williams did not answer at once, but Bobby thought that there was a relaxation in that tension of which previously he had been aware. It was as though some other question had been expected, one more disturbing, more difficult to answer. Desperately he wondered what it could be. Williams was looking, if anything, even more sulky than usual, but there began to die down that dark menacing glow in his eyes of which till now Bobby had been aware. Williams said presently:

"Tit for tat, that's all." He paused. He had his hands thrust deep into his pockets, his head bent forward, but with eyes and ears alert, almost as if he were listening for some message. Then he said:

"Well, why can't we chip in together?"

"In what way?"

"Same as you and Volny."

"What makes you think Volny and I have anything to do with each other?"

"Plain enough, isn't it?" Williams retorted. "Volny has been doing a lot of snooping round here. Began as soon as we got here. Didn't expect the old place to let so soon. Thought he was going to have it all to himself; and when he found he wasn't, tried to scare us off. That didn't work, so then he fetched you along, or maybe you were behind from the first. And soon as you turned up, Volny snooping around again and shots fired to see if that would do the trick."

"You admit now there was a shot?" Bobby remarked. "Why did you tell lies about it?"

"We didn't want a fuss; we didn't know then you were in it, too; we thought you and Volny being around together was coincidence. Of course, there was no coincidence about it. Was it you did the shooting or was it Volny? We wondered about that and I kept my eyes skinned. I saw Volny going off up in the hills when I knew he ought to have been at work in the fields and then I saw you follow. Plain enough, you and him going to have a quiet talk. Well, what I say is, how about a deal together, me and you?" It was a development that Bobby had never anticipated, though he had thought of many possibilities. He did not quite know what to reply and Williams continued:

"Where is Volny, anyway? What's the big idea, him dodging off? You haven't done him in, have you?"

"What? What's that?" Bobby asked, startled by the question.

"Have you done him in?" Williams repeated. He looked at Bobby closely, as if now attaching more importance to a question not at first meant seriously. "Well, have you?" he repeated.

"Is there any reason to think anything's happened to him? Do you know anything?" Bobby asked slowly, and a fear he had hitherto hardly been conscious of leaped in his mind to sudden life.

"Turned up missing, hasn't he? One party been croaked around here, why not another?" Williams asked, still with that new and strange expression of mingled doubt and wonder and suspicion in his eyes. "Looking a bit green about the gills, aren't you? Lumme, I do believe I've tumbled to it all right."

"Believe what you like," Bobby muttered, very well aware he might in fact be looking 'green about the gills', now that a new terror was slowly taking shape and substance in his heart.

"Where there's been one murder, sometimes there's another," Williams said.

"You mean Miss Polthwaite was murdered?" Bobby asked. "How do you know?" Then he said: "Did you murder her?"

"Don't you try to come that over us," Williams retorted, scowling. "We were nowhere near. In Paris we were. See?"

"You mean you've got an alibi?" Bobby asked. "Alibis need checking. That's my experience."

"What do you mean, your experience?" Williams said, mistrustful again. "Why don't you spill it?" he demanded, "What's your game? First of all we thought you must be a regular dick, but you can't be that very well, not out here, not in France; the Frenchies wouldn't stand for it. Are you a private man? Or just a blasted, interfering, meddling snooper? One thing's sure, you're no artist."

"Why not?" asked Bobby, a little hurt.

"Don't look it," said Williams briefly. "I've seen 'em, Chelsea, Soho, round there. You're as different as chalk from cheese, and you haven't got that silly lost look like most of them, either, just as if they were where they knew they didn't belong."

"In any case, you've no reason to worry about me," Bobby pointed out. "Take me as you find me. If you've any real reason to think there's anything queer about Volny's having cleared off, you ought to tell the police. It may be awkward, if I have to tell them, as I certainly should, that you had suspicions and kept them to yourself."

"Now, see here," Williams retorted angrily. "I know nothing about Volny, or about Miss Polthwaite either. We came here for a quiet holiday. My old woman's nerves were bad, she wanted a rest. And then we hear there's been murder done on the place and people come poking about wanting to look down the well and where it was done, and all that. Enough to upset any one."

Bobby wondered how much of truth there was in this. Possible, he supposed, the Williamses were simply on the spot by pure accident, and until their arrival had known nothing of the Polthwaite tragedy. Yet it had been widely reported and commented on in the press.

"Well, then," he asked; "if you're not interested, what's all this about working together and what for?"

"We've got interested," Williams said. "If there is anything here to show the old girl was really murdered and who did it, I suppose it ought to be turned up. We're willing to help. Why not? Only we've got to be sure first. Cards on the table and all that, open and straightforward and nothing kept back."

"You told Mademoiselle Simone you had proof of some kind?"

"Not me. I asked her if she thought there was proof hid here, not that we had it. It was her started it, asking questions when the wife was in that bit of a shop of hers. The wife was a bit curious, same as women are, and she asked the girl to come along and tell us all about it but it didn't seem she knew anything really, only wanted a peep down the well and then got scared. My own idea is she wanted photos of the well taken, so she could sell em to tourists and people. 'Scene of the tragedy.' Marked with an X. That sort of thing. I suppose it was her gave you that message?"

"I don't think it matters who it was," Bobby answered. "Frankly, Mr. Williams, I don't much believe you're putting all your cards on the table as you call it. You may be here by accident, but I doubt it. I do not believe Mademoiselle Simone was the first to speak to you about the murder. I don't believe she showed any interest in the well. My guess is you were trying to frighten her. I think you were trying to find out something you thought she might know. I think you are here not by accident but for some purpose and I wonder what that purpose is."

"Curiosity," answered Williams promptly. "Wouldn't you be curious yourself if you found you had come to a place where there had been a murder, and no one knew who it was, and people came snooping round all the time?"

"Your own affair," Bobby answered, "but I shouldn't try to play tricks with the French police if I were you."

"Same to you and many of them," growled Williams. "As you know such a lot about that Simone girl, ask her if it was her fancy boy did in Miss Polthwaite?"

"Who is her fancy boy?" asked Bobby.

"Volny, isn't it? Used to be young Camion but she gave him the go-by because they think in the village it was Camion did it. I don't."

"Why not?"

"No guts. All bounce and swank. Thinks about things, doesn't do 'em. Besides, why should he? He was getting all he wanted out of the old girl. Doted on him, they say. She was the goose laying golden eggs for him."

"There's that," agreed Bobby, though he thought such considerations overlooked the possible complications that might have resulted from Camion's realization of the false position he was in, or the even more possible results of some sudden outburst of anger or revulsion. "If it wasn't Camion, who was it?"

"Volny."

"I thought your idea was he had been murdered himself?"

"There might be a reason for that," Williams said. "It might be he knew too much, it might be he had really found out something. There's some one else likes to snoop round here. I've seen him. Told him to get out, too, and quick about it. But he's been back all right."

"Who?"

"An old blind beggar. I don't know his name. He's always about the village for what he can cadge. I happen to know he had a row with Miss Polthwaite. She said she would put the police on him. He didn't like that. Swore revenge. Very upset over being threatened with the police."

Bobby could believe that. From the little he had seen of the Père Trouché, he could well imagine that no threat would be more likely to rouse his ire.

"Hardly a reason for murder," he suggested, though his voice was uneasy.

"Might have lost his temper and hit out with that stick of his, knocked her out, then got scared and popped her down the well out of harm's way. They say in the village he's done a murder or two already. He pokes his nose into everything, gets to know everything, they're all scared of him for what he knows and might tell. Suppose he got to know Miss Polthwaite had—" He paused and looked sharply at Bobby—"had anything of value? Money. Jewellery. Anything. If he got to know and came snooping round and she spotted him—well, there you are."

"But you say he is still snooping round?"

"Perhaps he didn't get what he was after. Perhaps she had it too well hidden. What do you think?"

"It's possible," agreed Bobby. "So many things are, aren't they?"

"Another thing," Williams said. "I don't believe he's blind, not him, no more than you or me. Put on, that is. Ever seen the way he hops about? Blind, my hat." He added thoughtfully: "Might be Volny knew and suspected something and that's why he's been done in. Easy for a man you might think blind and wasn't, to do the job."

CHAPTER XV

HUNDRED-FRANC TEST

It was in a disturbed and troubled mood that Bobby slowly made his way back towards the village. The possibility suggested by Williams was one that had not before occurred to him and yet one he felt could not be utterly dismissed.

Especially disturbing did he find the suggestion that possibly the Père Trouché's blindness was only fictitious. Was that extraordinary dexterity and knowledge of his surroundings displayed by the old beggar really due to abnormal cultivation of his other senses or had he in fact, like other people, the use of his eyes?

Again, the old man boasted, and the claim seemed more or less justified, that he knew most of what went on in the neighbourhood. He might then very well have heard in some way of Miss Polthwaite's gift of diamonds to the curé, he might have guessed there were more where those had come from, and then what a temptation would present itself.

Bobby did not much like the look of things. True, the old man had boasted of his indifference to money, but was that indifference probable? Was there any one in all the world so totally indifferent to money? A voice broke in upon his thought, saying:

"You think then it is possible the story is true?"

Bobby gave a little jump. The words came strangely apt to his thoughts, and came from Père Trouché himself, sitting there by the road side, on a bank still only partially dried by the sunshine that had followed the storm, and so far hidden by a growth of bushes and a tall chestnut tree that Bobby had not noticed he was there.

"Oh, it's you," he said, standing still.

"That surprises you, Mr. Englishman," the old man said with his low, hoarse chuckle. "Indeed, it seems to me that it more than surprises you. Why?"

"I didn't see you," Bobby said. "You startled me."

"That is true but not all the truth," Père Trouché answered. "There was more in your voice than that, more than that, too, in your footsteps."

"What was in my footsteps?" Bobby asked.

"Perplexity, hesitation, doubt; all that was plain even to the ear of a child. I said to myself: The Englishman, too, has heard, and he, too, is troubled. But in your voice there was more also, a shade, a nuance that I did not recognize. What was it?"

Bobby crossed to where the old man sat, basking in the warmth of the strong sun and apparently quite indifferent to the damp its hot rays were drawing from ground soaked by the recent rain.

"Seat yourself then," the old man said with something of the air of a host putting his guests at their ease. "Here there is room for all. It is Monsieur and Madame Williams you have been visiting, is it not?"

"How do you know?" Bobby retorted, though, with more respect for possible rheumatic pains, he remained standing.

Père Trouché made so angry and impatient a gesture with his staff Bobby almost thought he was about to strike him with it, nor could he help the thought flashing through his mind that perhaps in some moment of irritation that gesture might well pass into action. Was that what had happened before in the Pépin Mill?

"But it is childish," the old beggar was saying, "you and your perpetual 'How do you know?' Do you not come from the direction of the Pépin Mill? Could I not hear your footsteps on the bridge? Do you not know that footsteps on a wooden bridge sound altogether differently from footsteps on a road? Soon I suppose you will ask me how I know there is a wooden bridge leading to the Pépin Mill? Why is it then that the good God has found it well to deprive some of us of all intelligence?"

Here the old man, in the classic phrase 'paused for a reply'. None came, for Bobby did not feel competent to offer any explanation, keenly conscious though he was of the implications conveyed by the last question. Père Trouché snorted and then continued:

"Evidently, then, the Williams ménage, they told you. Well, do you believe them?"

"I don't know enough yet to say," Bobby answered. "You know best what the truth is, I suppose?"

"That," agreed the old man, evidently pleased, "is the most sensible thing I have ever heard an Englishman say. They are not, I speak as between friends, a race of high intelligence. For me, I answer simply: 'No.'"

Bobby made no comment. He stood staring at the old man, wondering how to prove whether his blindness was genuine or assumed. One can test deafness simply enough by dropping a small weight behind the suspected person. If he seems to remain unawares, then he is certainly shamming, since a genuinely deaf person, though he would have heard nothing, would yet feel the vibration set up. But Bobby knew of no equally simple and effective test for blindness. He said abruptly:

"Tell me now, are you really blind or can you see?" Père Trouché laughed delightedly.

"Ah, that, it is often asked," he said through his mirth. "There are those who say I see as well as another. They do not believe that the nose, the ears, the touch, can tell as much and more, too, than the eyes. Whether I see or no, am blind or no, none will ever know for certain, and on my tombstone it may be written: 'Here lies the Père Trouché, who was blind or else perhaps he wasn't.'"

In a veritable paroxysm of laughter the old beggar rocked to and fro, and Bobby seized the opportunity to extract from his pockets both a cigarette and a hundred-franc note. He was certain that, absorbed in his eldritch merriment, the old man could not know, however keen his hearing, that both cigarette and hundred-franc note had thus appeared, nor yet be aware that the note had fluttered to the ground as if accidentally dropped. Yet if he had in fact the use of his eyes, he could not fail to notice that significant piece of paper. Hardly a conclusive test, but the best Bobby could think of. He said:

"I am glad you are amused. I did not think I was so pleasant as it seems I am."

This last phrase, a well known quotation from one of Molière's plays, caught Père Trouché's attention and stayed his mirth.

"Yes, yes," he said, "I have said that myself and it is often wisdom. Yet, too, in another sense, it is why I enjoy so much talking to others, for often they are amusing without intending it. But never mind whether I see or am blind. It is not of importance. Tell me, for it is of importance: How is it the Williams ménage has heard so soon?"

"How do you mean so soon?" asked Bobby, puzzled.

"I only heard myself this morning. The story has spread indeed, since all repeat it, but the Williamses have not been to the village to-day nor has any, I think, from the village, been to the Pépin Mill. How then have they heard so soon?"

Bobby felt puzzled and began to think that possibly they were talking at cross purposes. The old beggar went on:

"It is not possible that it is they who have invented the story? One would be glad to think so and yet it is not likely, for why should they? As for me, I am uneasy, for when such a story springs up on a sudden, well, it is often because it is true, or nearly true. Not, I think, as regards the young Camion, but for Volny—there I have a fear."

"Camion? Volny?" Bobby repeated, and this last name reawakened in his mind that unease of which lately he had become conscious. "What about them?" he asked "Volny has not returned yet?"

"But you have heard? It is what they told you at the Pépin Mill?" Père Trouché asked. "That Volny is dead and that Camion has killed him and hidden the body, killed for the second time?"

"That is being said?" Bobby muttered.

"You did not know? There is surprise in your voice? But assuredly you knew, or why was there such unease in your footsteps, such questioning and such doubt, you who generally walk so firmly and with such assurance?"

"You hear too much in footsteps," Bobby said. "You deceive yourself."

"Never," retorted the other. "Faces may lie. I do not know for I cannot see them. Yet it is probable, for faces, they are under control, they have been trained to deceive, taught to hide well what lies behind. But the footsteps —no. They are not controlled, they have not been taught to deceive. They tell always what they feel. Your footsteps told me plainly something had been said that disturbed you. What was it if it was not this story that all the village speaks of?"

"It is of no importance," Bobby said.

"You do not wish to tell me? Why? I warn you. I shall find out. I always do. What is told me, I respect. What I find out, it is mine to tell to others or not, as I choose. Also, it is not good when friends hide things from each other, and it is as a friend that I came here to wait for you."

"You were waiting for me, then?"

"But naturally, or why should I have been sitting here? They told me you had gone this way and so I waited your return. For, you see, Mr. Englishman, it is not pleasant, this story that is going about. And it is not pleasant that you and I, we heard a shot, a single shot. You remember?"

"I remember well enough," Bobby answered reluctantly.

"But you wish that you did not? I also, I have that wish. The memory has ruined my afternoon. In general, after a storm, it is very calm, very beautiful. One can sit quietly and listen to all those lovely sounds that make up the world. Eh, it is worth something then to be alive, to sit, to feel the warm sun, to hear and notice each little sound that tells how the good earth is alive again, strong and refreshed as if the rain were wine. For the rain, monsieur, makes glad the earth, as wine makes glad the heart of man. Eh, there is the veritable joy of life, the birds so busy, the buzzing of the bees, the song of the cigales, the air so richly full of every kind of scent from flower and herb, and then the air itself fresh as if just breathed from the lips of God. All that, monsieur, I have lost this afternoon, lost for ever, for the only thing that I have heard, it is the report of a pistol shot, fired once and not again."

Bobby asked a few questions. But the old man had no idea how the story had originated. It had seemed to be all over the village almost simultaneously. Possibly some hint Volny or Camion had dropped about their proposed duel had been remembered, repeated, and, in the light of Volny's disappearance, suddenly invested with significance. Père Trouché protested that he had breathed no word of that early morning scene when they found Charles Camion alone in the chestnut grove, and Bobby, for his part, declared that he had been equally reticent. To be assured of this, and to suggest that their silence should still be preserved, was, it now appeared, the real reason why Père Trouché had followed Bobby here. He was also very anxious to be further assured that Bobby had actually had a look round on that morning and had noticed nothing in any way disturbing.

"It is one of those rare cases," Père Trouché confessed with his usual reluctance to admit that the use of the eyes conferred any special advantage, "when to have sight is actually a help. A dead man makes no sound, does not move, and I might pass not far away and know nothing of it. But with the eyes one might, I suppose, note a dead body from afar. It is so?" he asked, a little as though hoping for a denial.

I had a good look round," Bobby said. "I saw nothing."

Père Trouché looked a good deal relieved. Changing the subject, he tried again to induce Bobby to tell him what Williams had said.

"For there was trouble in your footsteps, monsieur," he repeated, 'and since it was not because of this talk of Volny and the young Camion, what was it they said to you? Tell the old blind beggar," he said, falling into a kind of professional whine, "for there is so much he knows, so much he can explain to clear away troubles and misunderstandings."

"Very likely, but we'll leave it at that," Bobby said and went back to the village, leaving Père Trouché sitting there with in front of him that hundred-franc note of which so far he seemed quite unaware.

In the village when Bobby reached it, he noticed even more of the inhabitants than usual clustered in small groups and talking together. At the door of the shop kept by Lucille's aunt, Lucille herself was standing. As he drew nearer Bobby saw that she was looking at him and when he lifted his hat, she gave a slight bow in acknowledgement and went back quickly inside the shop. Somehow Bobby thought that an invitation was intended. He entered accordingly. Lucille was standing just inside and now that he could see her more plainly, it was easy to make out that she was looking very pale and troubled. She said nothing and he began to occupy himself with the postcards as if his sole purpose was to buy some more. She remained silent, though watching him intently, and presently he said:

"I hear, mademoiselle, that there is gossip in the village. One talks."

"It is not true," she burst out. "It is not true what they are saying."

"That Volny is dead?" Bobby asked. "I hope it is not true, but is there news of him?"

She shook her head and then murmured in a low, choking voice:

"I cannot believe that he is dead."

"Have you seen Charles Camion to-day?" Bobby asked.

"Ah, that, it is a lie," she cried. "Even if Volny is dead, it is not Charles who killed him. Ah, it is wicked that they should say such things. Monsieur, it is not true that you and Père Trouché—that you know, that you saw...?"

"Is that being said, too?" Bobby asked. "We only know what I suppose plenty of others know—that Camion went out early one morning. Why is every one so ready to believe such a story? Is it because there was a murder here before when also his name was spoken of?"

"They told lies about him before," she said vehemently, "and so they tell more lies about him again and then it sounds as if it must be true."

"What does Camion say himself?"

"Nothing," she answered. "He is mad. He wraps himself in himself. He says nothing. I do not think he understands that it is real."

"Perhaps that is it," Bobby said thoughtfully. Lucille's remark had flashed out suddenly, as if it had broken spontaneously from the depths of a half unconscious understanding, but it seemed to him that possibly it shed light on a good deal he found puzzling. But how it affected the main problem in his mind, he was not sure, for a man who dramatizes himself too much may sometimes dramatize himself in strange ways. He said presently as Lucille still watched him:

"Do you think Mademoiselle Polthwaite was murdered?" She became very pale, her eyes grew large and terrified. Though she did not speak, made no sign, he understood. He said:

"It is what I think, too."

"It was not Camion," she burst out. "He was foolish, he was worse, it was shameful what he did. I told him so. I said that never would I have more to do with him. It was a quarrel when we were both so angry that we did not know what we said."

"And now?" Bobby asked.

"Now," she said proudly, lifting her head, "now I have sent him word that if he wishes to, he can arrange our fiangailles."

She was less pale now. Her eyes had lost their fear and were bright and eager and defiant, so that for the moment it was a light, clear beauty that hung about her, like a garment. Bobby remembered a little sadly how often women had put in men they loved an eager faith for which there proved in the end to be but small justification. He did not say that, but watched her as she glowed there in her perfect trust and then he said:

"If Miss Polthwaite was murdered, some one murdered her. Who was it? To-day I have been told it was Père Trouché."

Lucille's surprise was evident. She forgot for the moment her anger and her fear over the gossip about Camion. She stared with open mouth and then she said:

"Oh, no, why should he? He is not like that, though he says himself that once—but others say it is only that he loves to boast."

"What is it he says?" Bobby asked.

"Those who follow the road," she answered, using the expression 'faire la route' Bobby had heard before and that perhaps is best translated by our expression 'tramp', "are angry if others, who are strangers, try to follow the same roads. Those who were the first think they have the best right and join together to drive away intruders. Père Trouché has always been jealous to allow no other on what he calls his territory. Years ago when I was a child a stranger tried to push himself in and presently he was found dead at the foot of a steep rock. It was thought that he had lost his way and fallen, but afterwards the Père Trouché boasted that he had struck him with his staff and then thrown him over. But some said it was only a story Père Trouché told to scare others away."

"That was a long time ago?" Bobby asked and before Lucille could answer old Madame Simone came in hurriedly.

"The commissaire of police has arrived," she said. "Look, there is his car. Monsieur Volny père rang for him on the telephone—eh, to think that in these days a functionary can be rung for like any maid of all work. Well, if the young man has been murdered, now we shall soon know all about it."

CHAPTER XVI
M. LE COMMISSAIRE ARRIVES

When Bobby went out again into the village street, he found it strange to see how great a change there was, how utterly the general atmosphere and feeling of the place had altered, how oddly visible was the uneasiness and common fear now prevalent. Even the children had ceased to play and run about and were gathered near their elders, listening and alarmed. No longer were the little groups of older people chattering together in pleasant and excited comment, each member eager to express his own ideas and to contradict those of others. Now for the most part they stood in silence, or exchanging only muttered observations to which most often no reply was made. But the eyes of all were turned towards the car standing before the door of the Hotel de la Belle Alliance, de la Victoire, et des États-Unis. What had been before a subject for amusing gossip or malicious speculation had now become a common dread, as into the general silence and reserve, as a stone into some deep and quiet pool, was dropped from time to time the one word: Volny.

In the distance, down a side turning, Bobby caught sight of Eudes, the schoolmaster. He was almost running, like a man pursued, and in his progress there was something, Bobby thought, that seemed furtive and alarmed. Eudes vanished from sight round a corner of one of the houses. Bobby turned and found he was not the only man who had been watching Eudes, for by his side was the curé. The curé said:

"That was Monsieur Eudes." Bobby made no answer. The curé said: "Monsieur the commissaire is here. That has not happened since Mademoiselle Polthwaite's death. Before that, never had it happened in living memory. Now he comes again. It is as though the reign of Satan had begun. It is because the teaching of the church is neglected and that of Monsieur Eudes and his like is preferred."

"Monsieur Eudes," Bobby remarked, "never I think received a present of diamonds from Mademoiselle Polthwaite?"

"It was not because he did not desire it, work for it," retorted the curé. "I know for a fact, because he had heard she was an artist, and therefore he thought she must be of a loose and careless life and an enemy of the Church, that he spoke of trying to obtain money from her. It was an intrigue he contemplated—ah, these intrigues that are the curse of France, that lead people astray before even they are aware of what they do."

"But surely," Bobby protested, "Miss Polthwaite was a foreigner here, she would never have given money for any political purpose?"

"Eudes schemed to secure it under pretence of educating children of special promise. It would have begun in a small way. It would have continued. It was to be in the end support of a weekly journal Eudes dreams of establishing. If ever he succeeds in carrying out his cunning schemes to publish here such a journal as a fresh centre of degradation and atheism—"

He paused, apparently unable to find words in which to express his horror at such a prospect, and then, without saying anything more, he walked away.

Bobby went back to the hotel. There was no one at the reception desk, no one in the entrance hall. A thing unprecedented. He went up to his room and sat for a time at the window, smoking a cigarette. When the hour came for dinner he went downstairs. There were fewer guests than usual. Curiosity, no doubt, was strong, but prudence was stronger still, and for that evening many had preferred to seek their evening meal elsewhere. At one table sat a man Bobby had not seen before, a small, stout, smiling man Bobby guessed must be the commissaire by his alert, authoritative air. He wore a close-cropped beard and had grown a little bald, and Bobby did not think that smile of his had much of mirth in it; assumed, Bobby thought, in an effort to put witnesses at their ease. He seemed to be enjoying his meal but behind his glasses his eyes were quick and watchful, and Bobby noticed, with little pleasure, that more than once they flashed a rapid glance in his direction.

"Going to put the hat on it," Bobby thought, "if I'm to be mixed up in a fresh murder mystery. I hope to goodness Volny turns up all right."

But he remembered with an inner chill how the name, Volny, had been whispered down the village street as in a kind of secret dirge.

The serving doors opened and Charles Camion came in, though that is but a tame way of putting it. Effected an entrance would be a more suitable description. Anyhow, there he was, drawn to his full height, fully aware that everyone was looking at him, himself looking at no one but with a stern and haughty glance fixed challengingly upon a spot several feet above the commissaire's head.

"The young ass," Bobby said to himself. "He's enjoying it."

An exaggeration, no doubt, and any enjoyment the young man felt was probably quite unconscious, more justly indeed to be described as a sort of profound inner satisfaction in a knowledge that it was about his personality that events were clustering. At any rate his whole bearing seemed to proclaim a kind of gloomy yet deep satisfaction in his knowledge that though Fate had chosen him to launch her thunderbolts against, yet none the less he was showing under that assault a proud tranquillity. The manner, too, in which he stood for a moment or two, quite still, then removed his eyes from the wall above the commissaire's head, gave a slow look all around, finally resuming his progress down the room, told clearly that his every movement was carefully, though perhaps instinctively, studied. Bobby found himself wondering what had happened to the limelight man, and had to check an impulse to applaud.

"Entrance of misunderstood and persecuted hero," he thought to himself. "Hang it all, the boy's a born actor."

Indeed the way in which Camion managed to suggest tragic innocence, the victim unjustly laid upon the altar of vengeance, and yet at the same time preserved the air of a desperado it would be imprudent to offend, was really magnificent.

"Monsieur is not content," he said once, bending darkly over a guest who had ventured some sort of trifling criticism; and the poor man went quite pale and hurriedly stammered out an expression of the most complete satisfaction to which Camion listened with an air of gloom that plainly said it was well for them both no complaint was intended.

"The young fool," Bobby muttered again, "he'll act himself to the guillotine if he isn't careful," and then was startled to notice the commissaire's alert, intelligent eyes turning thoughtfully from him to Camion and back again.

The commissaire was the first to finish his meal and leave the dining-room. Bobby purposely lingered over his coffee but when he went into the entrance hall he found the commissaire there, talking to the elder Camion. The hotel keeper vanished, the commissaire turned to Bobby, introduced himself very politely, and explained that there seemed to be a certain uneasiness over the disappearance of one of the young men of the village—'un nommé Volny, Henri'.

"His father," he explained, "the elder Volny, is not without his importance. He is in politics of the centre, a good republican, and a strong opponent of the Church."

"Oh, yes," said Bobby cautiously. "I know so little about French politics. Are all good republicans strong opponents of the Church?"

The commissaire waved this aside, and Bobby thought he looked a little disappointed as though he had hoped that this reference to the elder Volny's hostility to the Church might have elicited something interesting, though what, Bobby could not imagine. The commissaire went on:

"At present, I see no reason to open a formal inquiry. Often in these days young people and their elders have very different ideas. The old family tradition is weakening. It is a pity. Not so long ago a father could arrange his son's marriage and if the son ventured to ask for whom his hand was destined, the father could reply by telling him to mind his own business. To-day that young man in the question of marriage would say the same to his parents. Then perhaps a family scene. The young man—or sometimes the girl—takes himself off. Even with a daughter it might happen. The parents are in despair. They seek our assistance. What can we do? Presently no doubt the truant returns, or a letter arrives. Then all is well and our inaction has proved the best for all. Yet there is always the possibility that it is more serious; and it may be, monsieur, that I shall have to ask you for a statement, since it seems you and another were so uneasy one morning that you left your beds at a very early hour."

"I suppose Camion told you," Bobby asked. "We saw nothing of Volny, nothing of any interest."

"So I understand," answered the commissaire, "so I shall not bother you unless it becomes necessary to open an inquiry as I hope it will not. Indeed, I should not have troubled myself in the matter at all, only that one understands the anxieties of a parent, and if it were not that already one has heard of the young Camion."

"In connection with the murder of Miss Polthwaite?" Bobby asked, certain now there was more in the other's mind than he was allowing to appear.

The commissaire raised his eyebrows.

"Murder?" he repeated. "You speak of murder?"

"It is what I gather is the general belief in the village," Bobby answered quietly.

"Ah, the general village belief," repeated the commissaire. A delicate shrug of the shoulders dismissed general village beliefs. "It is I myself," he said, "who conducted the inquiry, and Monsieur Alain, the juge d'instruction, agreed with me there was no evidence to support any theory of violence, much to suggest that the poor woman destroyed herself."

"No doubt," Bobby answered. "It is, of course, understood that I speak only of what I have heard in the village."

"One understands that," agreed the commissaire, very politely, even with a little acquiescent bow, but none the less somehow making Bobby feel more uneasy still. "Monsieur is not at present thinking of leaving us?"

"Oh, no, I am expecting to stay at least another couple of weeks," answered Bobby, realizing that this meant no departure would in any case be permitted.

"For my part," observed the commissaire, "I trust our young friend will report himself in a day or two and then I trust his family will scold him well for the trouble he has caused. I shall pick a bone with him myself. One has work enough without false alarms." He added abruptly: "You are observant, monsieur. I saw you watching Charles Camion and I saw that you were interested. I should be glad of your opinion."

Bobby hesitated.

"My own impression," he said at last, "is that he is impulsive, well meaning, amiable, but here entirely out of place. He lives, I think, too much in his imagination. He ought to be on the stage, he is a born actor."

"It is interesting, that," the commissaire said thoughtfully. "You are perhaps accustomed, monsieur, to judging men? I think you may be right. But that type, the imaginative, the introvert, it has its dangers, too, for the comedy of the imagination may well pass over into the reality of tragedy."

He took his departure then; and when he left, it was as though a visible weight lifted from all the village. But not from Bobby, who had found that last remark profoundly disturbing. For a little he waited and then went out as if for a stroll. He took his way towards the Pépin Mill, and when he came to the spot where earlier he had talked with Père Trouché, he looked to see if the hundred-franc note he had allowed to fall and had left there was still in the same place. But there was no sign of it and Bobby was looking more worried than ever as he turned back towards the village. It was late now but the little postcard shop was still open. Bobby entered and Lucille appeared from the room behind. He said to her:

"You know the commissaire has gone?" When she nodded an assent, he added: "I think he will be coming back before long."

"Charles says he is sure Volny will be heard from in a day or two," Lucille said, but not with complete confidence. "For me, I do not know why it should be supposed that anything has happened to him."

"If Volny returns, so much the better," Bobby said. "The commissaire asked me questions, too. He spoke about the death of Mademoiselle Polthwaite."

"It is why you are here, is it not?" Lucille asked. "To find out what you can."

"What makes you say that?" Bobby asked, disturbed by this fresh confirmation of his fear that his errand was generally suspected.

"All the world," she answered, "knows that it is for that Monsieur Williams is here. He has said himself that he is from your Scotland Yard. Then you came, and you, also, you began to ask about the Pépin Mill. It is thought that you are here for the family."

"Oh," said Bobby, still more disconcerted. "I don't see why any one should think so. I don't see why most people wouldn't be interested in the Pépin Mill. What happened was in all the papers. People are curious about such things. Naturally."

"They do not all ask such questions as you do," Lucille answered. "Many in the village say it is right for you to make your inquiries; above all, if it is for the family. They think there will be no good luck here till the truth is known."

"Well, anyhow," Bobby said, deciding it best not to pursue that aspect of the affair, "I'll tell you one thing. I don't believe Williams has anything to do with Scotland Yard. If he has any special reason for being here, it is for his own purposes."

"Some say that if there was murder done, then he is the murderer," Lucille said. "It is said, you know, that a murderer cannot stay away from the scene of his crime."

"He would hardly go so far as to want to live where it happened, would he?" Bobby asked. "There may be some other reason. Some idea of hiding something, of preventing some one else from finding it. But that is merely guessing."

"He is trying to find out something," Lucille insisted, "and it is something he thinks I might know. That is why he asked me to go there, why he and his wife—Madame Williams I do not like, she is more terrifying than he, it is she who made me afraid—why they were so disappointed when I said I knew nothing, why he made me go to look at the well to frighten me."

"If he wants to find out something, it can't be the murderer's name if he is the murderer himself," Bobby said thoughtfully. "There may be something quite different, though."

"It is not Père Trouché at any rate," Lucille said with a faint smile. "Of that I am sure."

"There is something else I wonder if you are sure about," Bobby asked. "Are you sure he is really blind or is that pretence?"

She looked startled at that. Then she said:

"There are some who think that no one who is blind could do what he does. Sometimes he hints himself that perhaps he can see more than is known. But for my part I think that is only talk, for he loves to talk, he loves also to impress."

Bobby said nothing about his test with the hundred franc note. He had not yet quite made up his mind what to think about that. After a pause he went on:

"Mademoiselle Lucille, will you tell me all you know about Charles Camion and Mademoiselle Polthwaite? It may be useful. It may be more than that. I have heard a lot but it would help if you would tell me what you think and know yourself. Also it seems to me possible that Camion may soon have greater need for help than he understands at present."

She made no answer for a minute or two and he waited patiently, knowing she was trying to decide what she could tell him, how far she could trust him. At last she said:

"Very well, I will tell you what I know. It is not much. It is not pleasant to have to talk about such things to one who is a stranger. But I think you have a reason why you ask and you may be able to help, and then there is your fiancée who trusts you, and I think her photograph you showed me was of one who would not trust too foolishly. When Mademoiselle Polthwaite came here first, she stayed at the hotel, and she made herself very friendly with

Charles. When she moved to the Pépin Mill, she asked him to help her to install herself. Next it was his portrait that she wished to paint so that he was often there and each day after she finished working, she kept him to talk to her and do little jobs and help her with her French. She made him tell her his plans, she even made plans for him he had never dreamed of, she talked of founding for him a great chain of hotels—the Camion hotels—and she promised him money to help him to begin. She seemed to think it might be a way to place her funds, for she spoke occasionally of having a stocking that was very well filled. Well, in the village they began to talk. There were many who were jealous of what seemed his good luck in becoming a favourite of a foolish rich old woman. A fortune for him to pick up, they said. But then they began to whisper, too, that it was not without a reason that an old woman had so often a handsome young man at her house. A gigolo they called him behind his back. It began to be said that a love affair is all natural, but that there is nothing natural when it is a question of an intrigue between a woman of that age and such a boy as Charles. Charles had only contempt for such talk. He said it came from minds already poisoned and evil. In reality, he was blinded by his ambitions she wakened in him, by the hopes of becoming great and famous she gave him. I was angry with him, oh, more than angry. I could not bear it that he should allow such gossip to continue. There was a scene between us—oh, such a scene. He said to me: If I thought such things of him, he would make them true. Since I spoke so readily of degradation, very well, so it should be, and when I thought of him in that degradation, then I was to remember that it was I who had driven him there. Oh, he said many things, and also he said that now he would marry her, old though she was."

She paused, and Bobby had a clear vision of the young man dramatising himself and his emotions and thoroughly enjoying picturing himself as a lost soul destroyed through a great, misunderstood love.

"If you ask me," he said, speaking with great deliberation, "I should say that young man was about the most foolish young man who has ever set foot upon this earth."

"It may be so," she agreed gravely, "but really it is only that he is very young and I think he always will be. Always he will be the child. But also you cannot imagine how dear he is and also how intelligent. Then she said: "I think sometimes he does not live in the same world as we others."

"Perhaps not," Bobby agreed in his turn, "but unluckily ours is the world in which things like guillotines exist. Do you know what happened after?"

"After our quarrel? That same evening a note came, asking him to come to the Pépin Mill and to stay there the night. What could one think? Ah, it was ridiculous. It would have been a comedy of the first order had it not become a tragedy. The poor Charles, he went then to the Pépin Mill. Mademoiselle Polthwaite was waiting. She was excited, nervous, hysterical indeed. She complained that he had been so long and that he should have come the moment he received her note. He answered that previously there had been need to reflect but now he had made up his mind to accede to her wishes. Well, it seems that when she on her side understood what he meant, what he thought she meant, she raged—oh, a formidable anger, a scene more frightful than can be imagined. A comedy, for each had so entirely misunderstood the other and both of them because of it so utterly furious they were entirely beside themselves. A comedy without doubt and all the time a tragedy that waited. She cried to the heavens, was it not possible for a grown woman to take an interest in a young boy, a mere child, without it at once turning him into a beast, a veritable beast of the fields? She screamed that and much more, and he shouted back to know why then had she sent for him to come and sleep there that night? She told him then, quietening a little, that she was afraid. She told him that she believed herself to be in danger from an assassin and that she had sent for him to be there to protect her, since she believed, she said, that her life was threatened by this unknown."

"She did not say who it was she feared?" Bobby interposed quickly.

"Charles did not ask, did not listen, he thought it was what you others, English, call to 'bluffer'. Lucille used the word 'bluff' as the verb into which it has been turned in French. "He was too angry to listen, for he felt that he had been made to look ridiculous, and if those in the village came to know of it, they would never stop laughing at him."

"All is there," Bobby muttered, "if only we knew who it was she was afraid of. He has no idea?"

"No, he did not take her fears seriously. He said to her that she might be visited by an assassin every night of the week for all he cared, and the sooner the better. The last thing he shouted at her from the door as he rushed away was that he would like to murder her himself and perhaps he would."

"It happened that night?" Bobby asked.

"Yes," Lucille answered in a voice so low he could hardly hear what she said. After a long pause, she added: "The worst is, the note she wrote asking him to come to the mill to sleep there, the police found it. Naturally, they put upon it but one interpretation."

"I suppose so," agreed Bobby, not at all sure indeed that such a letter would not have been considered by many courts as strong presumptive evidence of guilt.

Only presumptive though, and apparently there had been little confirmatory evidence. He suspected, too, there had probably been no great anxiety to press the case and also no great likelihood of obtaining a verdict of guilty from any jury.

"There is even worse, but that the police never knew," Lucille said suddenly. "Their quarrel was overheard. The threat he shouted but never meant as he rushed away, that was heard."

Bobby looked grave, for there it seemed was the very kind of confirmatory evidence calculated to appeal to the official mind.

"Who heard it?" he asked.

"The curé. And another, too. The curé was returning from visiting a sick woman and he heard as he was passing. He said nothing. He was not asked. None knew he had been near and he did not speak. But he sent for Charles and he made him go to the bishop to confess. I think the curé felt the responsibility was too great for him. I think perhaps—" her voice faltered—"I think perhaps he was not very confident that Charles had no concern in it."

"Who was the other who heard?" Bobby asked. "Père Trouché."

"He has kept silent, too?"

"He promised me."

"How did he happen to be there?"

"I do not know, perhaps he had heard about Charles and Mademoiselle Polthwaite and was watching to find out the truth. He is like that. Always he must know. He is not malicious, but he wishes always to know. And then, why should he not have been there when he is always everywhere? He says himself that he shares with the good God both omniscience and omnipresence, but not omnipotence."

"I wish I knew how far one could trust the old man," muttered Bobby, who did not much like this story, for it seemed to him Père Trouché might have had his own reasons for his reticence. "He told you though?"

"I asked him. Charles had seen him. He told me, and so I asked Père Trouché what he had heard. It was then he promised to say nothing."

They talked a little longer and later Bobby went back to the hotel. There he told how he had lost a hundred- franc note and how he would share it equally with any one who found it and returned it. Monsieur and Madame Camion thought this a very generous offer and promised to make it widely known. They also produced a letter that had arrived earlier for Bobby, but that had been overlooked in the general excitement caused by the commissaire's visit. It was from Olive, in part of purely private interest, but also giving the information that the bottle and glass he had secured from the café and had sent to her, had been tested by the finger-print people at the Yard, as he had asked her to get done for him. Of various finger-prints found, one set had been clearly identified as belonging to a man known as William or Joseph Weston or Williams, real name unknown, who had served various sentences for assault, for burglary, and, in addition, one for a not very serious assault on his wife. He was regarded as a violent and dangerous criminal, and Bobby whistled softly when the further information was given that though Williams seldom did any honest work, he had at one time secured a position as porter at the branch establishment of Messrs. Polthwaite, Ltd., in Paris. He had worked there, giving full satisfaction for nearly a year. He had left of his own accord. A month later an audacious attempt at burglary there had been fortunately frustrated. There was no evidence whatever against Williams, but the coincidence had been noted and he had been traced and questioned, but entirely without result. For one thing, he had a perfect alibi. There was also reason to suspect that he had been concerned in a notorious gang murder that had taken place in Soho some years previously. For the actual murder he had again an unimpeachable alibi; on this occasion, that of having been at the time under arrest on a charge of 'drunk and disorderly.' All the same, there was reason to believe he had planned the murder though someone else had carried it out. Who that someone else was had never been discovered or even suspected.

"And now he is here," Bobby mused, "here where there was a murder not long ago, the murder of a woman who bought most of her store of diamonds through a firm he had worked for. He might easily have got to hear of her purchases. Only again it seems he has an alibi."

CHAPTER XVII
BOBBY WRITES

The next day or two Bobby spent on the slopes of the Bornay Massif, ostensibly sketching, though in reality he hardly touched brush or pencil, but sat idly, or else walked to and fro, trying to compose recent happenings into some sort of consistent pattern. When his tired brain refused to work any longer he refreshed it by long and often difficult and always tiring walks across the Massif as far as that great crevasse which cut it in two and made further progress too difficult. He made friends also with one or two of the neighbouring farmers, from whom he learnt more of the topography of the district, and from one of whom, much to the worthy man's amusement, he bought a supply of binder twine. Bobby needed it for an experiment of which the vague and doubtful outline was beginning to appear at the back of his mind, but the farmer thought it merely another instance of the well-known eccentricities of the 'artiste-peintre', and Bobby did not try to enlighten him, could indeed hardly have done so, since his own mind was as yet not clear. In any case the purchase provided an excuse for a chat about the Massif and its desolate and waste expanse, which the farmer, a man of some intelligence and education, had certain plans for bringing into use. They were plans, Bobby learnt, that, some two or three years previously, had nearly cost the farmer his life, when, in pursuing his explorations of the Massif and its possibilities, he had lost his way in that bewildering maze and had only been rescued when in a state of almost complete exhaustion. It had been a lesson to him, he said, to treat the Massif with more respect, and his use of the word 'maze' in speaking of it, interested Bobby greatly. It might all prove, Bobby told himself, valuable in one way or another, or else of no value or interest whatever, and certainly so far he saw no way of fitting the things he knew or suspected or believed into a coherent whole.

Much depended, for instance, on the significance to be attached to the disappearance of Volny, a matter of which Bobby felt too little was at present known for any clear opinion to be formed. Was it voluntary, and, if so, what was the reason? Funk? A desire to avoid the duel to which Camion apparently had challenged him? Or a deeper fear for another reason? Or if there were a darker reason for his disappearance, then again what was that reason and who was responsible?

Rumours, of course, were current all the time in the village that Volny had been seen in Paris, recognized in Marseilles, heard of in Cherbourg, but these were silenced when again the smiling commissaire of police appeared in the village asking more questions and bringing with him once more a sentiment of foreboding and unease. The same day Bobby heard another piece of news, overshadowed indeed in the village by the proof that the authorities were still concerned about Volny's disappearance, but one that Bobby found of curious interest. It was to the effect that sudden and important business had summoned Mr. and Mrs. Williams to Paris. They had departed at once, though expressing the hope that they would be able to return to finish their holiday, as they had taken the Pépin Mill for the whole summer.

The next morning Bobby, instead of going out to sketch as usual, announced that he had letters to write, and settled himself with pen and paper in a shady corner on the hotel 'terrace'. In every case that so far he had been connected with, it had been his practice, indeed his duty, to submit a full report to his superiors, for them to consider, and, if they thought fit, take action on. This time he had no superiors to satisfy. He did not wish to say too much to his direct employers, Lady Markham and her relatives, till he had arrived at more definite conclusions. He fell back therefore upon writing a long letter to Olive, since he had always found it useful to clarify his thoughts and his impressions by putting them upon paper. More than once indeed as soon as he had arranged all he knew in orderly fashion on paper, in black and white, then the truth had seemed to leap upon him from the written words, as though in pen and ink there were some kind of magic to reveal it.

From what he wrote the private matter may be omitted and indeed there was but little of it, for chiefly he concerned himself with the tangled and troubled problem he saw at the moment small hope of solving.

'I am beginning to wish,' he wrote, 'that I had never touched the case. It has more points than a hedgehog and all of them liable to prick. And then what seemed to afford a chance of a promising beginning was knocked on the head from the start when I got here and found the Pépin Mill in the occupation of some one else. I thought a careful examination of the locality was sure to help, but the Williams couple got in first and I didn't much think by chance.

'It is hard enough to get at the truth in the ordinary way when you are right on the spot from the start. After all this long delay it looks pretty hopeless, like trying to solve a crossword puzzle with all the clues destroyed. Then, too, I never realized before what a difference there is between playing a lone hand and having a big organization behind you. Mere matters of routine inquiry in London, if I were working on such a case there, are hopelessly out of my reach here.

'Every trail is dead cold. If any material clues ever existed, they have long ago vanished. I have to depend entirely on memories months old. I have no chance of examining official records. Nor did I understand before I got here how much more difficult it is to judge people of another country, with an entirely different background, than it is to form an opinion of your own countrymen. There are so many differences, often quite tiny differences, in habit and outlook. In London I can almost always tell whether people are telling the truth or not. Here, I simply don't know.

'One difference is that I am probably the only person here able to believe that Miss Polthwaite's interest in young Camion was entirely innocent. I'm not saying that psycho-analysts couldn't dig down to all sorts of hidden motives, all disreputable. If there was any such hidden motive, I am quite sure myself it was only sexual in the sense that it was maternal. But I'm jolly sure you would never get the average Frenchman to understand how entirely the cruder sex emotions are sublimated—I think that's the correct word, anyhow it sounds rather good—by the habitual self-restraint and self-respect of most of our unmarried women, by the armour of their respectability, if you like, and never mind how big a sneer Bloomsbury and Chelsea put into that word. And if you could persuade the average Frenchman to believe it, he would remain quite unconvinced and merely murmur to himself something about British hypocrisy.

'So there, you see, we start from entirely different standpoints—I mean myself and the official investigators. They were as convinced of one thing as I am of another.

'I am sure not a soul here believed there was, or could be, anything innocent in the relations between Camion and Miss Polthwaite. I think the whole village was inclined to be shocked—there is a strong Puritan strain in the Frenchman though it works differently from ours. The difference between their ages was disliked; and I think Camion was aware of this general disapproval and yet I fancy he did not choose to try to explain the true position, because then he would have risked being laughed at and youngsters like Camion face moral disapproval more easily than ridicule.

'So I am putting aside any suggestion that Miss Polthwaite committed suicide, since the only motive suggested is disappointment or quarrelling in a love affair with Camion that I am perfectly certain had no existence.

'Taking it for certain then as I do that murder was committed, there are the usual questions to be answered: Who? How? Why?

'The "How?" is plain and unimportant. She was thrown down the well, unconscious, one hopes, but certainly, by medical evidence, while still alive. The bruises on the face and body may have been caused by the fall down the well or inflicted beforehand. I don't know if expert medical examination could have told more. The examination made at the time was only superficial as suicide was taken for granted.

'The "Why?" is equally clear, since I'm not having the illicit love motive. Robbery. It had got about that she possessed what one calls here a "stocking". Lucille Simone knew. And the curé knew she had a store of jewels, since she had given him several of the stones. No doubt there was general gossip in the village.

'The conclusion I draw, therefore, is that the murderer was not in any way a stranger but some one who in some way knew something.'

Bobby paused here and laid down his pen. Then he took it up again and wrote slowly:

'There is a formidable list of possibles, most of them probables as well. Here they are:

Charles Camion,

Henri Volny,

The Abbé Granges, curé of the village,

Shields, Miss Polthwaite's friend and art teacher,

Eudes, the village schoolmaster,

The Abbé Taylour,

Père Trouché,

Williams,

Mrs. Williams (or do they count as one?),

and of course the inevitable and possible but improbable X no one knows anything about.

'Anyhow, for my part, I am fairly certain I have written above the name of the murderer of Miss Polthwaite and it's no "X".

'But which among the nine, for you'll see there are nine in all, and a very nasty number, too, when you remember that the last case I had anything to do with had just that same number we had good reason to suspect and that the truth only came out by the accident of a blunder the murderer made. But if in this case whoever's guilty made any comparable blunder, what chance is there of finding it after all this delay?

'The evidence will have to be largely psychological, and what jury in England or France or anywhere else is going to convict on purely psychological evidence?

' Of course, if we can trace the stolen diamonds— supposing they have been stolen—to the possession of any one, that any one will have some questions to answer. But it's a kind of vicious circle. Not much use looking for the culprit till you know who stole the diamonds. Until you know who stole them, not much use trying to prove who is guilty.

'Take them all in turn.

'To start:

Charles Camion'.

Carefully and in full detail Bobby wrote all he knew and had observed about the young man. He dwelt, too, upon the explosive stage at which the relations between him and Miss Polthwaite seemed to have arrived and on the proof that there had been a violent quarrel and threats, overheard by two witnesses, just previously to her death and caused by the queer misunderstanding between them. It was at least possible that Miss Polthwaite's fury of indignation at Camion's misconception of the meaning of her invitation and desires had led her to say things that might in turn have roused in him an equal fury. And with two people in a fury anything may happen. Then, too, there was the fact that Miss Polthwaite had excited his ambitions, had promised him help to realize them, and that their quarrel would put an end to any such hopes. Camion was again the last person known to have been in her company. His statement that she had told him she was afraid of some other, unknown, person rested only on Camion's word, and might easily bear the explanation of an attempt to divert suspicion. His romantic, undisciplined and emotional temperament, as shown also by his challenge to Volny to meet him in a duel, suggested, too, a tendency to resort too easily to violence. Then in addition there was the odd incident of the visit to the bishop of the diocese, since a bishop alone can give absolution in cases of murder. Was it possible a confession had been made to the curé with a view to closing his mouth, since what has been learnt in confession must not be revealed, and had therefore the curé insisted on the confession being repeated to the bishop?

Bobby laid down his pen once more and looked grave. It seemed to him that under motive, association, opportunity, temperament, a formidable case existed. He felt that in England he could have submitted it with some confidence to Treasury counsel.

Yet he reflected, too, that there was no material proof. Romantic and emotional temperaments are precisely those that shrink from cold-blooded murder, they are inconsistent with such brutality as the throwing of a still living woman down a well.

'If Miss Polthwaite had been found with her head bashed in, I could have believed it of Camion more easily,' Bobby wrote, 'though of course he may have been quite off his head with fear and fury, and when, and, if he threw her down the well, he may have thought only of concealment and not realized she was alive. But all's conjecture."

Bobby shook his head again, ill-satisfied, and wrote slowly the name of the next upon his list:

'Henri Volny'.

Again he wrote all he knew and had observed about the young man, the state of poverty in which he was kept by his father, his ambition to become a first-class boxer, his need of funds for the preliminary training, his attempt to drive away Mr. and Mrs. Williams from the Pépin Mill and his secret association with the

Abbé Taylour, his tendency to resort to violence when he felt himself of superior strength, as when he had threatened Bobby after the visit to the Abbé Taylour he was apparently anxious should not be known. Finally Bobby dwelt upon his recent disappearance that seemed to suggest guilty flight. There was, too, the fact that he was a rival of Camion's for Lucille's favour, and that rivalry might possibly have been a motive urging him to try to get hold of the cash Miss Polthwaite was contemplating giving to Camion, so putting him in a favourable position for urging his suit with Lucille.

'Jealousy, poverty, rivalry, all strong motives,' Bobby wrote, 'but again no material proof, though Volny's disappearance is suspicious; and it is clear he knew or suspected something or why was he trying to chase away the Williamses?'

Once again Bobby laid down his pen and once again took it up.

'Père Trouché'.

He wrote, and wrote of him at length, for the old blind beggar interested him and of him, too, he felt doubtful, suspicious even, finding it difficult to come to any decided opinion about him.

'An old scamp,' he wrote, 'but what kind of old scamp? and is he really blind? There's my hundred-franc note test, of course, but that can't be full proof unless I can trace it back to his possession. Some one else may have picked it up. He is said to have had a grudge against Miss Polthwaite for her threat to complain to the police about him—and he is not a man to forget a grudge in a hurry—and by his own admission he was on the spot on the night of the murder. If he heard Camion's threats, he may have thought them good cover for himself. He boasts himself indifferent to money, and perhaps that is suspicious, too, for is there any one really indifferent to money? I think there's a case against the old man. On his own showing, he is fond of revenging himself on people who happen to offend him. Apparently, too, there is a record of violence and at least a suspicion that he has already killed. He seems, too, to know so much of what goes on, that almost certainly he would have heard talk of Miss Polthwaite's supposed hoard.'

The next name Bobby wrote was:

'Basil Shields'.

Of him, too, Bobby wrote in great detail, dwelling on the terms of intimacy on which he stood with Miss Polthwaite, the likelihood, therefore, that he knew a good deal of her private affairs, on the significant fact that he had acted as her art teacher. Then, too, he had kept up his connection with the village in a somewhat marked manner. Bobby went into specially full details of his own first encounter with Shields when Shields had talked pointedly about 'coincidence', as if he had felt it necessary to explain his reappearance in the district.

'Is there anything,' Bobby wrote, 'in Shields's friendship with Eudes? On the face of it, they would not seem to have much in common. Why was Shields interested in my arrival? Simply because he had heard I was a fellow-countryman and a brother artist? Is that likely? Or had he been warned by Eudes, and was his visit to make sure that I really was what I seemed to be—a casual tourist fond of sketching? If so, then he and Eudes are partners—and partners may mean accomplices. Yet if they are guilty and are in possession of Miss Polthwaite's valuables, I still do not see why the mere appearance of a stray Englishman should so much upset them when the authorities appeared satisfied.

'Again is Shields as successful as he claims to be in selling his stuff? He boasts of a very comfortable income from his sales and yet does not seem to spend much money—economy or scarcity? Shields is certainly not a really well-known man, but then I believe some artists have private connections they do well out of. He seems, too, to have been the chief suspect of the French police till his apparently impregnable alibi satisfied them. Personally I don't like alibis, seen too much of them. Every rogue is of the elder Mr. Weller's opinion. Even a grave in the churchyard alibi may be a fake—twin brother perhaps.'

It was some time before Bobby roused himself from the deep thought in which he now became lost and wrote down the next name on his list:

'Eudes'.

Of the schoolmaster, Bobby had less to write. The association, perhaps suspicious, perhaps innocent, with Shields he had already dealt with. Now Bobby noted his undisguised eagerness to secure money for starting his projected journal from which he hoped such great things and the fact that such fanaticism as his may easily take a man far.

'Anti-clericalism,' Bobby wrote, 'is itself a kind of religious fanaticism, and religious fanatics are unpredictable. Of course, starting a paper in France is much easier and simpler than it would be in England, and is often an ambitious politician's first step. Eudes is ambitious enough, that is fairly evident, and very likely he sees his paper as the first step to high political office. Though he would need very much less capital for the enterprise than would be required in England, it would still probably be very much more than he would have any chance of raising in the ordinary way.

'You have to remember, though, that he is one of the three suspects with an apparently sound alibi, since he was attending a political conference at the time at Dijon. I suppose one can slip away from political conferences and Dijon is not so far from here, but I take it his alibi was checked at the time, though goodness knows how carefully.'

Of the next name Bobby put down:

'Abbé Taylour',

there was even less to write. He was one of the three who had an alibi, since apparently he had been ill at the time of the murder. But he himself had said that his fever had gone by the time a doctor saw him and it is not difficult to sham a few symptoms that a doctor with no reason to be doubtful, would accept as genuine. The sole ground for suspicion in his case seemed to be that he was a somewhat mysterious person come suddenly to live near where a mysterious murder presently occurred. Bobby was conscious, too, of a vague feeling that in some way the regular hanging out of a lamp at night was somehow of importance and yet he could not think how that could be. No possible connection, it would seem, between a lantern high up upon the hill-side and a murder occurring in the valley far below.

Next was written:

'Abbé Granges, curé of Citry-sur-l'eau',

and there, of course, what Bobby emphasized was the fact that the curé was actually in possession of uncut diamonds that once admittedly had belonged to the murdered woman. True, he said they had been a free gift, but of that there was no proof. Again he had been upon the spot about the time of the murder, he had apparently overheard the quarrel and Camion s threat, and, as in Père Trouché's case, might have seen the opportunity to use such threats as cover for his own contemplated crime. Was it possible, too, that the visit he had induced Camion to make to the bishop had been for the purpose of diverting any possible suspicion from himself? A far-fetched notion, perhaps, and yet in such a mirk of fog and doubt one had to consider every possibility. Remarkable, too, that living in such extreme poverty as seemed to be the case— even as Bobby had heard, taking long walks in the winter to keep himself warm so as to save fuel—he yet spoke continuously of his project for restoring the Citry church to its former glory. There was his tale of 'l'oncle d'Amerique' certainly, but that might well be merely a blind. Bobby shook his head as he put all this down. It was at least susceptible of being interpreted as evidence of guilt.

Finally Bobby wrote the names of

'Mr. and Mrs. Williams',

He dwelt on their tenancy of the Pépin Mill which he did not believe for one moment was merely a coincidence, but added that on the theory of their guilt their sudden departure seemed hard to understand since no fresh threat to them had appeared. If they were innocent, though, they might well have decided that they didn't want to have anything more to do with the Pépin Mill and its mysteries. Bobby dwelt, too, on all the many odd and suspicious facts about them he had noted, their attempt to bully Lucille, their attempt to drive him himself out of the village, and other such details.

'They were at the Pépin Mill in my belief,' he wrote finally, 'neither for health nor for holiday, but for some purpose of their own, and, in view of their record, probably a criminal purpose. Is it the diamonds supposed to have been in Miss Polthwaite's possession that they think are still somewhere in the garden or on the premises and are trying to find? If so, how do they know about them? Why do they think the stuff is still there? If they do think so, are they right? If so, have they found it and is that why they cleared out in such a hurry? Did they commit the crime, and did they know the diamonds were still somewhere in or near the mill for the very good reason that they had failed to find them? Apparently they were never seen in the village till they rented the mill and they claim they were in Paris at the time of the murder. But I suppose that alibi was not checked, since, when the investigation was on, they had not been heard of—they were then in fact in the position of the unknown "X", a detective has always to keep in mind. In any case I still stick to it that alibis, like promises and piecrusts, are made to be broken.'

He paused and for a long time remained frowning and deep in thought. Then he took his pen again and wrote more slowly:

'Well, to sum up, this is how it stands.

'Take motive first:

I. GREED.

A. Camion.

Camion needed money to realize ambitions Miss Polthwaite had herself aroused. She had promised him money and after their quarrel might have refused it.

B. Volny.

He was kept short by his well-to-do father and had talked about going to America to train for professional boxing.

C. The curé.

He needed it and apparently expected to procure it, to rebuild his church.

D. Eudes.

He required it to start his projected paper and realize his political ambitions.

2. ALIBI.
Alibis, by implication or directly, are claimed by Williams, Eudes, Shields, the Abbé Taylour.

3. IDENTITY (of time and place).
Camion, the curé, Père Trouché, are known to have been near the mill at the time of the murder.

4. ILL FEELING.
A. Père Trouché had been threatened by Miss Polthwaite with the police and boasts of revenging himself on those who offend him.

B. Camion is known to have quarrelled with Miss Polthwaite that night and to have uttered violent threats.

C. Volny is said to have resented her show of friendship towards Camion.

5. CHARACTER.
Both Camion and Volny have shown a tendency to resort to violence, Camion when he felt his "honour" injured, Volny against those he believed weaker than himself. Both conditions apply. Père Trouché boasts of his revenges and is under some suspicion of having killed already. Williams has a criminal record.'

Bobby once more paused to re-read what he had written and frowned again to contemplate so many indications all pointing different ways. Then he wrote:

If you look at and read everything from the very beginning over again carefully, you will see—it is of course perfectly obvious, even a child at school couldn't miss it—that the murderer's name may be there on record, staring us right in the face all the time. But even so, it doesn't help—not, I mean, from the official point of view which only considers the solid proof you can rub a jury's collective nose into. Still, there it is as, at least, a clear indication.'

But even yet he added a postscript. It ran:
'I am waiting anxiously for your reply about those broken bits of wine glasses I sent you. If my luck is in, and Records finds finger-prints on them, any finger-prints at all, I shall chance my arm and go to the police commissaire. Not that the finger-prints, even if found, will affect anything in this letter or any of my

previous ideas. But I shall gamble, I shall have to, on my other guess being right. Only if it's wrong, I shall probably find myself advised to return home by the next train and not meddle with other people's business. I shall be on the fidgets till your letter gets here.'

He had scarcely written these last words when Madame Camion came out from the hotel with a letter that had just arrived. He opened it eagerly and found within two sets of photographs of clearly defined finger-prints.

"That means me for the commissaire," Bobby told himself uncomfortably, "and quite likely me put on the train and packed off back to England for an interfering, fussy fool. Got to chance it, though."

He noticed that Madame Camion was lingering near. Evidently there was something she wanted to tell him. When she saw that she had his attention, she said to him: "There is news about that poor Monsieur Williams. It seems he is less sober in Paris than here, for now one hears he has been in trouble with the police and they put him in the shade for a day or two."

'In the shade' is French slang for prison, and Madame chuckled again as she moved away, for Williams had never been a favourite of hers. But Bobby's face was very grave, for to him it was as though all suddenly he had been aware of the chill presence of death passing slowly by.

CHAPTER XVIII
BOBBY TALKS

It had been not far from a full day's work to get down upon paper and to consider all the various details in all their different and generally doubtful implications, mere hints indeed, that in the end seemed to him to point so clearly in one unwelcome direction.

Nor did Bobby take immediate action when at long last this conclusion had become firmly established in his mind. For one thing, he was certain that if there were any justification for those chill fears Madame Camion's story of Williams's trouble with the police in Paris had put into his mind, then it was too late for that to be prevented which he so darkly feared. For another, he was very keenly aware of the heavy responsibility that would be his if he decided to inform authority of the conclusions at which he had now arrived. Once again he found himself remembering wistfully how much easier it had been when his sole duty was to place his views before senior officers, running no other risk than that of a snub if they decided that his theories were unwarranted and that his report had best go into the waste-paper basket.

Now, it was for him alone to decide whether to take action. Easy to keep quiet, to await events, to allow the official investigation to continue without knowledge of the facts that he had gathered. No one could blame him for failing in a mission so difficult, one in which the French police with all their advantages had not succeeded. Only then the guilty would go unpunished; and Bobby's looks were dark as he thought of the well at the Pépin Mill and of the still living, perhaps still conscious woman thrust down into those black depths. More important yet, suspicion would continue to rest here and there, and Bobby knew well how corroding can be the effects of unfounded suspicion upon all but the strongest characters.

Again, he had to remember that upon his decision rested any chance his employers, Lady Markham and her relatives, might have of recovering their lawful property.

On the other hand, he risked, if his theories and his deductions from the impressions he had noted, proved ill-founded—and that they were correct he had no firm, material proof to show, it was all a matter of argument and reasoning—he risked inflicting great, perhaps irreparable, harm on the person he would then have wrongfully accused. Incidentally it might also lead to unpleasant personal results, to his being asked to curtail his visit to France, to hints reaching Scotland Yard that one of their officers had been meddling foolishly abroad in matters that did not concern him. It would mean a big black mark against his name if that happened.

Yet it was perhaps this fear of possible personal consequences he felt he must not allow to influence him, that helped him in the end to make his decision. All the same he decided to wait till morning before taking the final step of communicating with the authorities. The delay would do no harm, and after a night's sleep he would be able to review his decisions and see if his resolve seemed weakened or strengthened.

He found it strengthened, but when he came downstairs for his morning rolls and coffee, he found also that his projected journey to Barsac would be unnecessary, for almost the first thing he heard was that once again the commissaire of police was in the village, that he had established himself at the Mairie, that, in spite of the early hour, he was already beginning to interview people. Of this, too, he had further proof when presently a message, extremely polite in form but all the same equally firm, informed him that Monsieur the Commissaire Clauzel would esteem greatly the privilege of a short interview with Monsieur Owen, at Monsieur Owen's entire convenience, at any hour before ten that morning.

Bobby sent back word that naturally he would be only too willing to attend as requested, and that, in fact, he believed himself to be in possession of certain facts he had already determined it would be well to place before Monsieur Clauzel.

"Monsieur Clauzel," Bobby said to Madame Camion who, pale, restless, and red-eyed, was wandering uneasily to and fro, between reception desk and door, "is the official of the police who was here before?"

Madame Camion promptly began to cry, slowly and with difficulty, for tears come less easily as the years pass.

"He searches my son for the guillotine," she said, a touch of wildness in her voice. "He hunts him down. Where is the good God that He permits such things? Since I swear to you that Charles is innocent, innocent as the blessed saints themselves."

"That is the important thing," Bobby said, though he thought he detected in the vehemence of these last words a dreadful fear in the mother's heart that possibly her son was in truth guilty. "The innocent have nothing to fear."

"The innocent have suffered before now," she answered with the same touch of wildness latent in her voice so that Bobby feared she might at any moment break down. "He is there at the Mairie, this Clauzel, he sits there and asks questions, lays traps, twists answers, makes things seem different, so that if a boy sharpens a knife, there is the proof that it is for murder. Next, it will be the juge d'instruction."

"They seek only to discover the truth," Bobby repeated.

"They have sent for you, they have not sent for Charles," the poor woman said, and evidently felt, as Bobby himself felt, that that was no good sign. She added: "Besides, for that matter, he is not here." Seeing that Bobby looked startled at this piece of information, she said quickly: "Oh, he has not run away. He went very early, before even Monsieur the Commissaire arrived."

"Do you know where he has gone?" Bobby asked, hoping that to all the other complication was not to be added yet another flight or disappearance.

"He did not say. I think it is in search of Volny fils. It was foolish, their quarrel. If it was for fear of him that Volny went, then Charles feels it is for him to get him to return. Oh, Charles will return," she added, for Bobby was still looking doubtful. "He went once before to try to find him and was back for the evening service. He promised he would try to be back to-day in time for that."

"Well, I hope he will," Bobby said. "It is not wise to be absent at these times."

"In the village they whisper, whisper all the time, but when I come near they are silent," Madame Camion went on. "They will whisper and whisper and whisper till they whisper us out of our minds. Charles, he is calm and proud, oh, so proud and calm—without. But within it is different. He said to me that none will be content till they have driven him to seek his own death himself. Then perhaps they will know remorse."

"Remorse?" repeated Bobby, startled and uneasy, for he felt young Camion was exactly the type to stage a dramatic suicide in a state of gloomy anticipation of how sorry every one would be when finally his innocence was established. "Not they, not likely. They would only feel how right they had been; and even if some one else were proved guilty, they would all remain quite sure he had been mixed up in it somehow. He is not going to give in so easily as all that, is he?"

Madame Camion looked impressed.

"I will say all that to him," she told Bobby. Then she added: "It has comforted me to talk to you."

With that she went off and Bobby retired to his room and collected all the material he had got together. When he came down Madame Camion was there again, looking more troubled than ever.

"Lucille Simone," she told Bobby, "is proclaiming to all the world that she and Charles are affianced. How can that be? To me, to his father, he has said nothing, and yet, she, a young girl, proclaims it aloud. What is one to think of such happenings?"

"Well, for one thing that Mademoiselle Simone is sure of your son's innocence," Bobby answered, but felt, too, that the girl's gesture had more than a touch of the defiant, of the melodramatic, not altogether consistent with assured and certain confidence in the young man's innocence.

He went on to the Mairie, where a curious group of spectators had collected, for to-day work in the village was very much at a standstill. His appearance and his admission by the gendarme placed at the door to keep out the unauthorized was watched with much interest. He was shown into a large, empty, sparsely-furnished waiting-room, its white-washed walls adorned with various notices and proclamations—including the latest speech delivered by the deputy for the district. Almost at once Eudes appeared from an inner room. He looked flushed and excited. He said indignantly:

"They are a pack of imbeciles, these officials. No wonder the republic is in danger when she is served by such a crew. For myself, I care nothing. My innocence proclaims itself. But when they seek to accuse others of the village, our cure for example, it is too much. Those black crows, it is the mind they seek to enslave and I resist them to the death. Corrupters of the mind, a thousand times, yes. Assassins in secret of the body, to think that is mere folly, and I say it, I, who have watched and fought the subtle trickeries of the church all my life. Bah!"

Whether this last angry ejaculation was aimed at the church or at the police, Bobby was not sure and had no time to inquire for he was hurriedly summoned to the presence of the commissaire. He found Monsieur Clauzel delivering an indignant harangue to an unfortunate official evidently held responsible for permitting a departing witness to meet and talk to one not yet examined. Bobby waited by the window till the storm should be over, and from it he could see at a distance down the street where Eudes and the curé were standing and talking together with every appearance of a mutual sympathy and understanding.

"You shall hear of it later," Clauzel was saying in low angry tones to his guilty assistant, "and in the interval, see that it does not happen again."

"I assure you, monsieur the commissaire," Bobby interposed, "no harm was done. Monsieur Eudes said only that for himself he was innocent and that none but"—Bobby hesitated, looked more embarrassed than he felt, went on—"imbeciles was, I believe, the word thoughtlessly used, only they could imagine for a moment that a curé could be also an assassin. It is an opinion, for Monsieur Eudes is, I believe, strongly anti-clerical."

Clauzel grunted and did not look either very impressed or much placated.

"Altogether irregular," he repeated, voicing an official's severest condemnation. "For that matter, priests have been also murderers before to-day, and I have known, too, the guilty protest furiously the innocence of others in order to impose a conviction of their own innocence." He grunted again and looked at some papers on the table before him. "As for that," he said, "the Abbé Granges was not far from threatening us with excommunication when we questioned him about the schoolmaster. Yet it seems they are bitter enemies and rivals, as indeed is only natural since it is war to the knife between them for control of the minds of the children."

"Enemies, perhaps, but loyal enemies," suggested Bobby.

"It may be," agreed Clauzel, "yet it would seem that both or either may be implicated, and indeed I thought we were to be faced with a confession when the good abbé began to speak of his guilt. But it seems merely that his conscience troubles him because he heard quarrelling and threats one night by the Pepin

Mill and yet because he thought it of little importance, and also because he had come far and was fatigued and it was late at night, he did not stop. Because of that he seems to think he is responsible in a way for the woman's death, since had he stopped to inquire, he might have prevented what was to happen. A sensitive conscience perhaps? One does not know. He admits, too, that he has in his possession uncut diamonds which he says, but has no proof, were given him by the unfortunate Mademoiselle Polthwaite. Then it seems the schoolmaster was trying to secure possession of the Pépin Mill garden. Was that to hinder investigation, to destroy any evidence that might still exist? Again, one does not know. Is it possible, one wonders, that these two enemies in public are accomplices in private? There is so much to be considered. For yourself, monsieur—"

He waved Bobby, who had been standing till now, towards a chair that Bobby had already noticed with some amusement was so placed that its occupant sat with his face in full light, while Clauzel himself, sitting at his table, had his back to the window. Routine, of course, in police work all over the world, but the first time, Bobby reflected, that he had been passive in it and not active. The only other occupant of the room was a clerk—the 'greffier'—sitting unobtrusively at a smaller table in one corner, in readiness to take down question and answer.

Bobby being seated, Monsieur Clauzel began on a most apologetic, friendly note. Infinitely did he regret that his duty compelled him to trouble a visitor, a guest of France, involved in these unfortunate affairs by the merest accident. All the same it was quite plain that a good many inquiries had been made about Bobby and his recent activities.

Clauzel, for instance, knew all about Bobby's recent long solitary days on the Bornay Massif, and had even heard of his chats with various farmers of the district and of his purchase of binder twine, which had evidently amused the commissaire almost as much as it had done the farmer himself. Not that he made much effort to question Bobby closely. He merely let it be seen that he knew a lot about him and he expressed once or twice his conviction that Monsieur Owen would realize how important it was in such an 'enquête' as this, that nothing should be over-looked. The tiniest detail had its importance, it might be its overwhelming importance. Unfortunately the affair of the young Volny was taking on an aspect of increasing seriousness. True, it might well turn out in the end to be no more than a youthful escapade, but still, there it was, the days passed, the uneasiness of the family increased, nothing was heard of the missing lad. So far as was known, he had only a little money with him. It was certain he had not his papers of identity, for all of them, including his 'carnet militaire', had been found in his room in his father's house.

Monsieur Clauzel paused to let this sink in, and Bobby understood how serious it was, for he knew that while sometimes it is possible to live without money, no one can exist for long in France without papers. It is of course possible to obtain false ones, but it is not easy; it requires time and knowledge. It was not very probable that a young countryman in Volny's position would have had much opportunity of getting hold of such forgeries. Nor was there, as Clauzel pointed out, any reason to suppose that Volny had been contemplating flight for any length of time.

"He may, of course," Clauzel admitted, "have found shelter with friends. It is a possible explanation, though we have made inquiries in every known direction without success. Comprehensible then that his family are very seriously alarmed. They have indeed," added Clauzel somewhat resentfully, "communicated direct with Monsieur the Deputy, as though we needed such pressure to carry out our duties."

"One must allow for the anxiety of a father," Bobby remarked. "Natural for parents to worry about their youngsters. Boys and girls generally turn up again, I know, when they get tired of playing around, but sometimes they don't. One's got to remember that."

Monsieur Clauzel agreed. He was happy indeed that Monsieur Owen understood so well, and then Bobby cut short further polite preliminaries by dropping his own little bombshell.

"I was in fact," he said, "about to ask for an interview. I thought you might perhaps find these worth attention." As he spoke he put on the commissaire's table the fingerprint photographs Olive had sent him, and the good man fairly goggled—an ugly word, perhaps, but expressive.

"But these, these are finger-prints," he stuttered. "I do not understand. Where do they come from? Whose are they?"

"As for whose they are, I do not know," Bobby answered. "They come from wineglasses taken from the studio of Monsieur Basil Shields, of whom you have heard. You will remember he was a friend of Mademoiselle Polthwaite's. He used to give her lessons in painting."

The commissaire continued to goggle. Never in all his official career had he been quite so utterly taken aback. He stared at the photographs, at Bobby, from one to the other and back again. He said finally:

"Yes. Of course, one remembers well. There were hints, there were suspicions. I considered them. There was no evidence. There was a strong alibi."

"You were not, however, fully satisfied?"

"One is never satisfied till justice has been done," answered Clauzel gravely. "But there was proof against no one and in the end a 'non-lieu' was returned." He was silent a moment and then said: "None the less we have continued to watch. It was said Mademoiselle Polthwaite had invested her funds in diamonds and other jewels. None were found after her death. If one of those concerned begins to show signs of possessing money not accounted for, or if we hear of attempts by such a one to sell unset or uncut diamonds, then there will be questions to be answered. We understand, for example, that Monsieur Shields will be visiting New York soon. We shall see that his baggage is examined with special care and in New York they will be warned of his arrival."

"Very wise," Bobby agreed, "but somehow if Shields is guilty and if he has the diamonds, I don't think he will be quite so simple as to carry them about with him."

"The most cunning criminal makes his mistakes, especially when he has begun to think himself safe," answered Clauzel, "but what has this to do with the Volny case? It is that we are concerned with at the moment. These photographs of finger-prints, whose are they?"

"I have no means of knowing," Bobby answered quietly. "I was hoping you might be able to identify them. I have told you where they come from."

Monsieur Clauzel set himself to examine them under a powerful magnifying glass he produced. With a muttered word of apology he left the room for a moment or two and when he came back he consulted with his clerk. Their heads were bent together over some papers Bobby could not see. Presently Clauzel turned to Bobby and said: "It cannot be considered fully established without a more complete technical examination. But there appears to be correspondence, as to one set of prints, with those Monsieur Shields was good enough to allow to be taken at the time of the inquiry into Mademoiselle Polthwaite's death. The second set appears to agree with those found in the bedroom occupied by the missing Volny. You expected that?"

"Yes," said Bobby. "It tends to confirm certain ideas of mine."

The commissaire was looking at him with a puzzled and, Bobby felt, slightly suspicious air. He said:

"Monsieur, will you perhaps be good enough to explain more fully?"

"It is quite simple," Bobby said. "You are aware that I knew there had been a quarrel, and even talk of a duel, between the two youngsters, Volny and Camion, and you heard how Père Trouché, the old blind beggar who seems a bit of an institution round here, hauled me out of bed to try to stop it. It was partly something I said that helped to start the row. Also he wanted it all kept as quiet as possible and I suppose he thought that as a stranger I should be less likely to gossip."

"I understand you yourself had been involved with Volny in a dispute of a serious nature?" Clauzel said.

"Well, hardly serious, but we did have a row. He seemed to think I had been spying on him and threatened me with a pistol. I managed to trip him up and got the pistol away."

"What did you do with it?"

"Threw it away, down a bit of a ravine near by," Bobby answered. He added after a moment's hesitation: "Perhaps I ought to say I saw it, or one like it, later on, together with a cap with bloodstains on it, in a drawer in the presbytery."

"Ah, it was you who saw it," murmured Clauzel, and Bobby knew very well he was thinking that perhaps Bobby had seen it there because it was he who had placed it there. "Unusual, perhaps, to find a pistol in a presbytery. Have you any theory to account for its presence?"

Bobby felt much inclined to retort that the curé was the person to question on that point. But he thought it more prudent to try to explain:

"It is only a theory," he said, "but Volny was friendly with the Abbé Taylour. I believe that he had even made his confession to him once or twice, and I don't think the curé here liked that one little bit. Poaching on his preserves. I expect he spoke to Volny père, and Volny fils had to promise to make his confession in the proper quarter for the future. If that was it, then the curé may have got out of him about his having threatened me with a pistol and may have insisted on the thing being handed over to him. As for the bloodstained cap—well," said Bobby, trying to keep every trace of satisfaction out of his voice, "I believe the chap's nose did bleed a bit."

"It is very plausible, it is very well thought out," agreed Clauzel with doubt in every syllable he uttered. "Proceed, monsieur."

Bobby felt his story was being accorded a somewhat sceptical reception. He had a vision of himself on trial for his life in a French court, and he made up his mind hurriedly that if he managed to get out of this business safely, never again would he undertake any kind of private mission. He knew very well that even an arrest, even though it never came to a trial, would put a very complete end to his career. After such a contretemps, the utmost he could hope for would be a transfer to the uniform branch, at the very best with permission to keep his rank as sergeant, but with all hope of further promotion for ever gone. However, he let nothing of that appear and continued quietly:

"Naturally, I heard, like every one else, that Volny had disappeared. At first I thought it was probably that he had thought the duel business rather silly and had decided to end it by going away for a time."

"I understand when you were out that morning you heard a single shot fired?"

"That is true," Bobby agreed.

"You attached no importance to it?"

"I could see no reason to."

"Camion's explanation is that he fired one shot to make sure his pistol was in working order."

"I may point out," Bobby said, "that if that pistol shot we heard, meant he had murdered Volny, the body must have been lying somewhere very near. There was no sign of it."

"The point has not been overlooked," observed Clauzel drily. "It might have been concealed and removed later. Proceed, monsieur."

"It seemed strange," Bobby continued, "that Volny did not let his friends know where he was. I knew there was a general feeling of uneasiness and I began to think there might be some ground for it. Monsieur Eudes told me he believed Volny had gone to visit the Abbé Taylour in that solitary hut up on the hill. But Eudes said he had gone off on his bicycle, and you don't use a bicycle to climb steep hills with no roads up them. I concluded Volny had meant to go somewhere else, and somewhere not far away, since it was within bicycle ride. I knew he was interesting himself in the Polthwaite tragedy. I knew he had been trying to get the Williamses away from the Pépin Mill. I supposed that was because he wanted a chance to visit it himself. That meant that either he hoped to find something to show who was guilty or that he had heard of the diamonds Miss Polthwaite was supposed to have had by her, and wanted to have a try himself to find them. I knew, too, for Eudes told me, that he was talking about the Polthwaite affair the night of his disappearance. I guessed the duel business might have made him keener on discovering something. Probably he believed Camion was the murderer—it seems the general idea in the village—and if he could find out anything to prove it, he would have got rid of a rival, since both he and Camion are trying to win Mademoiselle Simone's favour, and also any idea of a duel would have been put an end to. So I thought he might for both those reasons be specially anxious just now to do a bit of investigating on his own. But the only person in bicycle-ride distance, who could tell him anything about the Polthwaite affair, was Shields. It seemed a fair guess that Volny had intended to ride over to Barsac to see Shields with the idea of questioning him further."

"Volny is known in Barsac, there are relatives of his there," Clauzel interrupted. "We have made inquiries. He has not been seen."

"I wondered about that, too," Bobby said. "I took it for granted you had made such inquiries. I thought he might have slipped in without being seen, but not that he could be staying there without its getting known. That also I found disquieting. Shields had asked me to pay him a visit to see his work. I thought it would be a good time to accept his invitation. At Barsac I found Shields was out. I determined to wait and I got chatting to a man named Ducane who seems to work in the garden."

"He has been questioned," Clauzel remarked. "He spoke of your visit. You did his portrait, didn't you? An admirable piece of work, if I may say so."

"You are most kind," said Bobby, very pleased, though he knew quite well the portrait had been admirable only in a very special sense. "Of course, I pretend to be no more than a highly incompetent amateur. Ducane told me a few things I thought interesting. For example, that Shields was always reluctant to spend money. Therefore he was either miserly or hard up. He didn't strike me as the miserly type, so I concluded he was hard up. Yet the first time I saw him he boasted of his prosperity. I wondered why he wished to give that impression. I noticed there was a bicycle pushed out of sight behind some sacks of artificial manure in a shed where I sat for shelter out of the sun while I was waiting for Shields's return. Ducane's story was that Shields had blundered in giving an order for garden stuff over the 'phone, and had in consequence had delivered to him enough artificial manure for half a dozen farms and a whole bale of binder twine, instead of the raffia he wanted. Curious mistakes to make, I thought, but curious mistakes can be made over the 'phone, especially when one is talking a foreign language. I was interested though, and interested to see that the mistakes hadn't been put right. Instead the bale of binder twine had fairly well been used up so apparently some use had been made of it. I noticed, too, that the bicycle was not new and that the identification plaque was missing. Ducane mentioned that Shields had had his bicycle smashed up in an accident about the time of the Polthwaite affair and afterwards had bought a new one. He said, too, that Shields had gone into Clermont that morning on his bicycle. I concluded therefore that the bicycle pushed almost out of sight I had noticed in one of the outhouses was not his. For one thing, it was not new, and I did not think a man so careful of his money as Shields seemed to be would have bought two."

"Monsieur," said Clauzel, and still there was some suspicion in his voice, "you notice many things. I ask myself how that is, for so few people notice anything at all."

Bobby did not answer this question. He went on: "When Shields got back he asked me to come in and look at his work. I noticed in the studio a tray with two empty wine glasses on it. As I was leaving to catch my train, with no time to spare, I knocked over the tray and glasses. The glasses broke. I picked up the pieces, told Shields I would get him others that matched them, so as not to spoil his set, and rushed off to catch my train as fast as I could, leaving him no chance to object. It happens that the woman who generally cooks and cleans for him had been away for a few days, which is why the place was not over tidy and why the wine glasses had not been washed and put away."

Monsieur Clauzel had been listening to all this with great attention and the greffier had been writing at his best speed. Clauzel put the tips of his fingers together and said slowly:

"All that you have told me is of the greatest interest. I am sure the juge d'instruction will be of the same opinion. I will not ask you for the present, monsieur, why you have taken so keen an interest in these happenings. Without offence, you will permit me to observe that your story rests entirely on your own statements."

"Not entirely, surely," Bobby said. "It can be checked in various details. Also you have there the finger-print photographs. The broken pieces of the wine glasses are being returned to me. You will find they match with others in Shields's possession."

"Wine glasses of the same pattern are not uncommon," Clauzel pointed out, "and it would not be difficult to secure on them any finger-prints you desired by inviting such persons to share a bottle of wine with you. The point is not one that need be discussed at present. The urgent necessity appears to be a visit to Monsieur Shields. I will ring up Monsieur Alain, the juge d'instruction, and ask him to meet us there."

"A confrontation?" Bobby murmured, and Clauzel either did not hear or did not choose to answer.

"You will do us the honour to accompany us," he went on.

"Enchanted," Bobby said. "I am sure it is wise there should be no delay. I am not easy in my mind for I am afraid of further incidents."

"For what reason? There is something else you know?"

"Only that, as you are aware, Monsieur and Madame Williams have left for Paris. I expect you know also—I was told by Madame Camion—that in Paris Monsieur Williams got into some sort of trouble with the police. He had dined too well, apparently."

"In fact, we have official knowledge of that," Clauzel answered, smiling slightly. "I have had a letter from Madame. She was distressed. She seemed to fear the most serious consequences. She wrote from her hotel in Paris to ask if we would certify that her husband's conduct had always been exemplary here. It is of course unnecessary. Without doubt, Monsieur Williams has already been released." Something in Bobby's expression caught Clauzel's attention. "What is the matter?" he asked quickly. "What has all that to do with us?"

"I do not know," Bobby answered slowly, "but I do know that once before Williams established an alibi by getting himself arrested on a charge of no importance, and that while he was thus under arrest, and so possessed a perfect alibi, there took place the murder of a man with whom Williams was not unconnected."

"You mean by that...?"

"I mean only that in England, and I expect in France also, a criminal tends often to reproduce the exact methods that have been successful before."

Clauzel was looking at Bobby more doubtfully than ever.

"You reason well and with care," he said. "Not all the world would have reasoned where Volny was likely to have gone on his cycle. Not every one would have observed that it was little likely a man of economical habits should have provided himself with two cycles. But that, it is perhaps for Monsieur Alain to consider."

CHAPTER XIX
BOBBY NOTICES

As clouds were coming up and rain was beginning to fall, Bobby was allowed to return to his hotel for a mackintosh and umbrella, though he had a strong suspicion that discreet watch was being kept to make sure he did not seize the opportunity to disappear. When he came downstairs from his room with the mackintosh he had been to fetch, he found the two older Camions talking to a stranger in the entrance hall. Camion Père was silent, sullen and troubled, muttering only a word or two from time to time in support of his wife who was protesting with voluble indignation that she had not seen her son since first thing in the morning, that he was not a babe to be tied always to her apron strings, that he was a free citizen, that the police were, as every one knew, a pest, a disgrace, and a danger to all honest folk—but Madame Camion's opinion of the police force of her country cannot be given here since it would undoubtedly scorch any paper on which it was printed.

Bobby heard the stranger say he would report to his superior and then retreat in haste before a fresh outburst calculated to make any high explosive bomb confess itself a mere back number. Monsieur Camion said 'Pouf, Pouf', and Madame Camion collapsed, changing suddenly from a formidable and angry tigress into a tired old woman. Bobby said to her:

"Your son is making a mistake. Useless to try to avoid the police. It is almost a confession, to run away like this. Much the best plan to face things out—when you are innocent."

She did not answer, but at the last word she raised her head and looked at Bobby, and all too plainly he saw the awful doubt her eyes betrayed. She got to her feet and went slowly away; and about her was the dignity that there brings with it a suffering and a grief beyond the common knowledge.

Her husband looked pitifully at Bobby. He said:

"He is her son, her only son."

"Courage," answered Bobby. "Tell her to have courage and to hope."

But his own voice lacked confidence, and Camion shook his head and began to walk away, walking like a blind man. Once he paused and said over his shoulder:

"They do not believe us but it is true. We do not know where Charles has gone or why."

He walked on, disappearing into the back regions of the hotel, for at least there is always work to be done. Bobby returned to the mairie where the commissaire's car was waiting. The commissaire himself was standing near, talking to the maire. Bobby said to them:

"It seems Charles Camion is not to be found."

"He was told that I had come again," the commissaire said. "After that, he disappeared."

"It is a confession," said the maire. "Never would I have believed it. Yet I do not call it a murder when two young men quarrel and a life is lost. Young blood is hot, it acts without thought, without intention. It is not an assassination. In Citry-sur-l'eau, we do not breed assassins."

"There is also the affair of Mademoiselle Polthwaite," said the commissaire. "It seems there is a connection. I think they are close together as fuel and fire, as bud and blossom."

The maire made no comment but looked angry and went away. The commissaire and Bobby took their seats. The car started. Bobby noticed that another followed behind. It was growing late now, for all this had taken time, and they had to lunch 'on the thumb', as the French say. It was between two and three when they reached Barsac, and the commissaire, who had stopped twice upon the road for brief 'phone conversations, drove direct through the town to its outskirts where, backing on the bare and desolate slopes of the Bornay Massif stood the house occupied by Basil Shields.

Almost as they drew up, another car arrived, and from it alighted three or four men, one of whom, tall and severe-looking, wearing pince-nez through which he seemed to look suspiciously on all the world, was Monsieur Alain, the juge d'instruction, now in charge of an investigation the authorities were evidently beginning to take very seriously. He and the commissaire talked apart for some time while the others waited. Bobby sat on the footboard of the car and smoked a cigarette and wondered what the two officials were saying to each other. No doubt for one thing they would be discussing Camion's apparent flight, which to the official mind would certainly seem, as Bobby himself had said, almost a confession.

Presently they came back together and Bobby heard Alain say:

"It is all tied up together, it is all one affair, one proceeding from the other."

"Without doubt," answered the commissaire, "and when there is proof in the one affair, then also there will be proof in the other."

A third car arrived, following the one Bobby had noticed following their own; and from it, to Bobby's surprise, there alighted Père Trouché. As he moved forward he stumbled over a small obstruction in his path his groping staff had missed, and might have fallen, but that Bobby with a word of warning put out a hand to support him.

"Hé, it's you, Mr. Englishman," the old man said. He added challengingly: "I do not often trip but on a path one does not know, it is permissible, hein?"

"It is a thing that might happen to any one," agreed Bobby gravely.

"One has one's moments of carelessness," the old man confessed, still a little on the defensive, though evidently pleased by Bobby's acquiescence. He added: "It seems they mean to make us tell again our story of our little walk in the early morning."

There was no time to say more for there hurried up to separate them one or two of the several men in plain clothes standing near—police inspectors, Bobby supposed they were, the rank of inspector in the Sûreté Générale corresponding to that of constable in a British force. Père Trouché indulged in one of his eldritch chuckles.

"They do not wish us to converse together," he said. "The police, they are not very intelligent, you know. Have we not had time enough to invent our little histories, if we had wished to do so?"

"Is that what you have done?" asked one of the inspectors sharply.

"I do not say so," answered the blind man. "Perhaps yes. Perhaps no. It is for you to discover."

"It is for you to help the law," retorted the other.

"That's as may be," the old beggar said, "but see now, I confess I am not in a good temper. I do not know in fact that I am in a mood to help the law. I do not like it that I am dragged away from my affairs in this manner. For fifty years I have made my regular rounds. One expects me, wet or fine, storm or calm, war or peace—and in the war I deserved well of my country for everywhere I went I preached faith and the victory to come. You know that, you, my friend, who are of this countryside."

"It is true," the other answered, "but the war, that is long ago."

"It may be that another comes, and then again there will be need of old blind Père Trouché," declared the beggar with dignity and conviction. "Yet now I am dragged away from my work and all along the Bornay Road they will be saying: 'Hé, where is then the Père Trouché? Is it that he grows lazy and neglects us? It is inconceivable that he does not come,' and all the little gifts that they have put aside for me, perhaps they will not be there when I do arrive. It is probable I shall lodge a complaint. Intolerable that the work of a free citizen of the republic should be hindered through lack of intelligence and comprehension on the part of her officials."

Don't you go talking like that to Monsieur the juge d'instruction," the inspector warned him.

"Hé, why not, then?" demanded the old man. "Do you not know that to-day only the beggar can afford to say what he thinks?"

By this time the juge d'instruction and the commissaire had finished their colloquy and the whole party began to move towards the house. Apparently there had been some preliminary investigation for it was with a solemn air of formality that one of the plain-clothes men went up to the door and knocked, repeating at the same time, the formula:

"Ouvrez, au nom du loi."

There was no response and after repetition of the formality, a second inspector who had been standing near in readiness advanced and examined the door.

"Locked, not bolted," he announced; and, at a sign from Monsieur Alain, proceeded to force an entrance.

It was an easy task and once the door was open there entered Alain, Clauzel, and two inspectors, apparently senior men, one of them carrying a camera and the other apparatus for taking finger-prints. After a time, one of the inspectors came out with a message for Bobby. It seemed Bobby was the last person known to have been in the house, and the juge d'instruction would be glad if he would go through it and say if he noticed any change or any kind of difference or alteration. All the police examination already made showed was that there was no sign of any disturbance or of anything out of the ordinary. Nor was there anything to show what had become of Shields or why he had disappeared.

One or two letters had been delivered but none of any interest and only during the previous day and this morning, so there was no conclusion to be drawn concerning the date of his departure. He was not apparently in the receipt of much correspondence. There was food in the larder, and a general suggestion that absence had been intended to be only temporary. Impossible of course to be certain if clothing had been taken but so much was left that probably only what was being worn was missing. There was even a little money, though only an insignificant sum, in one of the drawers. What was evidently regarded as more important was that there was no sign of the carte d'identité issued to all foreigners resident in France for any length of time. Nor was there any sign of a passport, and these were facts to which evidently great significance was attached.

Under the guidance of one of the Sûreté inspectors Bobby made a tour of the house, including those parts he had not before visited, a fact of which the inspector assigned to him was fortunately unaware. But Bobby thought it might be interesting to have a general look round, and in the attics he noticed two rope ladders of the type nervous people sometimes keep in store as a means of escape in case of fire.

"Why two?" Bobby asked the inspector who shrugged his shoulders.

"It was perhaps an additional precaution," he remarked.

Bobby was careful not to touch them but he pointed out to the inspector certain tiny traces of earth and vegetation adhering to them both.

"They have evidently been used," said the inspector, slightly bored. "It is always wise to practise with such things."

"So it is," agreed Bobby and they went back to the dining room where Alain was very busy writing and where Bobby noticed a half-burned candle standing on the table. He wondered what it had been used for. He went across to the electric-light switch and touched it. The bulbs lighted, so evidently there had been no need to use the candle for illumination. Monsieur Alain looked up inquiringly from his writing and Bobby said:

"I am wondering what that candle was for."

"Why? what about it?" Alain asked.

"I like to know the reason for things, especially odd things," Bobby answered. He added uncomfortably: "I do not know why, but I do not like it. That candle, I mean. Who used it and why and for what reason?"

Alain shrugged his shoulders without making any attempt to answer. Evidently he thought the candle of small importance. Bobby gave an account of his tour of the house, admitted he had noticed little of interest, except the fact that there were two rope ladders in the attics. Alain was already aware of that fact. Monsieur Shields was evidently of a nervous type. Bobby asked if a gold pencil-case had been seen in any of the drawers examined. Alain said he believed there was one in the studio upstairs and Bobby asked if he could see it. He thought possibly it might be the one he had noticed Williams using and that that gentleman had accused him of 'pinching'.

"He talked about Volny at the same time so it is possible Volny did take it and brought it here to show Shields," Bobby suggested.

"Well, why should he?" Alain asked. "But we will go and look. Even if it is the same one, what will that show except that Volny was here once? And the question, Monsieur Owen, is not where Volny and Shields were once, but where they are now, either or both."

Bobby made no answer, for he did not wish as yet to explain what was in his mind. Alain led the way upstairs, and began to look for the pencil-case. Bobby had already been in the room with his attendant inspector but now he looked about him even more carefully. A half-finished painting stood on the easel, palette and brushes had not been cleaned, as though they had been put down only for the moment but then something had occurred to prevent their being picked up again. On the spot where Bobby had upset table and glasses, some fragments of glass had already been noticed, proof both that Bobby's story was true and that the floor had not been swept since. Again, as Bobby glanced round he was conscious of an impression he had felt before that here some slight change or alteration had been effected, though what he could not tell. Once more he looked carefully about him, and Alain, who had found the pencil-case, called to him to come and look at it. Bobby had not seen it closely enough before to be able to make a positive identification, but he could say that the resemblance was exact. Alain remarked that a mere opinion of a resemblance was not much use, and Bobby who had, while examining the pencil-case, given up thinking about the studio, gave a sudden exclamation as now there flashed into his mind an understanding of the cause of his impression that something here was different.

"There is something you notice?" Alain said quickly.

"Rather, it is something that I do not notice," Bobby answered, "but I can't think what. Only I feel that there is something missing that was here before."

"Try to remember," Alain urged. "In an affair so difficult as this, so puzzling, with so little to go upon, with so many complications and so few facts, even the smallest observation may have its significance."

"Yes, I know," agreed Bobby. "It is all very difficult," he added vaguely and then said: "Is it permissible to ask when Monsieur Shields left?"

"It is permissible to ask," replied Alain, "but it is not possible to answer. He has not been seen for several days but no one is quite certain when was the last time. There has not been much occasion for tradesmen to call, and if they came and got no answer they thought no more of it. Monsieur Shields was often out. The woman who cooked and cleaned for him has not been coming recently. She has not always found it easy to get her money, and when Shields paid her last she seems to have made up her mind to give him no more chance of getting into her debt. Ducane has been working in the garden but he has noticed nothing and he made no inquiry. Shields's movements were no concern of his. It almost seems as if you yourself, monsieur, were the last in the company of the missing man."

It was said very smoothly, but all the same Bobby did not fail to appreciate the suspicion latent in Alain's voice.

" It jolly well looks as if I'm going to be for it," he thought uncomfortably, and then abruptly there came into his mind a knowledge of what was the trifling change that had been made in the room since he had been here with Shields.

"What is it? You remember something?" Alain asked, noticing the sudden alteration in Bobby's expression.

"There was a small framed landscape on the wall there," Bobby explained. "Look, you can see where it hung. Now it has gone."

He did not himself understand the excitement that thrilled in his voice as he spoke. For a moment it was as though everything had somehow been made clear in one swift flash of revelation, and then once again the curtain fell and he knew no longer what it was that he had almost but not quite understood. Yet that the disappearance of this picture had its own significance he remained convinced, and there was still excitement in his voice as he said:

"It has been removed. Some one has taken it away. Why?"

"Do you mean that it was valuable? Was it Shields's own work?"

"Yes. It was signed. I noticed that. It couldn't have been of much value. If it had been valuable, one could understand why it has gone. It was called 'The Duel'. There were two men with pistols facing each other. Primarily it was a landscape. Shields was fond of putting figures into his landscapes. He thought it added what he called 'human interest'."

"Was it any place you recognized?"

"No, nowhere I had ever seen. Somewhere in this neighbourhood, I should say. It looked like that. The drawing was very bad. The two duellists had their pistols pointing yards away from each other. They would have hit a tree in the middle background or thereabouts." He was silent then, still dimly struggling in the recesses of his mind to understand why all this was of such supreme importance.

"For my part," said Alain severely, "I do not see how a missing picture concerns us. You say that it was of little value?"

"I doubt if any one would have given ten francs for it," Bobby answered. "Why did Shields have that special picture framed? There are plenty of other canvasses, as good or better, generally better, lying about unframed."

"An artist has his whims," Alain answered. "I do not see that it concerns us why Shields preferred to frame one of his works rather than another. Probably it appealed to him for some reason."

Bobby made no comment. He did not know himself why there was still struggling for expression in his mind a feeling that the disappearance of the picture had some deep and hidden significance. He did not yet see for that matter how it could have any such significance. He tried to put the idea out of his mind. He said:

"Has Shields's bicycle been found?"

"The garden and outhouses are being searched," Alain answered. "There is nothing here apparently. Not even," he added smilingly, "a small, framed landscape called 'The Duel', so we will see if anything of interest has been discovered outside—such as, for example," he added with another smile, "more half-burned candles, or even a pair of rope ladders."

He made no objection to Bobby accompanying him. A rapid but very thorough search of the garden and out-buildings had been made without much result so far. One of the searchers reported the discovery of a pile of artificial manure that had apparently been dumped in a heap in an out-of-the-way corner of the garden, between a tree and the garden wall. Some excitement resulted for a time from this discovery; but the stuff when cleared away showed ground beneath plainly undisturbed, and one of the police inspectors remarked that Ducane had expressed dislike and mistrust of all artificial manures, protesting that never would he use them since they did nothing but burn up the ground.

"He was given some and instead of using it he threw it away, most likely," remarked the inspector. "For my part, I confess I am also a little of the same opinion concerning these products of the factories. At any rate, that he should have thrown it away rather than use it, is of no importance."

It was in fact difficult to suppose that anything had been concealed, by burial or otherwise, in a garden where Ducane was constantly working and where any disturbance of the ground he would have been sure instantly to notice. Bobby was asked in which shed he had taken shelter and he duly pointed it out. The bicycle was still there, still hidden by the sacks of artificial manure behind which it had been thrust. One of the inspectors got it out and Alain and Clauzel gave it a minute examination.

"Identification will be difficult," pronounced the juge destruction. "It is like many others. Volny himself might be able to swear to it but hardly his family. It had better be placed in the shop of some dealer with the rest of his stock and then the Volny family can be requested to see if they can tell which it is. If they can, it will be important, but also it will be surprising."

Bobby thought it a test both severe and fair. He ventured to ask if Shields's other bicycle had been found and was told it was in the place where, according to Ducane, it was generally kept. He took an opportunity to point, too, to what was left of the bale of binder twine, and to remark that it had almost all been used.

"I am wondering," he explained, "to what use it can have been put. There must have been miles of it employed for some purpose or another."

"You ask a good many questions but you do not provide the answers," Alain remarked, a trifle impatiently.

"Questions are so much easier than answers," Bobby observed. "For example—those sacks of artificial manure.

"I notice that they seemed to interest you," Alain said. "Or is it something else? You do not," he added, again mildly sarcastic, "remark that here also there is a half-burnt candle or that a small framed landscape of the value of ten francs, has disappeared?"

"No," Bobby answered slowly, "but it is in my mind that when I came in here out of the sun that Sunday afternoon, it was on those sacks that I sat down to rest and smoke a cigarette."

"And that it concerns our inquiry?" Alain asked. "It concerns us where it was you sat that afternoon to smoke your cigarette?"

"It is only this," Bobby said, speaking now more confidently for the idea that had been struggling for some time in the recesses of his mind was slowly beginning to shape itself into a theory. "I chose them for a seat because they seemed less dusty than most of the rest of the stuff lying about."

"Well?"

"It suggests to me that perhaps they were less dusty because recently they had been moved."

"Evidently it is a reason," agreed Alain, still mildly impatient. "One even remembers that one of them must have been opened, since a part of its contents has been found thrown away in a pile in the garden."

"Surely it is unusual to open a sack for the sake of throwing part of its contents away?" Bobby said. "In these cases I do not like the unusual."

"You have something in your mind?" Alain asked. "There is something you notice?"

"Once more, there is something I do not notice," Bobby replied. "I do not notice that any of the sacks shows any signs of having lost any part of its contents. To me, they all appear well filled."

"That is true," Alain agreed, now staring at the sacks as intently as Bobby himself had been doing. "Yes, that is certainly true."

"I ask myself," Bobby said softly, "if when the contents of one of the sacks was removed, something else was placed within."

Alain looked quickly at Bobby, then again at the sacks piled there so competently, so naturally, so innocently. He went to the door. He called an order, and two of the Sûreté inspectors came hurrying up. Alain gave them brief directions. They began to lift down the sacks and to open them one by one. Those they came to first were evidently as they were when they left the factory. One had as evidently been opened and then refastened. It was dragged out into the middle of the floor and there reopened. Within was the dead, doubled body of Henri Volny, the artificial manure packed closely round it to give the sack containing it the same well-filled undisturbed appearance possessed by the others.

CHAPTER XX
BOBBY THEORISES

There began now just such a scene of busy, purposeful activity as Bobby had so often shared in. Photographs were taken, measurements were made, fingerprints looked for, consultations held, messengers came and went, doctors appeared, presently there arrived a stretcher and the sad relic of humanity just discovered was removed with all that careful respect always shown in France to Death, man's last hope and refuge.

All the time this was going on, Bobby stood quietly watching, taking a kind of professional interest in the scene and admiring the calm and unhurried efficiency with which everything was accomplished. He had a feeling, too, that neither Alain nor

Clauzel, even in the midst of all their busy preoccupations, had forgotten him, and that occasionally their brief consultations had himself for their object. Uncomfortably aware was he, too, that the glances occasionally sent in his direction were still not entirely devoid of doubt or even of suspicion.

Presently preparations were begun for clearing the shed and for putting in position the official seals. Bobby went outside accordingly. He saw Père Trouché at a little distance, the very image of eager and alert attention, giving himself entirely to the recording and the interpretation of every passing sound or other impression he received. Bobby began to understand how it was that the old man, though blind—if blind indeed he were—was yet able to know and to understand so much of what went on around him. Most men have eyes and see little, ears and hear less, nor to most of them does touch mean anything at all. This old man had no eyes perhaps, but to every difficult impression that reached him through the other senses he gave his full attention to wrest from it all its meaning and significance. But to the easy knowledge others gained with little effort, since it was there before their eyes as they were wont to say, they often gave little consideration and less thought. Bobby went to join him and the old man said as he approached:

"Hé, hé, the Englishman again, the Englishman who points out where dead men are hidden."

"You heard that?" Bobby asked.

"I have ears. By the mercy of God, I am not deaf," retorted the old man. "I can even hear what is in their thoughts, these good men of the police."

"What is in their thoughts?" Bobby asked.

"That it is easy for those who hide to find."

"Oh, that's it, is it?" said Bobby grimly, and the old beggar chuckled once more.

"That makes you angry and even a little uneasy," he said. "Above all, you say to yourself: 'Very good, very good, presently we shall see about that.'"

"You read a lot into what others say," Bobby remarked. "Does it ever strike you that you may be wrong?"

"I seldom find it so," the other answered simply. "When I was young perhaps, but not now. One learns in life." Bobby grunted, and after a time Père Trouché added: "They were going to confront us with Monsieur Shields apparently, but now it seems that will have to wait, for where is Monsieur Shields?"

"A good many would like to know," Bobby remarked.

"One disappears a little too frequently just now," Père Trouché said. "The young Volny, but then he has been found. The young Camion also, but of him one knows nothing?"

"Nothing," Bobby agreed.

"That one does not like for he is a youngster concerning whom it is not safe to prophecy. He needs always an outlet, he looks within always and then—a something gives way and there are happenings."

"Yes, I think he needs a vent," Bobby agreed again.

"There was hatred between them, those young men," Père Trouché went on. "Now one is dead and one has disappeared. It is a thing these good police will not over-look. But then also Monsieur Shields is missing, and Monsieur Williams—but he, Williams, he is in Paris, isn't he?"

"He was," Bobby said.

"Difficult to make of it sense that fits," said the old man. "No wonder you are so puzzled that you scratch your chin."

"How do you know what I'm doing?" Bobby asked, startled, for indeed he had not known it himself till his companion spoke.

"Psst," came the contemptuous retort. "Have you shaved so recently that there are no bristles on your chin and I cannot hear your nail scrape on them? Also you are uneasy and even perhaps afraid for your breathing is not as usual. You are longing to do something, you are worried that you have to stand and watch. That is why I hear your foot go: Tap, tap. And you feel that if only these fools of Frenchmen would take you into their confidence, you could help them. That I know because there is in you all the arrogance of the English who always think they can do everything better than any one else."

"We don't," exclaimed Bobby, quite indignant at what he felt a most unjust accusation.

"Hé, you are so sure of it, your superiority, that you do not even know your own certainty. But all this I am aware of only by reasoning, in the same way that I know you are furious because you feel they are idiot enough to doubt your good faith. For that, I have not the plain evidence of my ears, as I have for the rest."

"It's a good thing you aren't deaf as well as blind," Bobby growled, "or there would be no limit to what you knew."

Père Trouché considered this thoughtfully.

"No," he decided, "one must either hear or see. The two, they often cancel out each other so that both are poor and dim, but one or other is needed. And hearing is best, for all men are blind half their lives, in the dark, at night, asleep, but at night, in the dark, asleep, one can still hear—as I hear there is some one coming to you with a message."

One of the agents of the Sûreté was in fact coming quickly towards them. His quick, purposeful tread explained, Bobby supposed, why Père Trouché guessed he came with a purpose and probably a message. He said:

"Yes, a message, but why for me?"

"Messages are not sent to old blind beggars, they come and go without," retorted Père Trouché impatiently. "Therefore it is for you."

The inspector came up and proved the old man right. Monsieur the juge d'instruction would like the privilege of a few words with Monsieur Owen. Bobby obeyed the summons. Alain explained that now it had grown so late and darkness had fallen, further investigation would have to wait till the morning, but he would like to get a full statement from as many concerned as possible, including Monsieur Owen, whose assistance in the discovery of the body of the murdered Volny had been so valuable. But Monsieur Owen was probably needing food, in view of that very sketchy luncheon taken so long ago. Was it too much to ask that Monsieur Owen should consent to spend the night at Barsac? A room would be found for him in one of the hotels where also he could dine. Later they could have a little talk together, when certain points at present a trifle obscure could be cleared up, no doubt.

All this was put very politely, with an air in fact of requesting a favour, but there was also a very clear impression given that a refusal was not expected.

However, Bobby having no desire to make any objection, agreed readily to accept the guidance of one of the Surety inspectors to the hotel suggested. He said good night to Père Trouché, who had been standing near listening with his usual close attention to what the inspector said.

"Me, too," he answered Bobby now, "they are keeping under watch and guard. Even, they wanted to find me a room to sleep in, as though on such a night as this one might not as well be in a coffin as within four close walls. It is understood, of course, that one can train oneself to anything, even to sleeping indoors on summer nights. But I did not say 'no' to food and wine."

Bobby and the inspector moved away and the inspector said crossly:

"That old scamp, he has had it three times over—his food and his wine. One of our men gave him both. Afterwards he persuaded another who knew of the order to take him to a pub near. Finally he found yet a third—and that third," said the inspector ruefully, "it was me—to carry out yet once again the order to provide him with a bottle of wine and a little something to eat. He is a devil, that old man."

"Must have had a good appetite to get through three meals," Bobby remarked.

"What he did not eat, he pocketed," explained the inspector. "Those rags of his, they are all pockets. As for wine, they say he has bottles of wine hidden everywhere in holes and hollow trees."

They arrived at the hotel arranged for and Bobby was soon enjoying a good dinner and a rest he found very welcome. Then about ten o'clock another inspector came in a car to say Monsieur Alain would now be happy to receive him. Bobby was accordingly driven to Alain's temporary office and there the interview began with formal questions. Asked for his passport, Bobby explained it was in his bag at the Citry hotel, but judged it prudent to explain both his profession and his errand. Alain did not seem much surprised. Apparently he had either known or guessed the truth.

"Monsieur Williams, too," he remarked, "the tenant of the Pépin Mill, it appears he claimed to be an officer of your London police."

"Bit of cheek," explained Bobby and gave in detail the information he had received about Williams's past, explaining, too, how he had secured it by obtaining a specimen of Williams's finger-prints.

Alain nodded abstractedly.

"It is interesting, that," he observed. "You connected his departure from Citry and his Paris alibi with the disappearance of Volny?"

"It made me uneasy, I felt there was more than appeared," Bobby answered. "What we call in England the M.O.—the method of operation—gives a very good hint of what to expect, only this time the dates don't seem to agree. Williams's care to provide proof he was in Paris on one special night suggested something was meant to happen that night, but apparently Volny was killed about the time he was first missed? I gathered that from what I heard the doctors say, but if so, that was before Williams left the Pépin Mill."

"The medical evidence is a little doubtful as yet," Alain answered. "They are not very sure of the effect of the artificial manure on the body. Probably preservative. There are to be experiments."

"Volny had been strangled, hadn't he?" Bobby asked.

"There are heavy bruises on the head, a cord round the neck," Alain answered. "The assumption is that he was attacked, knocked senseless, strangled. A similar piece of cord was found in the house. It had been used for tying up a box. There is nothing to show what has become of Shields. A general inquiry for him will be made."

"Nothing has been heard of Camion since this morning?"

"Nothing. I should be glad to hear any observations you can make."

"I can only give you theories/' Bobby said slowly. "I have not been able to find any material proofs. I think perhaps none were left. I think it certain Mademoiselle Polthwaite was murdered, but murdered with a mingling of cunning and audacity that makes it difficult to find proof of the assassin's identity.

"In Volny's case murder is evident and I think has resulted from the previous murder. One can only reason from probabilities. My belief is that Volny at first thought only of searching for the hoard he believed might still be hidden at the Pépin Mill, grew to entertain suspicions of murder, heard of Williams's vague hints that evidence of some sort had been found in or near the Mill well, associated that story with the gold pencil-case in Williams's possession, knew or guessed that it had originally belonged to Shields, got hold of it somehow from Williams, brought it to show Shields and ask him about it, with the result that Shields, in an outburst of anger or of panic, attacked and killed him. Shields, of course, knew he was not exempt from suspicion, and in face of such an accusation he may have lost his head—innocent or guilty. Quite probably Shields mislaid the pencil on one of his visits to Miss Polthwaite and Williams came across it and thought it might be useful in some way."

"Volny's body may have been hidden where it was found without the knowledge of Shields, to throw suspicion on him," Alain remarked. "I may tell you that we have information now that Volny was seen in a small bistro near here soon after he left Citry and that a young man answering the description of Camion inquired for him there. One does not," he added, "even know if there is any truth in this story of Mademoiselle Polthwaite's store of hidden diamonds."

"In any case," Bobby said, "the story was current, and, it seems certain, provided the motive. I have proof that she was obsessed by fear of a world-wide revolution and that she invested her funds in the purchase of jewels, mostly uncut and unset stones easy to dispose of, impossible to identify, easy to carry away. The poor woman, trying to safeguard herself from imaginary dangers of revolution and what she called bolshevism, incurred very real ones. People like her get so used to their orderly, guarded existence, they can't imagine sudden incursions of violence. It simply doesn't happen in their experience.

"Obviously various people were open to suspicion. I believe they were all considered and all questioned by you at the time. Some of the suspects had alibis. Alibis are often suspicious. Shields was here in Barsac. The Abbé Taylour was under the care of a doctor. Eudes was away at a political conference. But the Abbé Taylour might have been shamming. He kept his lantern burning those days anyhow. Eudes might have slipped away from his conference without his political friends noticing it. Shields—I think his alibi was very closely examined?"

"Most carefully," answered Alain. "It was impossible he could have used a car which indeed he did not possess. Bicycling was equally impossible. The roads were being watched. One does not traverse the Bornay Massif twice during darkness unless one has wings."

"Camion and Volny, and the Abbé Granges, curé of Citry-sur-l'eau," continued Bobby, "were all admittedly on the spot. Williams, I presume, did not come under official notice at that time?"

"We had never heard of him," Alain answered. "His tenancy of the mill was remarked, but there seemed nothing to suggest any connection with the murder. It was known there were rumours that the dead woman had left valuables hidden in the Pepin Mill itself or the garden. A watch was therefore kept. In that connection, we knew also that Shields had spoken to Eudes and suggested there would be a large reward if any jewellery hidden could be found and restored to the family. It seemed to suggest Shields was innocent since he was still eager to find what presumably the unfortunate woman had been murdered to obtain."

"It was perhaps for that reason," Bobby answered, "that the suggestion was made. To create an impression of innocence and at the same time to keep up a connection with the village so that he might learn of any developments—as he learned quickly of my own arrival."

"You suspect then that Shields is the assassin?" Alain asked. "But there is also this Williams, whose appearance has to be explained. His movements at the time must be traced—though that will be difficult after so long an interval."

"I was inclined to suspect Shields from the first," Bobby said, "but only vaguely and suspicion is not proof. One oughtn't to suggest anything like that too quickly. It is easier to make mischief than to cure it and innocent people have a right to protection. They mustn't be implicated without good cause. So I held my tongue. But I noticed two things. Mademoiselle Polthwaite had a paint brush clasped in her hand when her body was found. Shields was the most likely person she would be talking to about painting. He gave her lessons and criticized her efforts. It was possible she was asking his advice when struck down. It was possible he was distracting her attention in some way. An indication only and even a faint one, but I noted it. I was told something else. An unfinished letter was found on her desk. It had only just been begun. She had apparently been writing when disturbed by the arrival of her murderer. Only the first sentences were written. They ran: 'J'en ai des écus jusqu'aux yeux, jusqu'en avoir peur.'"

"I remember," Alain agreed. "I remember even the phrase. But what is the importance? 'Avoir des écus,' it's a common way of saying that a person has more money than he knows what to do with, and apparently that was the case with Mademoiselle Polthwaite. Apparently also she was nervous, afraid, because of it—afraid of revolution, bolsheviks, what not."

"Monsieur," said Bobby gravely, "it may mean nothing and it may mean much, but the word 'écus' is, in English, 'shields', and Shields is the name of one of those suspected. Was it not perhaps Shields of whom she had had enough and of whom she was afraid that night?"

CHAPTER XXI
BOBBY REASONS

The juge d'instruction sat silent and thoughtful for some moments. He rose from his chair and walked to the window and then came back and sat down again.

"If only we had known that at the time," he muttered, half to himself, and then to Bobby he added: "But are you sure? Pardon. It is stupid to ask that. But you understand, I do not know a word of English."

"I can assure you," Bobby answered, "that 'Shields' is the English for 'écus'."

"If only we had known that before," Alain repeated, and went on apologetically: "You understand? There was not one concerned in the inquiry who had knowledge of English."

"Easy to overlook," Bobby assured him. "The word conveys the idea of money and one forgets the literal meaning is 'shield' which has no reference to money in English. Mademoiselle Polthwaite's family never noticed it, though some of them certainly speak French. I expect Mademoiselle Polthwaite meant to add something to make her meaning more plain. I imagine she very likely started to write just before Shields came, or even while he was there."

He paused. There seemed to rise a clear vision in his mind, a swift succession of vivid pictures as though he sat in a cinema and watched a film. He seemed to see Miss Polthwaite after her quarrel with young Camion hearing a step outside, a knock at the door; rising to open in the quick hope that Camion had understood at last and had returned, or else had sent some one else ready to stay with her through the night; finding herself instead faced there upon the threshold with the man she had begun to dread; concealing her alarm; asking him to enter; smiling a welcome; accepting easily whatever excuse he put forward for his late arrival; understanding that he only wished to assure himself she was alone, but smiling still; begging him to excuse her while she finished a note she was writing, resolute that if she were to die at least she would leave some clue to indicate her murderer; realizing almost at once that her purpose was suspected and for that reason wrapping up her meaning as best she could, so that even if he read it afterwards he might not destroy it; obliged to leave it uncompleted when he began to show a restless and horrible impatience; even then not despairing but beginning to talk of her painting; still striving to gain time; hoping still that Camion might return or another might come in his place; hoping perhaps that in talk of art and painting, their common interest, murder might be forgotten; hoping even that such an appeal to their common search for beauty in expression, which should make good comrades of all who share in it, might in the end turn the assassin from his purpose. Bobby seemed clearly to understand that that firm hope and will had never left her, and that, solitary, alone, and helpless, she had never yielded to despair, but had still fought on, thinking of death and chatting of art, paint brush in hand, till there crashed down upon her from behind the blow that had been the end.

Plainly, as plainly as if he had seen it all recorded on the screen, so clearly that it lives as vividly in his memory as though he had been a witness of the actual scenes, so clearly, plainly, vividly indeed that, remembering, he almost believes there was some mysterious, unknown power at work, conveying to him thus strangely what in fact had been, did Bobby see all this.

It passed. It was as though the series was complete, the reel finished, the message given. He stirred slightly in his chair and moved like a man awakening from sleep. He heard Alain draw in deeply his breath. There came to Bobby a memory of something said to him by the Abbé Taylour—that where the human soul once had fled in anguish and in terror, there the memory still lingered on the earth. The thought came to him that if that were true, then perhaps in some strange and unknown way there had been called up in his mind a recollection of a dreadful hour of the past. In a low and troubled voice, Alain said:

"It was as though just now I saw it all pictured there, like a dream, like a film at the cinema. Yet I was awake." To Bobby he said: "I cannot explain. You could not understand unless you, too, had seen."

"I did," Bobby said, but Alain shook his head. He said:

"It was like a dream, only more vivid. One does not share another's dream. Also I was awake. It would be impossible to make you understand or anyone. It is very strange for I am not of those who believe. Also," he added more briskly, "it is not evidence and so it is not of importance. Merely one's imagination at work showing how it might have happened."

"Yes," said Bobby. After a time he said again: "Yes." Then he added but more to himself than aloud: "I wonder."

Alain was busy, fumbling among his papers, once more the brisk, efficient magistrate. He said:

"All the same, she had courage, that one. She held out to the end. It is that that counts, to hold out to the end, no matter what end."

"Yes," said Bobby again. "Go down fighting," he said.

"All is there," agreed Alain. "Enough of that, though. What we need is evidence, proof. There are indications, certainly. In effect, good indications. But an advocate defending would ask: 'Where is the proof?' and a jury might listen. One could invent other explanations and, above all, where is Shields? It may be that once again he will produce an alibi to make us helpless. The night Mademoiselle Polthwaite died, it is proved he was here in the evening, proved he was here the next morning. How is it possible to persuade a jury that he crossed the Bornay Massif, there and back, during a dark winter night, when they could see for themselves that it is impossible? "

"I don't think it is in fact impossible," Bobby said. "I think it could be done. I think I know how."

"Yes. Well?"

"I expect you heard from Monsieur Clauzel that I visited a farm to buy binder twine," Bobby went on. "Monsieur Clauzel asked why. I did not want to explain then for I felt I had to be more sure of my ground and I wasn't pressed. I expect it didn't seem to matter. It was Volny's disappearance that I was being asked about and there didn't seem any connection. May I remind you of two things? Shields knows French well, he has lived long in this country and he speaks French fluently. It seemed to me odd he should make such a blunder as ordering a huge supply of artificial manure and, further, a bale of binder twine, instead of a ball or two of raffia. Odd things have sometimes explanations even more odd. I noticed that no use had been made of the artificial manure— at least, not until now. But the bale of binder twine had nearly been used up. It struck me that perhaps it was the binder twine that was really wanted and the other stuff only ordered for a blind. Then by a bit of luck I learned that Shields had seemed interested—even oddly interested —in a classical dictionary with illustrations by Gustave Doré."

He paused and Alain said:

"Monsieur Shields is an artist. It is not strange that he should be interested in Doré's work. It has its merits even though to-day it seems to us a little crude, raw even, without real depth or feeling. But what have Gustave Doré's illustrations of more than fifty years ago to do with murder to-day?"

"Apparently," Bobby continued without answering this directly, "there was one illustration that had interested Shields particularly, for that special page was thumb- marked and there was even on it a burn from a cigarette end. Naturally Monsieur and Madame Camion were annoyed. It is vexing to see treated so carelessly a book one values, and indeed I think Shields had been even more careless than he knew. Possibly as a request or warning to me to be more careful, the elder Camion showed me that page. You remember, monsieur, the story of Theseus, the Minotaur, the labyrinth, Ariadne? Doré's illustration showed Ariadne offering Theseus the ball of thread by which he was to retrace his steps through the labyrinth after slaying the Minotaur."

"I remember the story well enough," Alain said, "but still I do not understand."

"For Theseus, the hero," continued Bobby, "read Shields, the assassin. For the Minotaur, the monster, read poor Mademoiselle Polthwaite, who was no monster. For the labyrinth, read the Bornay Massif, almost equally difficult to traverse. For Ariadne's ball of thread, read a bale of binder twine."

"You mean," asked Alain looking very puzzled, "that Shields marked out paths across the Massif with binder twine and followed them so in the darkness at night. Is that possible?"

"Why not?" Bobby asked. "He was out all day and many days on the Massif during his supposedly sketching expeditions. He found the paths to follow and to mark them tied binder twine from bush to bush, or even between stakes driven into the ground. Then he had only to pick up the twine in one hand and follow it as Theseus followed Ariadne's thread. I imagine that on his way back Shields picked up the twine, made it into balls and threw them away. I expect a search would find some. I think, too, that is why he persuaded the Abbé Taylour to hang out a lantern each night, it made a most useful, almost a necessary landmark to guide him—a landmark of murder."

"It is a possible explanation," Alain admitted thoughtfully. "One had not considered it. Crossing the Bornay Massif at night seemed too impossible to be worth considering. It was intelligent of you, monsieur, to work out the possibility of such a method having been practised."

"I suppose it was chiefly luck," Bobby answered, "the luck of young Camion's father showing me that particular page in his dictionary. It was that started me wondering whether possibly Shields was more interested in Ariadne's trick than in Doré's drawing. I remembered Shields told me once he wasn't keen on the old style stuff and went out of his way to refer to Doré as being hopelessly out of date, and yet here he was taking special interest in his work. It didn't seem consistent, and when things don't hang together there's sometimes an explanation if you can find it."

"That is true," agreed Alain, "and it was certainly extraordinary good fortune that Camion père had the idea of drawing your attention to that drawing. I only wish that while the Polthwaite inquiry was going on, such a piece of luck had come our way."

He looked at Bobby enviously; and Bobby found himself suddenly and ruefully wondering if ever he would learn to wrap up his methods in suitable mystery instead of explaining them away. If only he had had the sense to hold his tongue and look profound, his little feat of deduction would have appeared in a light as exaggerated as now diminished.

He reflected that he must learn how to boost himself, though indeed to boost oneself is a gift like another and best not attempted by those to whom it has not been granted. Alain, who had been deep in thought, said abruptly: "But luck is only of value to those who know how to use it. Do not think, monsieur, that I undervalue the intelligence you have shown. It will, however, be necessary to test thoroughly your theory by actual experiment. For one thing, I seem to have heard that the Massif is crossed by a crevasse with steep, indeed precipitous sides. It would be impossible to climb them in the dark and binder twine would be no help?"

"I think," Bobby answered, "that explains the two rope ladders in the attics here. Unless I am mistaken they still show traces of earth and vegetation to show they have been used out of doors. I called the attention of your inspector to it. Possibly expert analysis would show if the traces I think I made out, correspond to the soil round the crevasse. Such ladders left in position and led up to by the binder twine trail would make it easy to get across, especially for a strong athletic man like Shields who, too, had cultivated a power of seeing in the dark. Shields boasted about that once to me. Possibly he had, too, a small electric torch to help, and certainly the Abbé Taylour's lantern would help to give him his direction. I know one of the police—the brigadier I think—saw his light go out in his bedroom at midnight as if he were retiring, but that could easily be managed by any clockwork appliance. I think it was to get that evidence, to make sure that police should be watching, that Shields manufactured signs of mysterious trespassing in his garden. At that time of the year it is dark early, and he could start by four in the afternoon. Allowing six hours to cross the fifteen miles of the Massif by the paths marked out, he would reach the Pépin Mill by ten. He could spend two or three hours there, leave about midnight, and be back at Barsac by six, before it was light or any risk of any one being up and about to notice his return."

"It is becoming plain how it could have happened," Alain agreed. "The proofs accumulate. Yet where is Shields? What has become of him? If he has yet another alibi as ingenious to offer us, our work will begin again. I ask myself, what has become of him?"

"I doubt if we are going to be worried by another alibi," Bobby said. "At a guess, I should say that probably he has already left France—and with the start he has, it won*t be any too easy to catch up with him. I expect he realized that after Volny's death flight was necessary. The body was certain to be found sooner or later."

"It might have been much later, even a year or two later, but for your gift of observation, monsieur," Alain admitted.

Bobby bowed acknowledgements.

"At any rate," he went on, "Shields could hardly hope this time to pass off what had happened as either suicide or accident. He had had neither time nor opportunity to make the careful preparations he carried out in the Polthwaite case. His only hope was flight and by this time he may be anywhere in Europe—or Africa either, for that matter, or on the way to America."

"We shall get him in the end, we always do," said Alain, though without too much confidence in his voice. "But it will not be easy. Most criminals are very stupid. It is why they are criminals. But this man is the exception. He is intelligent. It is probable he has had his plans prepared in readiness. The world to-day is full of fugitives, of refugees. They swarm. One more. It is difficult, even very difficult."

"There is perhaps one line that might be followed," Bobby suggested.

"Which?"

"The diamonds and so on stolen from Mademoiselle Polthwaite."

"The diamonds? Yes, it is true. Even so, it remains difficult. Many of the refugees, they have had the same idea as your Mademoiselle Polthwaite and have their capital with them in the form of jewels. It is easy to say to a jeweller: 'I am a refugee. That is why I have these stones to sell."

"I am going on a theory," Bobby said. "It is clear I think that Shields fled in panic after the murder of Volny.

I imagine he had the jewels concealed in some secure hiding-place. I think there is no doubt that his story to Eudes, his pretence of hoping to discover them, was partly to avert suspicion, partly for an excuse to keep in touch with Citry so as to get early warning of any possible new developments. The prompt way he turned up there immediately after my arrival, his talk about coincidences— I dislike coincidence, almost as much as I distrust alibis— all helped to confirm my suspicions of his guilt. Therefore I assume he had the jewels already and had them hidden in some secure hiding-place. Not, I think, in his house. That, I am sure, he would think too dangerous. Not in any bank or anywhere like that. He would be afraid. Hidden, then, in a secure hiding-place, but at a distance, where it would need a little time to recover them. I doubt if he would want to take that time now, after the Volny affair, when he would feel every minute counted. I reason therefore that the jewels are still in their hiding-place."

"Yes, it is possible; all that is logic," Alain interrupted. "But where? I ask you, where?"

"I tried to think that out," Bobby answered. "It seemed to me that in his place I should reflect that there was a secure hiding-place almost at my back door, so to say. The Bornay Massif. I think it would seem easy to dig a hole up there somewhere, to bury the jewels, to take a note somehow of the exact spot, and to leave them there, quite secure, till safe opportunity offered to remove them. All this case has shown that Shields understands the value of patience."

Alain was looking a good deal worried.

"All this is very well reasoned," he said, "but a search, it is impossible. How to tell where in all that wild wilderness of the Bornay Massif a little hole was dug six months ago? An army might search for a century and find nothing."

"I think it logical to suppose," Bobby went on, unheeding this outburst, "that Shields made some sort of note of the place, both for his own sake, to help his memory and guard against any forgetfulness, and also to provide against the risk of having to send some one else to get the stuff for him. If you throw your mind back, monsieur le juge, you will remember, I think, we have already some idea of the form taken by that aid to his memory."

Alain leaped to his feet in sudden excitement.

"Why, of course," he cried. "That is as plain as the nose on your face. Only—"

He paused, his enthusiasm suddenly evaporating. Bobby completed the sentence.

"Only now it's not there any longer," he said, and Alain nodded a gloomy acquiescence.

CHAPTER XXII
SEARCHING

It was late now—early perhaps would be a better word, since morning was not far away—and both Alain and Bobby were needing sleep. A few hours were all either could afford, and by eight o'clock Bobby was hard at work in Shields's studio, trying to reproduce from memory that framed landscape he had seen hanging on the wall, that now had disappeared, that both he and Alain had so suddenly perceived the previous night must show the spot where the stolen jewels had been hidden.

It was a simple deduction from the belief Bobby held that for every action there must be an explanation, difficult as it might be to discover that explanation.

"For every action a criminal takes, there must be an adequate reason, which it is the business of the detective to discover," he said presently to Clauzel, who had greeted this theory that the missing landscape showed the hiding-place of the diamonds with some incredulity.

Bobby believed, too, that the inaccurate drawing by which the two duellists shown in the picture seemed to be aiming, not at each other, but at some unknown object in the background, had been in fact not clumsiness but intentional, and that the spot where the lines of fire crossed, at the foot of a stunted oak, showed the exact spot where the Polthwaite treasure had been buried.

"In any event," Clauzel grumbled, "how can one hope to find one stunted oak, one overhanging rock, in a wilderness that is full of them?"

Bobby did not try to argue the point. He went on busily with his sketching, trying his hardest to remember how tree and rock and the general background had been related to one another, and Glauzel went off to join Alain who had secured a map of the Bornay Massif. Together they set to work to portion it out in sections for the search they were organizing, though indeed Alain fully agreed with Clauzel that it would be difficult to find in that vast wilderness of scrub and rock the one spot where a hole had been dug and the lost diamonds buried.

"Provided also," growled Clauzel, "that Shields has not already recovered them. For my part, I cannot imagine a man who has committed two murders leaving behind him precisely what he committed the murders for. I say, find Shields, find the diamonds."

"For my part," answered Alain, "I think, Commissaire, our young English friend is right and that Shields might easily think first of escape, hoping to return later or to send some one else to recover the diamonds. If so, that would explain why he took away with him the picture which we believe shows the actual hiding-place. In that connection, one observes," added Alain thoughtfully, "that the young Camion has also disappeared."

"It is a coincidence," agreed Clauzel, "it is even suggestive. Is there, however, anything to prove that this landscape does in fact represent a spot to be found on the Bornay Massif?"

"It seems likely," Alain answered. "Could one choose a better hiding-place? One hopes that if our young Englishman can reproduce the sketch from memory, then some one will recognize it. It is a chance."

Clauzel grunted again to show what he thought of that chance. Then he grumbled:

"That young man, he does not seem to me very intelligent. Yet it is certain that he notices things. Also he can reason from what he notices. It is something."

"It is even a good deal," observed Alain. "It is even possible that he is in fact intelligent—that is to say, for an Englishman."

They gave up discussing Bobby and continued with their work. After each man had been shown the sector to which he was assigned and before he was dispatched on his task, he was sent up to the studio where Bobby was trying so desperately to recapture his memory of Shields's sketch in successive versions of which about the only permanent features were a stunted oak growing before a steep, overhanging cliff, overhanging to such an extent indeed that the hollow beneath was deep enough to be called a cave, and a tall, isolated rock, of the shape of a sugar loaf, which he found himself unable to relate to the rest of the landscape in any probable connection, and so tried putting it in to the right and to the left, in the background and in the foreground without any satisfactory result.

"Hang it all, I don't see how the thing could be there at all," he told himself despairingly, and wondered if in fact it had been sketched in merely to deceive.

Yet he could not remember that in the glance he had given at the lost landscape he was trying to reproduce, it had seemed in any way incongruous.

His work was not helped nor his memory improved by the constant succession of interruptions to which he was subjected by the procession of prospective searchers who came to him all through the morning, all of them full of questions to which he could not reply, all of them declaring firmly that they had never seen or heard of such a spot as Bobby was trying to depict.

He was indeed thoroughly tired out and disheartened by the time noon arrived and with it an excellent lunch Alain had arranged to be sent in.

After that, he felt better, and was even allowed a little peace, since by now all Alain's men, recruited chiefly from the gendarmerie, were away searching the Massif. The moment seeming appropriate for a little more of that sleep of which the night had been so much curtailed, he put some rugs and cushions on the floor, lay down, and instantly fell fast asleep. When, late in the afternoon, he woke, sat up, and looked round in that kind of bewilderment which follows wakening from sound slumber in unfamiliar surroundings, wondering where he was and how he had got there, he heard a familiar chuckle. Opposite to him sat Père Trouché.

"Hé, hé," the old man said, "one takes one's ease, eh? Some work, it seems, and, my faith, it is work, out there running about on the Massif in the sun, and some slumber."

"And you," asked Bobby, getting to his feet and shaking himself, "what are you doing here? How did you know where I was?"

"I had only to follow the thunder of your snores," Père Trouché explained gently.

"I wasn't snoring, I never do," said Bobby, very indignantly.

"I hoped also," Père Trouché went on in a voice full of reproach, "to find a little left of that excellent déjeuner of which I smelt the savour as they carried it by. But it seems every plate is as clean as though a dozen starving men had been here. Fortunately," he added with his characteristic chuckle, "they were good to the old blind man last night, so that I have no hunger yet."

"Three parcels of food, three bottles of wine, I heard," Bobby remarked. "Two of them hidden away for another day perhaps."

"One must think of the future, it is fatal to be improvident," answered the old beggar complacently. "You have heard then of my little hiding-places? I learnt it from my father and he from his father, who exercised his profession at first in this district, for by origin we are of Barsac. In our metier, it is necessary to practise much foresight."

"So I suppose," agreed Bobby, looking thoughtfully at the various sketches he had produced, deciding that not one of them was really satisfactory, reflecting that this time sleep had not, as it sometimes did, brought good counsel.

"Though sometimes," Père Trouché added darkly, "scoundrels of an inconceivable baseness will watch for and discover the most secure, the most hidden reserves. It broke my poor grandfather's heart when after he had saved near here by his economy and care a whole winter's reserve of wine beneath an overhanging rock well hidden, some heartless and abominable rogues discovered it and removed all. Never was he the same man again; the injustice of it crushed him. Since then it is a tradition in our family never to reserve more than one bottle in one place."

"Under an overhanging rock? One not easily seen?" Bobby repeated and then reflected that on the Bornay Massif overhanging rocks are not so very uncommon. "Near here?" he asked; but what was the good of questioning a blind man? "If your grandfather were alive," he said, "it might have been worth while asking him to take us there."

"Useless," pronounced the other. "I have told you, every single bottle of wine was taken away by those who no doubt are now suffering torment where even a drop of water, much less wine, is denied them to cool their parched tongues."

It was a reflection that seemed to give the old man much pleasure. Bobby said:

"There's just a chance the stuff stolen from Mademoiselle Polthwaite was hidden somewhere near here under an overhanging rock. But since your grandfather is dead, one can't very well ask him to take us there, even though his overhanging rock might be the very one we want."

"Why not ask me?" inquired Père Trouché.

"Do you mean you could find it?"

"Why not? Since I had full directions from my father that he had received from his father. I have not forgotten them, for if one is to beg well one must forget nothing. Fatal to speak of three hungry little ones to-day, and of five starving the week following."

Bobby was looking and feeling a little incredulous. He had some experience of the old beggar's strange, uncanny powers, but that a blind man could find that one special spot in all the vast extent of the desolate Massif for which so many men with sight were searching, seemed hopelessly impossible. Above all, when apparently the old man had never visited it himself, but was relying solely on his memory of verbal directions.

"What were the directions?" Bobby asked.

"Already I have offered my help when I heard what it was they sought," Père Trouché said with dignity. "They laughed. Oh, very loudly they laughed. An old blind beggar man, what help could he be to those who had their sight and were still young? They laughed and went away. Well, do you too laugh and go away?"

"Not if you can help," Bobby said.

"Good," said the old man. "It is nearly five o'clock, is it not?"

"So it is," agreed Bobby, a little ashamed to think he had slept so long, though feeling all the better for it.

"Then the sooner we start, the better," said Père Trouché. "It was indeed to see if you were willing that I came to find you."

"Are you sure you remember the directions?" Bobby asked doubtfully. "Are you sure they are clear enough?"

"I remember them perfectly," Père Trouché assured him. "Also they are perfectly clear. It was thought at the time that our family might return to Barsac to practise here, but Barsac grew into a town, and in towns hearts are harder, the competition is greater, there is less need for news, so we stayed in the Citry district. Also in a town there are more gendarmes and such-like meddlers earning their own base living by preventing other folk from working for theirs. I tell you, Mr. Englishman, that I, I who now speak, I, the old blind beggar, I will guide you to this spot that others with their eyes they boast of, search for and will never find. You are ready?"

"Yes," Bobby answered, and knew enough of his strange old companion's whims to ask no further questions.

"Give me your arm," the old man said when they were outside in the garden surrounding the house, "for I have need of support on this ground that I do not know. Once I have traversed it, I know it as well as another, but the first time it is difficult."

Bobby complied though he felt a little foolish. He was not sure he was not being made a victim of the other's vanity and love of display. Absurd, he felt, in such a search as this, to trust to the guidance of an old, blind man. Père Trouché, with that uncanny instinct of his, seemed to guess Bobby's thought, and said with his accustomed chuckle:

"The blind leading not the blind but the seeing, and where shall that end?"

"Not in the ditch, I hope," Bobby grumbled.

"There is a gate at the back that gives admittance directly to the Massif, isn't there?" Père Trouché asked. "We leave by that."

Two gendarmes had been left in charge, chosen for an age and corpulence that did not suggest them as very suitable explorers of the Massif. They watched with a good deal of amusement the departure of the blind beggar and the young Englishman, but as good soldiers—the gendarmerie is supposed to be a military, not a police, force—they made no attempt to interfere, since they had no orders to do so. One of them did indeed ask if there were any message for the commissaire, and Bobby said 'No', and Père Trouché said:

"Tell him there are times when the blind can find where those with eyes seek in vain."

Outside the garden, on the bare slope of the Massif, here rising fairly steeply, Père Trouché said:

"It is five o'clock, you told me? Exact? Good. Then at this time in the evening, at five, that used once to be four before our good officials decided to issue regulations for the clocks as well as for everything else, it needs the sun directly on our backs." He turned a little. "So," he said. "One feels it. The shadows straight in front, aren't they? The sun exactly behind? Good. Forward."

They walked on, Bobby more and more inclined to ask himself why he had embarked on this preposterous search under the guidance of a blind man. The blind leading not the blind, but a fool, he feared. Yet the old man had a brisk and confidant air, his features were alert, he carried his head a little forward, turning it quickly from side to side. Easy to imagine he was in fact sensitive to a thousand subtle impressions that passed others unperceived or that they failed to interpret. Abruptly Bobby said:

"Are you really blind or can you see like another, and is your blindness merely professional?"

"It is a foolish question," the old man answered, "the question of one who thinks that the eyes are all, who does not know that we can hear and taste and feel as well, who does not understand that when God takes away, then at the same time He gives. But without doubt you are thinking of your hundred-franc note you dropped so cunningly in order to make sure, wasn't it?"

"You know about that?" Bobby cried. "Then you can see, you lying old fraud."

"Hé, hé, less language, if you please," retorted Père Trouché. "What does that prove if I know about your tricks of a little child, of a little child of limited intelligence, for that matter? Could not another have found your note you dropped so cleverly, so cunningly, there by the roadside. And if another found it, should I not hear of it? I, who hear of all things? Ah, bah, my friend, all that was not very well imagined."

Bobby said nothing and felt rather suppressed. The old man indulged again in his usual chuckle.

"Good sight, poor sense," he said and added in a different tone: "Yet, my friend, I would willingly know what is this thing they call 'light' that they all talk about and yet that none can describe. If indeed the sun has, besides its heat, something called 'light'; well, then, tell me what it is, this light."

Bobby had no answer, for he knew he had no words in which to tell of light, loveliest of all things here below.

"You, too, you cannot tell me," the blind man said. "I think myself there is no such thing or, if there is, that it is without importance."

Bobby made no attempt to answer. They were walking on, at a brisk pace, keeping always the sun directly at their backs, Père Trouché, with the help of his staff, keeping his footing wonderfully, though several times he would have tripped and fallen on unexpected obstacles but for Bobby's strong, supporting arm.

"We are growing near," Père Trouché said. "The ground is level now, we have ceased to climb, haven't we? It is level or nearly level for about half a mile before it begins to rise again? The edge of the ridge is clearly marked on our right?"

"Yes," agreed Bobby.

"It is as my grandfather said. Then we must move along to the right, along the edge of the ridge, till presently we come to a small gully, the bed of a dried-up stream, gravel now and hard to walk on. We must follow it."

Before long they found the little gully, evidently, as Père Trouché had said, the bed of a small, dried-up stream. For a distance they followed it, and Bobby noticed that Père Trouché was counting his steps. Presently he said:

"Soon the gully we are following will take a turn to the right. Tell me when you notice that."

In another few minutes Bobby was able to say that a sharp turn in the direction indicated was just ahead.

"Because before us is a wall of high rock changing the course of the stream?" asked Père Trouché. "The rocks go on a long way without any sign of a break, do they not? That is how my grandfather described it."

"There doesn't seem to be any break," Bobby agreed. "It is like one long wall with no opening."

"Hé, but my grandfather, he was to be trusted," said the old beggar proudly. "Now, my friend, for once your eyes may be useful. Tell me, can you see a grove of trees and just beyond them a tall rock standing by itself in the shape of a sugar loaf? I think you can, for I feel there is an excitement in your arm where I hold it. The blood runs fast, hein?"

"It is all there," Bobby said. "The rock you speak of is like the one in Shields's sketch, only he altered its position. That's what bothered me so."

"It is there," Père Trouché said, "that the wall of rock goes back to form a kind of bay. One cannot see that till one is near and at the right angle. It is why my grandfather chose it for a hiding-place he thought secure. Monsieur Shields also if he found it, as he might well, since so often he was here and hereabouts looking for subjects for his pictures, he too may have thought it a good place for hiding what he wished to hide. Yet it is not a place of good fortune, as my grandfather found when he was so shamefully robbed. For it is said that once murder was done there."

"What murder?" Bobby asked, a little startled.

"That I do not know for it is not told," the old beggar answered. "But also it is said that when the day of judgment comes to the Auvergne, after, it is understood, all other peoples have been dealt with—here it will be delayed because we are the oldest, descended as we are from the men of Troy who were old when the Greeks were young—then it is there that 'Le Vilain' will sit and wait for his own."

"Nice reputation to have," Bobby said smilingly, "but I think we must risk 'Le Vilain'."

"It is still day, the sun is still warm," Père Trouché said and Bobby was surprised to notice that there seemed a real fear in his voice, "so perhaps there is no danger. Yet I remember my grandfather said it, too—to enter there is like entering the tomb."

CHAPTER XXIII
FINDING

They had by now left behind them on the one hand the tall, sugar-loaf-like, isolated rock, and on the other a grove of low, wind-driven trees that between them guarded this indentation in the wall of rock they were approaching and that, grove and rock together, hid its entrance so well that only from one or two points was that entrance visible; or indeed any sign to be perceived to show that such a break existed anywhere in that long line of almost perpendicular cliff.

When they had passed between the two jutting points of rock that approached each other so closely and yet allowed passage, they found themselves within a kind of bay or enclave, still surrounded by the same high wall of cliff. Some far-off contortion of the young earth struggling to assume a settled shape must have been responsible for this odd and as it were secret formation, one that seemed as if it had been prepared from the beginning for dark and hidden deeds. Here the fresh winds of heaven penetrated never, here the rays of the sun came only at high noon. Now it lay in gloom, heavy and desolate and sullen, the air damp and stagnant. A few struggling, sickly bushes, the one stunted oak tree Shields had shown in his sketch, grew here, but little other vegetation save in one corner where a slimy and unpleasant growth of some sort sprawled beneath a portion of the rock down which water trickled to form a small shallow puddle that never got any bigger but seeped away continually into some underground reservoir.

On one of these stones that lay half in and half out of this puddle, a small toad perched and watched them from its small and beady eyes. It was the only sign of life visible. It vanished suddenly. Bobby thought that never had he seen a more forbidding spot and his glance went towards that cavity beneath overhanging rock at the further end which Shields had shown so clearly in his sketch. In that darkness Bobby felt monstrous things might lurk and yet he remembered that the line of fire from the pistols of the two duellists in the sketch had seemed to meet behind the stunted oak tree, between it and the cavity or cave whereof the mouth gaped at him with so dark and menacing a threat. Possibly, he thought, Shields had avoided the cavity beneath the rock as being too obvious a hiding-place and had chosen instead to bury his booty, assuming he in fact possessed it, behind the oak as being a spot less likely to attract attention.

Swift, eager, and attentive had been the gaze whereby he had noted all these things, and now he noticed, too, that the old blind beggar at his side showed just the same attitude of tense and eager attention, his face a little raised and turning quickly from side to side, his lips parted, his nostrils twitching as he sniffed in the dank and heavy air, his whole being and existence as it were concentrated into the single act of listening.

Yet there was no sound that Bobby could hear in that heavy, muffling atmosphere. Even the water trickling down the side of the rock ran not freshly and brightly as spring water should but in a furtive, silent manner as though it had some errand it dared not let be known. The darkness, silence, stillness, of the spot filled him with a curious dislike and mistrust, though he did not understand why his blind companion should be affected in the same way. That he was so, seemed plain, and Bobby was hardly surprised when almost to himself the old man muttered:

"Here there is a smell of death." After a time when Bobby made no answer, he said again: "I do not like it. It is as though one entered in a tomb."

"It is a bit like that," Bobby said and found himself shivering. "It's the damp, mouldy atmosphere," he said.

He went forward a little. His companion followed, feeling his way carefully with his staff. Bobby noticed that his walk was more hesitating and uncertain than ever it had seemed to be before. He was muttering some-thing to himself but Bobby could not hear what he said. Bobby's eyes were growing more accustomed to the sort of perpetual twilight that reigned here. He said:

"It's the place all right that Shields made his sketch of. Everything agrees except that rock outside. He moved it right round, some idea of further concealment most likely. He didn't show that grove of trees either. Same idea, I expect, to make identification more difficult. If he really hid Miss Polthwaite's diamonds here, it ought to be behind that tree according to the sketch."

"It was under a great rock, in a sort of cave beneath it, where my grandfather kept his wine he was so treacherously robbed of," Père Trouché said. "There is such a rock here?"

"Right in front," Bobby said. "There's a tree between us and it. Come along."

He took the old man's arm and guided him, for the ground exactly before them was rough and stony, round by the cliff wall and on behind the tree.

"I can smell fresh turned earth," Père Trouché muttered. "I have smelt it like that before—in the Citry cemetery when there was soon to be a burial. Or when there had just been one."

"Oh, shut up," growled Bobby, who, too, was beginning to feel an odd strain and nervous tension.

But he saw now freshly disturbed ground, between tree and rock, where evidently digging had taken place only a short time before and he did not like what he saw and somehow he liked it still less when he noticed a spade lying on the ground at a little distance. He went across to it and picked it up. When he came back, he said:

"Well, some one's got ahead of us and that's that."

Père Trouché had been feeling carefully with his staff the extent and texture of the disturbed soil. He pushed his staff through the loose earth and drew it back quickly. He was muttering to himself again but still inaudibly.

"Looks as if the diamonds had been there all right but now they'll have gone," Bobby said, though in his mind there was another thought.

"Some one has been digging and then has been filling it in again," the old beggar said. "If it was only the diamonds, why, when they had taken them, did they fill in the earth again?"

"I suppose we must make sure," Bobby said, "but it looks to me as if Shields had been before us."

Père Trouché was still busy with his staff. He said:

"It is two metres long where they have dug. It is less than one metre wide. That is much for the concealment of a packet of diamonds, but not too much for another purpose."

"We must make sure," Bobby repeated.

"It seems to me that most likely you are right and Monsieur Shields, he has been here before us," Père Trouché said.

Without answering, Bobby began to dig. The task was neither long nor difficult, for when he had removed but a bare six inches of the loose earth, he found reason to lay aside the spade and to begin to use his hands. Père Trouché said:

"It is not surprising that when we entered here there was a smell of death in the air." Then he said: "It is Monsieur Shields, is it not? They have buried him there where he had his diamonds buried. In effect then, he was here before us?"

"It is Shields all right," answered Bobby, who by now had uncovered enough of the hastily-buried body to be sure of its identity.

He removed a little more of the earth and paused and then continued and then once more he paused and scrambled to his feet. Père Trouché said:

"What is it now? Why are you so disturbed?"

Bobby had straightened himself, moved away a few yards. He said below his breath, three times over:

"My God! My God! Oh, my God!"

"What is it? Tell me, then," Père Trouché repeated, his voice high and shrill. "What is it that is so disturbing? Have you then never seen a dead man before?"

"Yes," Bobby stammered, his voice not quite under his control, "but not like this. There's... there's..." His voice trailed away. Père Trouché said sharply: "Well. Well, what then?"

"There are burns on the face, on the arms, burns... the half-burnt candle was used for that. The hands— the finger-nails—"

"Ah, torture, they tortured him," Père Trouché observed calmly. "It was to be expected. It was known he had the Polthwaite diamonds hidden. He was visited when he was alone in his house, he was taken unaware, he refused to tell, means were taken to make sure that he did tell, and since he was a strong man and an obstinate, doubtless he held out as long as was possible. But pain, when it is carefully and skilfully applied, will break down any man's resistance. Except indeed when there is a living faith, for that—that is stronger than all things, than death or than pain. But diamonds and a living faith, they are very different, and so Monsieur Shields he would not be able to hold out for long. Then they brought him here to make sure he spoke the truth and when they found he had done so, then they shot him—naturally. One would feel more sympathy for him had he not already killed an old and helpless woman who was his friend and trusted him. On the whole I do not greatly regret that he in his turn also suffered."

"Yes, but you can't see him," Bobby muttered. He moved a few yards farther back, nearer the entrance, avoiding instinctively that part of the cliff where the water dripped and made a small puddle on the ground. He wanted to lean against the rock, for he had an odd feeling that presently his legs might refuse any longer to support him. Where the cliff was drier he supported himself against it. Père Trouché followed, but groping with his stick kept more in the centre of the enclave and found himself caught in that tangle of loose stony and difficult ground that lay in front of the oak and between it and the entrance gap. He stood still and Bobby said again:

"You couldn't see him and I wish I hadn't."

"There are times when it is better not to see," agreed the old man. "But I also, I do not find it agreeable here. It resembles too closely to a tomb."

"Look out, look out. Quick," Bobby screamed. "Lie down."

He had glanced towards the entrance gap. A low sound from that direction had caught his attention. There, poking round a corner of the rock, showed clearly the long muzzle of a pistol, a point forty-five automatic, probably. It was aimed straight at the old beggar. Bobby himself was out of the direct range. Père Trouché answered peevishly:

"Why should I lie down? When I cannot see, how can I look out as you call it?"

He was standing quite still, upright and motionless, directly before that dark menacing pistol muzzle that he could not see, that was aiming directly at his heart, that he made no effort to avoid, since of its presence and its threat he was equally unaware. Even as he spoke, before Bobby could shout again or move, the clamour of the discharged pistol filled the little enclave, thrown to and fro from its high, echoing walls. The old man sat down and began to cough.

"Well, now, what is all this?" he said bewilderedly.

Bobby sprang forward instinctively. That brought him into the line of fire. A bullet whizzed past so near that he heard its shrill snarl as it went by. Instinctively again he sprang back and more quickly still. Another shot was fired, this time again at Père Trouché. He sank slowly from his sitting to a recumbent position, turned a little to one side and lay quietly, like a man asleep. With quick decision Bobby saw where lay his only chance of safety. If he stood where he was, if he tried to seek shelter where shelter there was none, his fate would be certain. He could hope for nothing but to be shot down at the convenience of their unknown assailant. He was still holding the spade with which he had begun to dig and that he had laid hold of for support in the first moment of the shock of his discovery of Shields's mutilated body. Brandishing it as though it were sword or battle-axe he ran at his utmost speed straight for the opening where the assassin hid, no sign of him visible save only that continually threatening pistol muzzle, the faint thread of smoke ascending in the air, the clamour of the echoing shots still being tossed to and fro from one cliff to another.

The hope in Bobby's mind, the forlorn desperate hope, was that the unseen murderer, seeing him charging thus, would hold his fire for the moment, meaning to make sure when he was nearer and could be shot down at ease. Moreover a man running at full speed, especially when running forward, is not so easy a target as one who is standing perfectly still. One shot indeed was fired, but hit not Bobby but the whirling spade he brandished and so was deflected to splash harmlessly against the rock, and Bobby hoped desperately that further shots would be withheld in expectation and anticipation of the ease with which any one could be shot down from one side or the other as they blundered through the narrow entrance gap out into the open.

But that formed no part of the intention behind Bobby's swift and desperate rush. One of the two rocks, that on the west or right hand from within, jutted forward in such a way as to provide behind it a sort of niche or shelter, so that any one standing there, as it were behind a door, was covered and would indeed have good opportunity to strike first at any attempting to pass. It was this kind of niche or crack in the rock that Bobby was aiming for, and when he reached it, he stood still, spade lifted, ready to strike, fairly safe so long as he stood just where he was and yet knowing that to move even an inch would be to expose himself as an easy target to the assassin, waiting unseen indeed but so near.

Indeed of that he soon had proof, for when presently he moved, though only very slightly, there was instant reaction in the shape of another shot, and a bullet that struck splinters from the rock not more than an inch or two away. Presently, too, the pistol muzzle appeared, groping and pointing in an effort to twist round far enough to bring him within its orbit. This Bobby had expected, and indeed had hoped, might happen, for he thought that so might be given him his best chance of escape. But he blundered, perhaps because his nerves were not so completely under control as he believed. At any rate when he struck out with his spade, he struck too soon, even though he had waited as long as he dared. Anyhow his blow miscarried, the pistol was snatched away, his hope of knocking it out of the other's hand and so getting on equal terms had failed. Nor was it, he supposed grimly, very likely that such an opportunity would be offered him again.

"Who is it?" he shouted once, but got no response.

In his mind, as he stood there flattened in his protective niche, knowing that any movement to relieve his cramped muscles would almost certainly bring him within range of the assassin's pistol, he went over the list of those who might be waiting there, recent murderers of the unhappy Shields who had paid so terribly for his crime, and now determined that those who had discovered so much must not be allowed to continue to live.

He supposed that the murderer or murderers of Shields, lingering near—Bobby wondered why and wondered also whether the answer to that question he would ever know—had seen his approach and Père Trouché's across the bare, and, at this part, nearly level expanse of the Massif, had marked their entry into the enclave, had realized what they must find there, had followed them in the resolve to make the secret safe by two more assassinations.

One they had already successfully accomplished and Bobby was inclined to think that the second would not be very long delayed, for he did not feel that he could sustain his present cramped position very much longer. His enemy had only to wait till hunger, thirst, exhaustion, compelled him to make some movement that would bring him within range of the questing pistol muzzle that more than once he saw again come pushing and seeking round the edge of the rock sheltering him, though never far enough or near enough to give him another chance of striking at it.

Again and again he found himself trying to think who it could be who thus was waiting to kill. He wished somehow very much that he knew. He had the idea that knowledge would make endurance easier, as the anonymity of the peril made it worse, and he found himself envying old Père Trouché who lay there so peacefully on his side, like one quietly sleeping. Once or twice he shouted out threats or questions or taunts, but got no reply. But a movement he made drew swift response in the shape of a bullet that actually tore the cloth of his coat sleeve, though without inflicting any wound.

What it was that presently and quite suddenly impressed upon his mind a conviction that the danger had passed and that now no one was waiting there, that he was no longer under watch and menace, he never understood. Perhaps his sense of hearing, keyed to a pitch of intensity inconceivable at other times, wrought indeed to some such keenness beyond ordinary human capacity as Père Trouché seemed somehow to have reached, had warned him sub-consciously of tiny sounds of departure; perhaps that extremity of peril in which he had been placed had opened in him other avenues of knowledge, of which, at ordinary moments, the ordinary man is unaware, something of the nature of that strange power by which it is said primitive people have almost instantaneous knowledge of far-off happenings.

In any case, whatever the explanation, and he himself had none to offer, abruptly he knew—knew beyond doubt or question—that now he could come out from his shelter with perfect safety.

He flung down the spade he had been holding and ran forward into that open where a little before to show him-self would have meant instant death. On his left was the tall, isolated sugar-loaf rock; on his right the grove of tangled close-growing trees and bushes, wind-swept and dwarfed; between them, but nearer to him, a figure was running. It shouted something and then dived in between the trees. Bobby's sight of it had been too brief for him to be able to say who it was. He stood still, hesitating. From the midst of the trees, muffled by their close growth, came the fresh report of a pistol shot. Instinctively Bobby dropped to the ground. He had no love for the role of target and he thought the shot had been aimed at him. He heard fresh shouting and, raising his head and looking cautiously, he saw several of Clauzel's men running quickly towards him. Evidently the recent shooting had been heard—indeed the reports would have carried far over that wide and empty space, caught up and echoed as they would be by the adjacent rocks—and rescue and help were coming. Bobby decided to stay where he was till that help was nearer. He had no wish to tackle, alone and unarmed, a desperate murderer who had already given such dread proof of readiness to kill. When the gendarmes arrived, it would not be difficult so to surround the trees as to make escape impossible and then to take such steps as might be necessary to force the fugitive into the open.

The gendarmes were quite close now. Bobby recognized Clauzel as the foremost among them. He shouted a warning. It was heard but not heeded. Clauzel shouted back something Bobby did not quite catch to the general effect that there had been quite enough of this sort of thing and he wasn't going to waste any more time—automatics or no automatics.

Bobby would have liked to reply that that was all very well, and no one was more tired of it than he was, but automatics remained automatics, and why run unnecessary risks? Clauzel, however, evidently had no intention of delaying and was running straight towards the trees when from the midst of them appeared a man, holding a long-barrelled point forty-five automatic in one hand. The commissaire, who himself held an automatic, though one of smaller calibre, promptly fired, though more in warning than with deliberate aim. The other ran forward, waving his own pistol in the air but not firing. Clauzel shouted to him to surrender. At the same moment as Clauzel called to him, the newcomer caught his foot in the rough ground, pitched forward violently, striking his head against a stone. The pistol jerked from his hand. He lay sprawling and quite still.

When Bobby came up he found Clauzel and two of the gendarmes standing round the still unconscious man.

Bobby recognized the young Camion.

Clauzel said to him:

"Eh, well, Monsieur Owen, who would have expected him?"

CHAPTER XXIV
CONCLUSION

It was some minutes before Camion recovered consciousness, for his fall had been heavy. There joined Glauzel and Bobby a middle-aged civilian whom Clauzel addressed as Dr. Mendel. Bobby, understanding that the new-comer was a medical man, explained hurriedly that Père Trouché had been shot, was lying at a little distance, and ought to receive attention at once.

"Though I'm afraid it's too late to help him," he added. "I think he was hit twice. I think he was killed on the spot."

"I had better go and see," Mendel said and was starting off when Clauzel stopped him.

"Just take a look at this fellow first," he said, nodding at Camion. "I do not want him to cheat the guillotine."

"It is nothing," Mendel answered at once, and indeed Camion had opened his eyes now and was struggling into a sitting position. "It is only that he was 'knock-outed.'"

Mendel used the English word 'knock-out' that has now become a French verb—like 'interviewer'. Camion, looking up at them, said:

"She put the pistol in her mouth and then she fired. It was as though the top of her head leaped off." He began to shudder violently. "I heard some one scream. I think perhaps it was me. I think I ran. It was an awful thing to see and I think I screamed and then I think I ran."

"What's all that? What do you mean?" Clauzel demanded while the others gaped. "What 'she'?"

"I ran after her, I saw her running and I ran after her," Camion explained, still in the same half-dazed manner. "I shouted to her to stop. I shouted that the gendarmes were all around and she could not escape. She looked at me and then she put the pistol in her mouth and fired. It was an awful thing to see. She fell down and so did the pistol and I must have picked it up and then I think I began to run, but I do not know why, except that I wanted to get away."

"All this, I do not understand it," Clauzel said bewilderedly.

"Who do you mean? What 'she'?" Bobby asked.

"But I am telling you," Camion answered impatiently. "Madame Williams. Do you want me to go on repeating to you again and again what I shall see to the end of my life?"

Alain had come up now and had been listening quietly. He said:

"Come, doctor. Let us look for ourselves."

Followed by one or two of the gendarmes who had also arrived by now, the juge d'instruction and the doctor disappeared amidst the trees. Bobby said to Camion:

"How did you come to be here? What are you doing here? Why did you clear out from Citry?"

"I wanted to find Volny," Camion answered. He seemed more composed now and talked quickly and volubly, as if in the flow of words he could forget the awful scene he had just witnessed. "I knew I was suspected. It was absurd, for there had been no duel, we had not fought, but I had no wish to go to the guillotine because of the folly of the ideas of others. It was because Volny did not wish to fight our duel that he went away, and I was very glad, because I also, I had no wish to fight."

"Did you see anything of him that morning Père Trouché and I followed you?" Bobby asked.

"No. He sent me a note to say that he was not going to make a fool of himself and he was not going to keep our appointment. I was very glad, but then I thought perhaps it was a trick to keep me away so that he could say he was there but I had been afraid. That I could not have endured. So I went to the place we had agreed upon and I waited, and when Volny did not come, then I fired my pistol in the air to show that I at least had sustained my honour.'

An action typical, Bobby thought, of the boy's leaning to the dramatic, not to say the theatrical. Probably when he discharged his pistol in the air he had felt himself truly heroic. All the glory of the duel and none of the danger. And yet just now he had shown a genuine and cool courage in following a criminal taken in the act, armed and desperate.

"It would have saved a lot of trouble if you had told us all that at the time," grumbled Bobby.

"I saw no reason to," answered Camion with something that at another time might have been a swagger. "Père Trouché could tell any story he liked. Why not?"

And Bobby divined a secret hope that Père Trouché would have spread a story in which Camion himself would figure as something of a hero and Volny as something quite different.

"Wasn't it a bit dangerous following that woman when you knew she was armed and had been taking potshots all round?" Bobby asked curiously. "She had just killed poor old Père Trouché," he added.

"A Frenchman does not permit himself to be afraid," answered Camion.

"No permission required for this Britisher," grunted Bobby. "If my hair isn't as white as the usual driven snow to-morrow morning, it won't be for lack of funk."

"Each has his qualities," said Camion kindly, and then in a burst of candour added: "All the same, as I ran, my very skin sweated terror. But do not tell any one," he added quickly.

"Not me," Bobby assured him and they shook hands solemnly. Bobby added: "You didn't find out anything about Volny?"

"I found he had been seen in Barsac, but no one seemed to know where he had gone or what had become of him."

"What made you think he might be here?" Bobby asked.

"There are some of his cousins he might have gone to. Also he had asked questions about Monsieur Shields and he had said there were other questions he would like to ask Monsieur Shields. It seemed to me he might have thought it an opportunity. If he had been able to find out anything about the Polthwaite affair, then it would have started people talking about that once more and they would have forgotten about our duel. I knew Volny believed Monsieur Shields might be able to explain certain things."

"Do you mean he suspected Shields of the murder?"

"But no, how could that be when Shields was in his home at Barsac on the night of the assassination? No, but he believed there might be points which Shields could explain. So I thought I would ask him if Volny had been to see him, but the good Monsieur Shields he had dined too well that night, he was in no state to answer questions even of the most simple."

"Why do you say that?" Bobby asked.

"It was not difficult to see. When I knocked I got no answer so I went round to the back. Monsieur Shields heard me and came out of one of the sheds in the garden. He had gone there to drink all by himself for he had a bottle of brandy in his hand and he drank before he spoke a word—-drank deeply, too. His clothes were all over dust. He said he had been sitting on a bag of chemical manure and it had burst open. Most likely he fell and upset it, he was not steady on his feet. He was quarrelsome, too. He would not answer my questions. It is useless to talk to a man who drinks brandy from a bottle as he speaks."

Bobby was looking at Camion with a kind of wonder. It seemed certain the boy had interrupted Shields in the very act of disposing of the unfortunate Volny's body.

"Did you say anything about Volny?" Bobby asked.

"I asked him if he knew where Volny was or if he had seen him. He drank the last drop of his brandy before he answered. Then he said if I would come into the shed with him he would show me something. But it was evident to me that he wished to quarrel. I felt that if I went with him, before long I should have that brandy bottle he flourished thrown at my head. So I went away. I thought I would return another time. As I was going I saw Monsieur and Madame Williams. If they were intending to visit Shields, they also must have found him in the same state."

"I expect they did," Bobby said slowly and wondered if ever before so strange a tale had been told so simply and so innocently.

He wondered, too, if ever before a murderer had been interrupted in the very act of concealing his victim's body by an inquiry as to that victim's whereabouts. A dramatic scene, Bobby thought; the body of the dead Volny in the adjacent shed; the murderer seeking support in his bottle of brandy, and going out of his way to account for the condition of his clothes; Camion asking his innocent and unsuspecting questions. Bobby wondered, too, what would have happened if Camion had accepted the invitation to enter the shed. Not that there could be much doubt. A second murder, a second body to be concealed, would have been the inevitable sequel. Camion had been nearer death then than he had ever dreamed. The condition of Shields that evening, as reported by Camion, explained, too, the ease with which the Williamses had been able to carry out their project, for Shields had been a strong and desperate man. Probably, however, he had awakened from a drunken stupor to find himself helpless in their hands, bound hand and foot very likely.

"Did you go back again?" Bobby asked.

"Yes, later, but there was no one there. I knocked and waited but no one came. It was a little curious though that once I thought I heard a sound like some one moaning. But it must have been imagination, for though I waited quite a long time I heard nothing more. So I went away." Bobby thought to himself that from Camion's point of view that had been just as well. Had he attempted to pursue his investigation, then again his life would probably have paid the forfeit. The moaning sound he heard must have been the wretched Shields from whom the Williams couple must even then have been forcing the secret of the hiding-place on the Massif. Again Camion had been near death, for very clearly had the Williams couple shown how ruthless they could be. Probably Camion had left only just in time to save himself.

"How did you happen to be here this evening just in the very nick of time?" Bobby asked.

"I thought it might be out here on the Massif that Volny was hiding," Camion explained. "I knew that he had been in Barsac, but then he had vanished, only I was sure he could not be far away. Also I was worried because I had seen Monsieur and Madame Williams again. They had come from Paris by train and I wondered why. I thought possibly Volny had found the things Mademoiselle Polthwaite was said to have hidden and that he had asked the Williamses to help him to get away to Paris with it to claim a reward there. I found out that Monsieur Williams had been trying to hire a car, and that he had specially asked for one that would stand up to rough ground. So I guessed that he meant to drive out somewhere on the Massif to pick up Volny."

"I daresay it was a bit like that," Bobby said, "only not Volny."

Alain and the doctor came back. Alain gave a few orders to his men and Bobby told as briefly as possible both his own story and the gist of Camion's.

"Looks to me," he said in conclusion, "as if, after they had dug up the Polthwaite jewellery from where Shields had it hidden, and after they had shot him and buried his body, Mrs. Williams remained hidden in this grove while Williams himself went off to get the car Camion says he had been bargaining for. I expect they thought it would be safer not to go back through Barsac, especially while in possession of the jewels. Unfortunately for them the search you organized upset their plans altogether. Williams wouldn't dare show himself in a car while your men were all about. He would have been seen at once and asked for explanations. It must have been a bit of a shock to him when he found he couldn't get back and was cut off both from his wife and from their loot, and he must have wondered a good deal what the search of the Massif would reveal. Mrs. Williams most likely didn't realize there was a general search taking place. She would only see Père Trouché and me making for the very spot where Shields was buried. She would realize we were bound to find his body and then

I suppose she decided their best chance was to stop us reporting it. She would think it might be weeks before our bodies were found, and she and her husband could be anywhere in the world by then, South America, China, anywhere. Her bad luck, that the firing was bound to be heard by your men, Monsieur Alain, though as it happened Camion heard it first. It must have been another shock for her, and the worst of all, when she realized that her pistol practice had brought down all your gendarmes on her. No wonder she made up her mind to end it."

"There was an old leather valise near the body," Alain said. "It is full of rings, brooches, unset stones in handfuls. Gold cigar cases, handbags in gold mesh, and so on, too. It had evidently been buried for some time, it was damp and covered with earth. It's a good weight. They would want a car to take it away in, if only to avoid attracting attention."

Darkness had been increasing rapidly while all these things were taking place and by this time was nearly complete. The doctor had been making out a brief written report as best he could and now was ready to listen to Bobby's request that he should see to old Père Trouché, who in the midst of so much excitement, with so much needing swift and instant attention, had been almost forgotten.

"Yes, yes, I go, I go at once," Mendel answered a fresh request from Bobby, "but if the man is dead, there is nothing I can do."

"I thought he was hit right over the heart," Bobby said.

Together they started off; Clauzel, to whom Bobby had also spoken, promising to follow immediately with two of his men as soon as they had ready the improvised stretcher he set them to construct.

The distance was only short but in the intense, impenetrable darkness that had now set in, no stars showing, the moon not yet risen, progress was both slow and difficult over the rough, uneven ground, covered with tangled vegetation, here and there with loose stony patches where sometimes big boulders lay. The battery of Bobby's torch had run down, the doctor had none with him, their only light came from an occasional match one or other of them struck, though even between them they had so few they were obliged to be economical in their use. Once indeed the doctor, who had stumbled several times and once fallen full length, refused to go on, protesting that it was useless to continue.

"We shall be breaking our necks," he complained. "Already I am covered with bruises. Also if the man is dead, then a doctor is no longer of any use."

"Two shots hit him," Bobby said. "He never moved after the second shot. Only it does not seem decent to leave him lying there."

As he spoke there came an instant response, from out of the heart of the black night, as a voice that Bobby knew well called softly:

"Hé, Mr. Englishman, is it you? What is it that has happened and who is that with you?"

Bobby, after a moment of blank amazement, began to run, then stood still, bewildered by the darkness. He struck one of his few remaining matches and held it up. Instantly a puff of wind, though the air had seemed calm before, blew it out. He called:

"Where are you? It's dark. I can't see a thing."

A familiar chuckle answered him.

"Now it is you who cannot see," the voice from out the darkness said. "Eh, well, that is amusing. Forward, march, but more to your right. No. More still. That's it. I am here but be quick for I think that I am dying though I do not understand why."

Bobby made his way on through the dark night he felt like a hostile force, holding them back, impeding them, that was almost like a palpable thing, hindering every movement. Behind him he could hear Dr. Mendel, stumbling and grumbling, but no longer thinking of turning back, now he knew a living patient might need his care. Behind them the darkness was broken by an increasing glow where some of the gendarmes had heaped together dry wood to make a bonfire that would give at least a little light. Bobby called again:

"Where are you. I can't see. I can't see a thing." Once more there sounded that familiar chuckle. "But I am here," came Père Trouché's voice. He said compassionately: "No doubt it is difficult when one is not accustomed to the dark. Tell me then, what happened? I remember only that I fell down and then I think I must have fallen asleep for when I woke I was alone. I tried to find you but it tired me to walk and presently I began to understand that I was dying. It is surprising, for I do not seem to remember having been ill."

Bobby, groping desperately, stumbling forward, striking now and then a match that was of little use, came at last to where the old man lay, propped up against one of the boulders that were scattered around.

"It was the Williams woman," Bobby said. "She fired at us. I thought she had killed you. Now she has killed herself. Doctor, he's here." He stood up and lighted another match that was of small service, so small it seemed in the vast, enveloping, tremendous darkness that was as though it covered the whole earth, as though nothing else existed save eternal night. "Doctor, here, he is here," he called again.

"You have brought a doctor?" Père Trouché asked. "A doctor for the old blind beggar? It is very good of you, but also it is useless."

"It's so dark, black as pitch. There is no light anywhere," Mendel's voice came complainingly.

"That is difficult for you others, is it not?" Père Trouché commented, "but for me, it is nothing, for I have always lived in darkness all my life and now it is only natural that I should die in it. Only I wish that I could just once have known what is this light that people talk about so much. Always, I have wondered."

Doctor Mendel came up at last, to join them.

"Ah, there you are," he said, "but I have used my last match and what can I do in this darkness?"

"Darkness? Here is no darkness," Père Trouché said in a voice louder than any Bobby had ever heard him use before. "There is only light, light everywhere, shining all round; oh, how lovely a thing is light."

He slipped away from the half recumbent position he had held before. Bobby thrust into Mendel's hand his few remaining matches. Mendel struck them one after the other. He said:

"The man's dead." A moment later he said: "He has been shot twice, right over the heart, through the heart. He must have died on the spot. It is inconceivable that he lived more than a moment or two." He stared up at Bobby, the light of the match he was holding flickering uncertainly on his face, on the face of the dead man. He said: "He was shot clean through the heart, twice. Well, after that, how could he walk and talk?"

Bobby had no answer to make. Mendel got to his feet, mechanically trying to brush dirt and earth from his clothing. He muttered:

"What was all that about light? It's black as pitch all round."

Again Bobby made no attempt to answer. Help came. Improvised torches of dry wood and brush gave uncertain illumination. The body of the old blind beggar was placed on the rough stretcher that had hastily been put together and was carried away. Bobby, conscious now of an immense fatigue, followed slowly. Clauzel said to him:

"Well, now it is finished. Shields has paid for his murder of Mademoiselle Polthwaite, of the unfortunate Volny. The Williams woman has escaped us. True, there is still Monsieur Williams to deal with but we shall soon put a hand on his collar."

In this, however, Monsieur Clauzel was mistaken, for from that day to this nothing has been heard of Williams. Evidently he took the alarm in time and in the car he had succeeded in hiring he must have escaped across one of the frontiers—possibly by means already prepared in advance for his and his wife's escape with their projected booty.

From his own private point of view, Bobby was not sorry, since it saved him from being involved in long legal proceedings and a sensational trial that might have dragged on for months. As it was, nothing could be done and nothing more was required from him except a long statement to be added to the enormous dossier of the case.

Of the others who had played their part in working out the drama to its end, there is not much to be told. The reconciliation between the Abbé Granges and schoolmaster Eudes still holds good and Citry-sur-l'eau remains one of the few places in provincial France where church and school work together in their common task of showing youth how to attain the good life. Charles Camion, cleared of the suspicions of which he had so long been the object, and finding himself as a result ceasing to be so generally of interest, made up his mind at last to leave Citry. By help of the publicity still attaching to his name, and with the aid of introductions given him by some of the journalists who came to hear his story, he was able to join a small travelling theatrical company. There he found his own special niche in life so rapidly that already he is becoming known, if not yet to the public, at least in the profession, and he has even had the good luck to get work on the films. The contract he secured made his position seem sufficiently sure, especially as his parents' hotel was beginning to do well again, to make possible his marriage with Mademoiselle Simone. It is likely to take place very shortly, and Bobby, returning to England, in the hope both of claiming the reward due to him and of securing the appointment promised, felt that now he ought to be able to induce Olive to follow so admirable an example.

THE END